Her Mentor

Isobel was giving Lord Christian something besides money—a piece of her mind. "It is most improper, most unacceptable of you, my lord, to attempt to pay for my lessons, and I will not have it . . . I cannot allow myself to be indebted to you; so I have come to return to you the cost of my lessons."

"Of course you must pay me back."

The thick, dark lashes fluttered in surprise. She had not expected him to give in so easily. "But it will not be with money. I will take more than money." A slight blush tinged her cheeks.

"You must tell me what I may do."

He could tell from the rapid pulse at the base of her throat that she was afraid to hear what he would demand in payment. Christian took one gloved hand and raised it gently to his lips. "Believe me, your happiness is all the payment I ask."

She had the oddest urge to pull off her glove and trace the hard, square line of his jaw to feel the strength of him. What was she doing? She had come to repay her debt to this man, to rid herself of all obligation to him so that she would never have to see him again, and now she was practically falling into his arms.

"Thank you," she whispered. . . .

Scandalous Secrets by Patricia Oliver

Years ago, Lady Francesca St. Ives was divorced, and cast out of her family amid scandalous rumors. Now, she has returned home to make a new life for herself—without the aid of a man. But a little girl who needs her help—and the child's handsome, intriguing father—may slightly alter the lady's plans...and her heart....

0-451-19886-7/$4.99

The Barbarian Earl by Nadine Miller

The unscrupulous Earl of Stratham has offered his illegitimate son Liam a generous inheritance—if Liam marries the noble Lady Alexandra Henning. But an arranged marriage is an affront to Alexandra's romantic sensibilities—unless Liam can find the way to her heart—and perhaps open his own as well....

0-451-19887-5/$4.99

The Scottish Legacy by Barbara Hazard

Clear-headed Lila Douglas never believed in love at first sight—until she fell hopelessly in love with her dashing second cousin, Alastair Russell. Ever since, she's dreamed of future meetings that end with happily ever after. But can her romantic fantasy withstand reality—not to mention a most unexpected rival?

0-451-19888-3/$4.99

To order call: 1-800-788-6262

My Lady Nightingale

Evelyn Richardson

A SIGNET BOOK

SIGNET
Published by New American Library, a division of
Penguin Putnam Inc., 375 Hudson Street,
New York, New York 10014, U.S.A.
Penguin Books Ltd, 27 Wrights Lane,
London W8 5TZ, England
Penguin Books Australia Ltd,
Ringwood, Victoria, Australia
Penguin Books Canada Ltd, 10 Alcorn Avenue,
Toronto, Ontario, Canada M4V 3B2
Penguin Books (N.Z.) Ltd, 182–190 Wairau Road,
Auckland 10, New Zealand

Penguin Books Ltd, Registered Offices:
Harmondsworth, Middlesex, England

First published by Signet, an imprint of New American Library,
a division of Penguin Putnam Inc.

First Printing, November 1999
10 9 8 7 6 5 4 3 2 1

To B.
Ten years and
still my romantic hero

Chapter 1

Slowly, deliberately, he climbed the marble steps to the imposing mansion in Grosvenor Square. It had been five years of fighting and marching in the heat and dust of the Peninsula, five years of living in tents or the occasional farmhouse, of wondering if supply wagons would make it across the rough terrain to feed them, five years of tension, exhaustion, and fear. It was odd that here nothing seemed to have changed at all, but then, his brother would never change. Albert was as staid and unchanging as the English countryside and as steeped in tradition as the monarchy itself.

The paneled mahogany door swung open to reveal Grinstead, more cadaverous than ever, but no less imposing. "Lord Christian!" The butler's hatchetlike face broke into something approaching a smile. "Welcome home, my lord. It is good to see you."

"Thank you, Grinstead. Is my brother home?"

"His Grace has gone to see Lord Liverpool."

"And the duchess?"

"Her Grace is at Madame Celeste's and some other establishments on Bond Street."

"Lady Sophia and Lady Augusta are at home, I trust?"

"That they are, my lord. Shall I tell them you are here?"

"Please." Christian handed his greatcoat and hat to the butler. "On second though, Grinstead,"

"Yes, my lord?"

"Do not tell the girls who it is. Inform them simply that they have a visitor."

Again Grinstead betrayed the faintest glimmer of a smile. "Very good, my lord."

Christian wandered around the drawing room after the butler had left. As he had suspected, there was absolutely nothing different about it. The same Hepplewhite chairs were placed in precise groupings. The damask draperies hung in carefully arranged folds. The portrait of his father, the fifth Duke of Warminster, still frowned down at him from its place on the wall opposite the fireplace. The same looking glass over the mantel reflected the scene it had reflected five years ago. Only the face looking back at him had changed. There was still the same fire in the gray-green eyes, but it was tempered by a somber expression as though the eyes had witnessed too much, and there were fine lines at the corners from years of squinting into the bright Peninsular sun surveying the countryside for enemy activity. The high cheekbones were even more pronounced than they had been and the lean face, which had lost all the softness of youth, was deeply tanned. It was a face that had seen a great deal.

The tinkling sounds of a pianoforte broke into his reflections. Grinstead must have been mistaken in thinking that the girls were upstairs; they were in the music room. All the better, it would be even more of a surprise if he appeared unannounced. A voice was now mingling with the sound of the pianoforte. It was a rich voice and surprisingly strong for a young girl.

As Christian moved closer he could make out the words *"meine Tochter nimmer mehr"* followed by a brilliant trill. No, it could not be Augusta or Sophia. No young girl would attempt, much less succeed, in singing the Queen of the Night's demanding aria of revenge from *Die Zauberflöte*. In fact, not many adults would have the temerity or the range to do so. Now that he thought about it, Christian realized that he had never heard it sung so well.

Intrigued, he crept closer and peered carefully around the French doors that opened into the music room. From his vantage point he could see a slim woman seated at the pianoforte, her hands moving over the keys with assurance, her head tilted slightly as the liquid notes spilled from the slender, white column of her throat. Christian stood spellbound as the music carried him away into another world, a world which, despite the dire words of the song, was one of wonder, harmony, and beauty.

The music stopped. With a sigh and a little shake of the head the singer played the opening notes of the song again. What could have possibly displeased her with what had appeared to him to be a perfect performance? She must have talent indeed to think she could improve on what he had just heard. The beautiful sounds poured over him and he leaned against the door allowing her song to carry him into another realm, washing away the images of war and destruction that had been part of him for so long, and gave himself up to the power of music.

The exquisite moment was brought to abrupt conclusion by a loud bang that echoed around the room as the door against which Christian had been leaning slammed back against the wall behind him. The singer leapt up, nearly upsetting the bench on which she had been sitting, and turned around to face him, her dark blue eyes wide with alarm. As her gaze fell on Christian, the slightly guilty expression on her face turned into one of intense annoyance.

"How dare you, sir, a stranger, intrude without the decency to announce your presence!"

Christian grinned appreciatively. She was as lovely to look at as she was to listen to and in her anger she was magnificent. It would be too bad to quell that anger by offering an explanation. "I was not aware that *I* was the stranger here."

"And how, who . . ." The singer rose in a stately manner prepared to launch into a stinging retort and then apparently thought the better of it. After all, if one was not certain of someone else's identity, it was better to exercise a little caution, no matter how provoked one might be. "Well, whoever you are, you are a stranger to *me* and it is exceedingly rude of you to intrude upon what is obviously a private moment." The frostiness of her expression, which conveyed to him so eloquently that she considered him nothing but a barbarian, her icy tone, and the haughty lift of the head told him more clearly than she could have said that this was a person accustomed to commanding respect. But who was she?

She was too young to be a friend of the duchess's, too old for Sophia and Augusta, and she was not a cousin or a niece, for he knew all the cousins and nieces. And she was not a servant, of that he was quite certain. The accent, though it was a little difficult to place, was refined and the proud carriage was definitely not that of a servant.

"Rude, perhaps, but you must blame yourself for it is the fault of your exquisite music." His eyes drifted over her, admiring the tall, slender figure, the generous bosom, and the long line of leg hinted at ever so slightly under the walking dress of cambric muslin. "And your even more exquisite person that have made me forget my manners entirely."

As Christian had anticipated, the delicate color that rose in her cheeks at this deliberately provocative remark made her a picture to behold and emphasized the deep sapphire of eyes that blazed with barely repressed anger.

The singer snatched at her music and stalked toward the door. He realized that he had gone too far. "Forgive me, I . . ."

He was interrupted by the sounds of running feet as two golden-haired girls attired in matching white frocks came racing into the room. "Uncle Christian, Uncle Christian," they cried in unison as they flung themselves at him.

Grabbing each of them in one strong arm he laughed and swung them off the floor. "Sophia, Augusta! And what would your mama and papa say if they saw their precious young ladies acting like perfect savages?" Both girls laughed as the elder replied, "Mama would not mind. She would be so glad to see you herself that she would give you a big hug."

"And Papa?"

"Oh, Papa"—the younger sister dismissed the Duke of Warminster with a shrug of her slight shoulder—"he is an old stick, and besides . . ."

"Gussie! You are dreadful! You must not say such a thing." Sophia was horrified.

"But it is true. He is always so proper and he never lets us have any fun or laughs with us the way Uncle Christian does, does he, Uncle Christian?"

Appealed to directly, Christian was at a loss for words, but Sophia came to her uncle's rescue. "You know it is not polite to ask questions like that, Gussie. Now, Uncle Christian"—she adopted her most grown-up tone of voice—" do tell us about your trip here. But first, has anyone offered you any refreshment?"

"Nnnnno." Christian's lip quivered. Sophia was the image of her mother. A quick glance at the singer whose eyes were dancing, informed him that she too was amused by the resemblance and he decided to seize the moment to his best advantage. "Thank you; I have just had a very hearty breakfast at my own lodgings, but you could do something for me."

"What?" Two pair of blue eyes turned toward him.

"You could introduce me to this young lady here who sings 'Der Hölle Rache kocht in meinem Herzen' like an angel." Christian observed the young lady's look of surprise with smug satisfaction. So she had not expected him to recognize the aria, so much for her dismissing him as a complete barbarian.

"Oh, we are being most unmannerly," Sophia apologized. "This is Mademoiselle Isobel de Montargis. She comes to teach us French and music."

"And her father is a French duc whom the revolutionaries wanted to put to the guillotine, but he escaped with the family in the middle of the night in their carriage and went to Switzerland, until they came to England, that is," Gussie informed him with bloodthirsty relish.

"Hush, Gussie. It is not polite to say things like that in public."

"But I think it is very exciting and Mademoiselle Isobel is very brave and her story is very romantic."

"Nevertheless, it is possible that Mademoiselle does not want her history told every time she meets someone. Do you, mademoiselle?" Sophia appealed to her instructress.

Isobel was at a loss for words, but help came from an unexpected quarter. "I expect that Mademoiselle would prefer to be introduced as the talented artist she is rather than having her past related to a perfect stranger. Sophia is in the right of it, Gussie." Christian laid a comforting hand on his youngest niece's shoulder. "It can be rather uncomfortable to have such personal things made known to a perfect stranger no matter how interesting those things are. And I"—he bowed to her, an ironic gleam in his eye—"am the Duke of Warminster's brother, Lord Christian Hatherleigh."

He smiled at Isobel. "Therefore, forgetting entirely that I heard a single word of what Augusta related, let me say that I am delighted to make your acquaintance and to thank you for providing me with the most tranquil, uplifting moments I have known for some time."

"Yes. Uncle Christian has been away in the war forever. He has been in all sorts of battles and Mama says he was a great hero at a place called Vitoria. Sophia and I have been writing to him for ages."

"There you go again, Gussie." Sophia was clearly disgusted with her irrepressible sister. It was Christian's turn to look just the slightest bit self-conscious at his niece's loquacity.

Isobel quickly repressed a smile at the man's obvious embarrassment. She was still annoyed at him for catching her unawares at her practice and she was even more annoyed at him for looking at her in that bold manner, his gray-green eyes sweeping over her from head to foot as though she were some delectable morsel of patisserie. The fact that his gaze had been so obviously appreciative only added to her irritation. She wished she had dared to do the same to him, to make him see how it felt to be stared at in that odious fashion, but she was certainly going to do nothing more to increase his conceit. The lazy, impudent smile had warned her at the very beginning of her encounter that he was a man much accustomed to being the object of female attention. Isobel had seen enough of that self-satisfied air among the courtiers who were her father's friends not to recognize it instantly for what it was.

But in this man's case, she admitted grudgingly to herself, it was deserved. She was a tall woman, but he towered above her. The severe cut of his coat and his total lack of ornamentation or affectation in dress, so different from the émigrés' more elaborate costumes, only emphasized the broad shoulders and slim hips, the sinewy strength that was so apparent in every movement and every gesture. While the men surrounding Louis XVIII, the Comte d'Artois, the Duc de Berri, and their entourages were soft and languid, this man was hard and alert. From the lean, tanned planes of his angular face to the well-shaped hands with their long, capable fingers he was a powerful figure, exuding an energy that could quite take one's breath away, if one were susceptible to that sort of thing. But Isobel was not. She had lived long enough among men who exuded that self-conscious charm, men who had charm and nothing else, to be the least bit taken in by it. Still, she could not help being gratified that he had identified the aria that she had been practicing and recognized it for the challenge it presented to even the most skillful singer.

"We are so glad you are home safe, Uncle Christian. Papa was very worried when he read in the dispatches that you had been wounded." Sophia's voice brought Isobel back to the moment at hand.

"Was he now? He need not have concerned himself, 'twas only a scratch."

The sarcastic tone surprised Isobel. She stole a glance at him under her lashes. The cynical twist of his lips and the ironic glint in his eye puzzled her. Was it not natural for one relative to be concerned for the safety of another?

Gussie, completely unaware of the change in her uncle's voice continued, "Yes, that is what he said at first, but then Mama told us that in foreign countries sometimes even the slightest wound can bring on a putrid fever and he began to fret."

"That is true enough." It was spoken almost as an afterthought and Isobel was not even sure that she had heard it or observed the bleak look that had crept into his eyes and was so quickly banished as he leaned over and tugged on one of Augusta's blond curls. "But that is of no account now. Tell me what you have been doing with yourselves since your last letters, and how are your new ponies?"

The girls launched into such a voluble description of riding lessons, the spaniel's latest litter of puppies, and excursions to such London landmarks as the Tower and Astley's that their uncle was obliged to protest. "Whoa, whoa, one at a time. Let us beg Mademoiselle de Montargis's pardon and then you sit on one side of me, Augusta, and Sophia on the other side. Now, tell me one at a time, or I shall never be able to keep it all straight." He winked conspiratorially at Isobel as he took his place on the sofa opposite the pianoforte with a niece snuggled on either side of him.

Isobel was at leisure to observe him as he sat there, his auburn head bent over first one little girl and then the other as he listened to their latest trials and tribulations, the most recent joys and sorrows in their lives. He was a strange mixture of qualities, she decided at last—impudent yet understanding, teasing yet compassionate, and though she took herself severely to task for it, she could not help but be curious about him.

It was this curiosity that made Isobel stay even though she told herself that it was merely good manners. If she had left the minute his attention was focused elsewhere it would have seemed pettish. She could easily have bid them all adieu, for she had finished her lesson and her practice session afterward, but bold and unmannerly as her employer's brother had been and as annoyed as she was by it, she could not help thinking that he was like a breath of fresh air in her circumscribed existence and she found herself listening to his tales of adventure in the Peninsula with the same breathless eagerness as her pupils.

Chapter 2

For all that Augusta made a drama of Isobel de Montargis's life, Isobel herself considered it to be sadly flat. She had been too young to understand anything when her parents and her brother Auguste had fled France in their lumbering traveling carriage, journeying in the dead of night until they had reached the safety of Switzerland. A child of two could not remember much except a series of unfamiliar rooms, all of them cramped and dark, as they had settled first in Basle with the Comte d'Artois and the Comte de Provence where the Duc de Montargis had joined the army raised by the royal princes. After the army's defeat in the Vendée they had moved to the small and quiet duchy of Brunswick and finally, after five years of wandering aimlessly across Europe, they had come to England. This last part of their journey in their now broken-down carriage and across the stormy channel Isobel remembered well. At age seven, never really having known a home, she could not understand why the tears had rolled down her mother's cheeks as the shores of the Continent faded from view, but she was old enough to recognize the Duchesse de Montargis's distress and to cling to her in the vain hope of offering comfort.

Upon their arrival in England their life had become more peaceful if less exciting. The duchesse's old friend, Charlotte, Countess of Barford, had offered the Duc de Montargis and his family the dower house on their estate in Buckinghamshire for as long as they cared to use it and had invited Isobel to join her daughters Jane and Emily in all their lessons.

Swallowing his pride, the duc had accepted the offer, relieving the stifling inactivity of the countryside and keeping the spirit of the emigration alive by corresponding continuously with the Comte d'Artois, the Prince de Condé, the Comte de Provence, and other members of the exiled court. Auguste, as befitted a young French nobleman, had been sent to join the sons of other émigré families at Stonyhurst, the school kept by refugee Jesuits in Lancashire, and the family had settled into a life which, though it was at last safe, was routine and limited pretty much exclusively to the company of the Lord and Lady of Barford Court.

Isobel, who for years had only enjoyed the companionship of her family and one doll given her by the Duchess of Brunswick, blossomed in the company of Jane and Emily. Full of energy and possessing a quick mind that was rendered even quicker and more observant by her tumultuous existence, she had thrown herself into her lessons, especially those taught by Monsieur Verbier. The Monsieur had been a noted performer on the violin and pianoforte in his day, but rheumatism had ended his career and forced him into teaching music to the children of the aristocracy. He was a kind man, genuinely interested in bringing the love of music to all his students, talented or not, a gift that made him admirably suited to teaching. His newest pupil rewarded this interest by demonstrating not only a natural aptitude for the study of music, but by possessing nearly perfect pitch and a voice that the music master insisted was a gift of the angels. So delighted was he that he donated many hours of lessons beyond the appointed ones in order to develop her talents to the fullest.

But, with the exception of these lessons, Isobel's life had been quiet in the extreme and she longed to know the world beyond the green fields of the Barford estates. In spite of Jane and Emily's teasing her for her bluestocking tendencies, she devoured the books in the library at Barford Court, but voyages of the imagination could not replace the real thing and she envied the worldly experience of her own brother Auguste, and Robert, Jane and Emily's elder brother. Whenever either Auguste or Robert was at Barford she would listen with rapt attention to their tales of schoolboy pranks, trips to London, or a day at Newmarket watching the races.

To Isobel, anything beyond the tidy flint cottages in the village or the rolling hills around the estate was new and exciting, but she alone of all Barford Court's residents felt this way. The earl and countess, imbued with the ancient sense of a landowner's responsibility toward land and tenants, a responsibility that passed from one generation of Barfords to another, had no wish to indulge in the delights of the fashionable world and therefore remained in Buckinghamshire even during the height of the Season.

The Duc de Montargis, who spent most of his days at his desk immersed in correspondence or his memoirs, was too wrapped up in the glories of the past to wish to learn anything more about the present, and his wife, exhausted by years of travel, and worn out by anxiety for the safety of her loved ones, was too fragile to do much more than work on her exquisite embroidery or take the occasional walk in the countess' rose garden.

So Isobel, born with a passionate soul and an inquiring mind, was left to her own devices to satisfy as best she could longings that were more appropriate to an adventurous lad than to a gently born young lady. It was not unusual for her to wish that the Duchesse de Montargis had provided Auguste with a younger brother instead of a sister. However, it was not in her nature to complain, and for the most part, she submitted to the dullness of her fate with good grace and a certain degree of wry humor, channeling all her energies into her school lessons and her music.

It was her music, however, that truly brought meaning to Isobel's life, providing an outlet for her abundant energy and an opportunity to pour all the passion of her vibrant soul into her singing. She would spend hours seated at the pianoforte in the music room at Barford Court going over a particular passage again and again, straining to reproduce the perfect pitch and rich timbre in her voice that she heard in her head. This search for perfection in her music was the only challenge to which she could devote herself in a way that satisfied her craving to do something extraordinary in her life, to be something greater than herself, much the way her noble ancestors had sought glory on the field of battle. Her father never tired of recounting the valiant deeds of the de Montargis who had been winning honor for their name since the time of Charlemagne, distinguishing themselves from Tours to Jerusalem even at the disasters of Agincourt and Crécy. Isobel had sat at his knee listening to these stirring tales and longing with all her heart to be part of this noble quest for fame and glory, but there was nothing heroic about life around Barford. No particular skill or daring was required for country walks with Jane and Emily, and the only bravery she was asked to demonstrate was to endure the stifling boredom of the hours spent trying unsuccessfully to learn the delicate needlework of which her mother was justly proud.

It was only in her music that Isobel could strive after something grand, something that lifted her above her mundane existence, and she threw herself into it with her entire being. It was only her music that allowed her to dream of making a life for herself that was very different from the one that either the inhabitants of the genteel, pastoral world at Barford Court or the closely knit group of noble émigrés in and around London could possibly conceive. There was no one who would understand or sympathize with these dreams, especially her dearest dream of all, that of becoming an opera singer. No one she knew could have conceived of the notion that a well-born young lady would wish to become an opera singer, even a singer of the caliber of Catalani. But Isobel's dreams extended even further than that, for she aspired not only to rival Catalani, but to surpass her, to have not only London, but all of Europe, at her feet. She knew very well that her parents, especially her father, would expire with horror at the notion of having a daughter on stage. The entire émigré community would disown her. If they had divested one of their poverty-stricken members of his Order of St. Louis simply because desperation had driven him to become a servant in order to support himself, what would they say of a woman who displayed her talents in public in order to earn a living? The Duc de Montargis and his coterie would sooner condemn her to a life of aristocratic penury than have her become an *actrice de l'opéra*, but Isobel, who had never derived any benefits from her aristocratic heritage except a life of exile and dependence on the kindness of others, did not agree with this philosophy. To her, being able to support oneself by one's skills was far more honorable than relying on the glories of a past lost beyond redemption to win pity and support from the sympathetic English.

Supporting herself and her family had become Isobel's goal and to that end she had devoted herself to her studies so that she could become a music teacher as Monsieur Verbier had done. She had been right to do so, for just at the time when Emily and Jane had begun talking about their come-outs the Duchesse de Montargis had succumbed to the wasting disease that had plagued her for so long and the duc, who had only accepted the Barfords' charity for his wife's sake had insisted on moving to London to be near the rest of the émigré community. However, his pension from the British government had barely allowed them to survive and Isobel, forced once again to accept the aid of the Countess of Barford, had been most grateful for her suggestion to her cousin Lavinia, Duchess of Warminster, that Isobel de Montargis would make an ideal music teacher for the duchess's daughters, Augusta and Sophia.

The Duc de Montargis was horrified at the idea, but necessity was a stern taskmaster and he was able to assuage his injured pride somewhat with the thought that even though his daughter was perilously close to holding a servant's position, it was in the household of one of England's most respectable families and she would be consorting with persons of the highest quality. Still, this did not keep him from shaking his head sadly every time Isobel returned home from giving lessons.

The duc would have preferred her to earn a living in the company of others of her kind working in the ateliers along with the Comtesse de Sallanches, the Marquise de St. Veran, and other noble ladies who spent their days bent over fine needlework, but Isobel had no skills along those lines, for which she was immensely grateful. The idea of spending her days listening to the gossip of these former aristocrats chatting of bygone days and the doings of their own narrow circle was stifling in the extreme and she constantly blessed her fingers, so clumsy at embroidery and so skillful on the pianoforte, for saving her from this restricted little society.

She continually promised herself that she would break away from it all. She would fulfill her dream to become a singer of incomparable renown, so sought after and so admired for her voice that none of her society's petty rules would apply and she would be free to live her life as she wished, to travel and bring music to admiring audiences all over the world.

Isobel was thinking of this dream now as she hurried down Duke Street toward their lodgings in Manchester Square. She was late, having allowed herself to be beguiled by Lord Christian's stories of the Peninsula, and now her papa would be wondering what had become of her. It had only been the strident chime of the music-room clock and the appearance of Sophia and Augusta's governess that had brought them all back to the present, so immersed had they been in descriptions of the rugged Pyrenees, beautiful Spanish senoritas, bold Portugese guerrillas, long marches over impossible terrain, and daily life in camp.

Lord Christian had a gift for making it all come alive, reminiscing about curious characters and local color in a half-mocking, half-humourous tone that made it all seem like a glorious adventure. The little girls had been spellbound, and Isobel, too, had been drawn in to it all, but she was drawn for entirely different reasons. There had been an undercurrent of pain that occasionally crept into his voice, a sorrow that darkened his eyes. His words had spilled over one another in such a way that Isobel sensed that the telling of it all somehow released him from an unbearable pressure that he had been suffering. What had caused that pressure, what memories were behind that pain? She could not help wondering at it, at the contrast between the teasing ironic gentleman with the rakish airs who had intruded into her practice session and the indulgent uncle who regaled his nieces with stories, between the dashing soldier and suffering man she had sensed under that handsome, bold exterior.

Rounding the corner into Manchester Street, Isobel pushed these intriguing thoughts from her mind, slowed her vigorous stride into the smooth graceful pace demanded of a well-bred young lady, and composed her features into the quiet, submissive expression of a dutiful daughter; not those of a young woman who had been relishing visions of herself performing before adoring crowds or who enjoyed an invigorating walk from Grosvenor Square, and certainly not one who had traded gibes with the dashing and impudent uncle of her pupils.

Chapter 3

The Duc de Montargis was to be found, as usual, at his desk in the corner of what he called the drawing room, though its size more nearly resembled that of a small sitting room. The duc had debated with himself for some time over the placement of the desk, for by rights it should have been in the room below and at the back of the house, which had clearly had been designed for that purpose. But in the summer the windows of the drawing room afforded him a glimpse of green and trees in the center of Manchester Square. Even now, in the pale January sunlight it offered a vista more similar to the one from his own library at the Hôtel de Montargis in the Faubourg Saint-Germain, and it allowed him to forget from time to time that he was no longer looking out over his own beautifully tended formal gardens in his beloved Paris, but a square in a foreign city. Steeped in tradition as he was, he had even felt the need to defend this unusual arrangement to his daughter, but she had laughed indulgently at his concerns, pointing out that all of their neighbors, the Comte d'Artois, the Duc de Berri, were making do with vastly reduced spaces themselves and were not likely even to notice that he was putting the room to such unconventional use, and even less likely to call attention to it. "You must sit and write in the spot most conducive to your inspiration, Papa," she had replied, planting a kiss on his worried brow.

So it had been settled and the desk had been placed in the drawing room, but the duc still suffered the occasional pang at having his working space taking up a room that should have been devoted to purely social gatherings until Isobel had had the brilliant notion of asking the Duchess de Gontaut to paint a screen that could hide the offending area from the rest of the room whenever guests were invited.

"*Bonjour*, Papa."

The duc looked up to see his daughter, bonnet dangling in one hand, illuminated by a weak ray of sunlight slanting through the window. With her exquisite features, the finely chiseled nose and chin, the beautifully sculpted lips, the delicate dark brows, she was almost as lovely as her mother had been, and the image of all that was grace and feminine beauty. She should have been the doyenne of her own chateau by now, or at the very least, the focus of a group of admiring courtiers. Instead she was here in this poor excuse for a drawing room, her music tucked under her arm, checking on her papa before going below stairs to help Marthe with the preparation of their plain, but nourishing dinner.

The duc sighed and laid down his pen. He knew he should be grateful that he was alive, that his daughter was alive, that his son—the duc stifled the thought. He would not think of Auguste now. He never thought of Auguste anymore if he could help it.

"How is it going, Papa?"

"Ah, I did not feel up to working on it today. I had no heart for it, *ma fille*, so I have been writing instead an article for the *Courrier d'Angleterre* which Monsieur Fauche-Borel assures me is distributed on the Continent so that all the world can see what we suffer at the hands of those regicides who call themselves Frenchmen. *Naturellement* I do not hold Monsieur Fauche-Borel in high esteem, for no one who was a true gentleman would act as an agent for any government, but if Lord Grenville, who *is* a gentleman, has convinced the British government to pay for the printing and distribution of the paper then I feel I must do all I can to support the endeavor."

"And I can think of no one who could write more convincingly for the cause than you, Papa. Did you attend Monsieur's drawing room today?" Sensing her father's melancholy mood, Isobel did her best to turn his mind to a more cheerful topic. The Comte d'Artois's weekly receptions for the few surviving members of the court, though a poor substitute for the elaborate functions he had once held at Versailles, never failed to restore her father's dedication to the members of the royal family and to rekindle the hope that one day they would again all be gathering at Versailles or the Tuileries.

"*Mais certainement.* I should never miss attending one."

"No, of course not. And who was there?"

"Oh, the usual, Uzès, Choiseul, Castris, FitzJames, though, now that I think of it, FitzJames was not there. I believe he and the duchesse were visiting the Condé at Wanstead."

"Yes. The other evening at Madame de Sallanches's the duchesse mentioned that they would be going to the country. And now, Papa, I leave you to your writing for I must go help Marthe."

Her father sighed. "I wish you would not. It is not fitting that a daughter of the house of de Montargis . . ."

"I know, Papa." Isobel hastily stemmed the lament she knew was about to begin. "But I like being useful. I know that Marthe can prepare dinner by herself, but I have nothing in particular to do and I like to help. It makes the task that much quicker and easier for both of us."

"*Useful!* A lady is not supposed to be useful—charming, yes, and decorative, *absolument*, but *useful*?" The duc shook his head and went back to his writing. His daughter was right; they *had* been over this many times before and she always overruled him. She had inherited the strong will of her grandmother, the Duchesse de Châlet-Gonthier and the pride of the de Montargis which, in spite of her gentle manner, made her a force to be reckoned with, but who could have thought that these patrician traits, passed through the blood of generations of aristocrats, would have manifested themselves in a desire to be self-sufficient and self-supporting? It must be the cold, damp air of England that was responsible for this odd state of mind, otherwise there was no accounting for it. It was a strange climate, to be sure, and only the strong survived. His sainted Louise had struggled against it for her children's sake, but in the end she had succumbed to its unhealthy fogs and incessant rain.

The duc had no doubt that the weather was somehow to account for his daughter's insistence on dragging herself to Grosvenor Square every day all for the sake of a few *sous* when she could have remained at home living on the pension he received from the British government. To be sure it would be rather a restricted living, for their rent was seventy pounds a year and his pension as a former senior officer in the army a mere ten guineas a month, but it would have been possible to survive gracefully enough as all their friends were.

There was simply no explaining his daughter's passion to be doing something except the climate which had made the English themselves into such a dull, industrious race. Of course her exposure to the Barfords had also contributed to it, for if one had not known that they were the owners of Barford Court and much of the surrounding countryside, one would never have guessed that the Earl and Countess of Barford belonged to the nobility, so hard did they work at tasks that should have, in the duc's opinion, been turned over to an able steward. Nor did they participate in court life or evince the least interest in it; instead they demonstrated an almost unnatural concern for local affairs, engaging themselves in the most pragmatic manner by writing letters in support of various causes or journeying to Parliament to speak to certain issues and then returning immediately to the country without spending any time in London. There was no wit, no dash, no spark of gallantry in their conversation or their lives and sadly, his daughter seemed to have absorbed this same mania for being productive rather than decorative.

To be sure, Isobel, graceful and lovely as she was, always attracted a crowd of admirers at the weekly salons held at the lodgings of one or another of their acquaintances, but all too often she would try to beg off an invitation, complaining to her father, "All they do is talk, Papa, and I would so much rather be doing. If only they would talk about something useful I should not mind it, but they talk of nothing at all. They do not wish to convey ideas in their conversations as much as they wish to demonstrate their own cleverness. I would so much rather stay at home and read a book; at least that way I would learn something."

And when he in distress would protest, "But, *ma fille*, how will you ever find a husband if you shut yourself up at home?" she would only laugh.

"And what would a husband bring me," she would ask, "more faded glory and a smaller pension than the one on which we now live? You see, Papa, it is far better for me to stay at home and practice my singing so that I might become a better music teacher. That would do more for me than a husband would."

The duc would shake his head in resignation. He knew there was no changing her. Even as a child Isobel had been the serious one, working doggedly at her lessons or whatever task she had put her mind to. She could not be distracted until she had completed the particular project to her satisfaction. It was his son, Auguste, who had shown the natural sparkle of a courtier, who had flourished in their small, select society and had distinguished himself among the young gentlemen of his coterie for his gaiety and wit. Given the opportunity to join in a social occasion, he had no difficulty in laying aside whatever he was doing in order to take part in the merriment. Yes, Auguste could be counted on to seek out other gallants in any group and become the most gallant of them all. But, he told himself, he would not think of Auguste.

The duc gathered together the papers he had been working on. He had had too much for one day. It was time for his walk, time to bow to Monsieur in his carriage as he returned from his visit to Madame de Polastron, and perhaps time to encounter Monsieur's son, the Duc de Berri, as he made his way to dine at his father's house. The regularity of the Comte d'Artois' existence made it possible for all of them, not just his son, who could count on his returning home for dinner from Louise de Polastron's at precisely the same time each day, to feel as though some semblance of order and of the French court still remained in this barbaric land.

While her father was doing his best to ignore thoughts of his son, Isobel was doing nothing of the kind. In the kitchen Marthe produced from the pocket of her apron, a grimy, creased letter that looked as though it had passed through many hands and been secreted in many a pocket. "Jacques, Monsieur's coachman, brought this for you. He said it had been given to him by a man who came from the Continent to visit Monsieur."

"Thank you." Taking the letter, Isobel dragged a stool underneath one of the two windows, at the far end of the kitchen and sat down. She smoothed the letter in her lap and began to read aloud while Marthe peeled potatoes and chopped onions, sighing gustily all the while.

"Ma chère soeur," it began. *"Je t'embrasse . . ."* By the time she had finished reading Isobel too was sighing and blinking rapidly.

Marthe wiped her eyes with the corner of her apron. *"Mon pauvre petit, mon brave."* She sighed again. "What will become of him, off fighting wars for that, that . . ."

"But, Marthe, when Monsieur Bonaparte became first consul and granted amnesty to some of us, Auguste and the Comte de Neuilly and the others had to return to France to see what they could do to reclaim some of our property. Auguste is not your *petit garçon* anymore. He is not even a young man any longer, but someone in the prime of his life. It has been years since you last saw him. This letter speaks of the army being at Château Thierry, so at least he is now back in France and no longer in the Peninsula."

"But to be forced into the army when all he wished to do was to claim his birthright—it is too terrible," Marthe moaned.

"Calm yourself. He would have been in the army even if there had not been a revolution in France. After all, Papa was in the army."

"But Monsieur le duc was an officer in the *king's* army."

"True, but war is war, and a dangerous proposition no matter whose army one is in. Until now, the only difference between being in Monsieur Bonaparte's army and being in the king's army is that Auguste was less likely to be killed under Monsieur Bonaparte who has, until recently, been far more successful than the king's armies have been."

Marthe shook her head and sighed again lugubriously. "It is only because that Corsican monster signed a pact with the devil that he was able to conquer so much of Europe, but you see, *le bon Dieu* is on our side and Bonaparte is losing now. But to think of my poor Auguste in his clutches and risking his life for a man who is not even of noble blood, that . . . that . . ." It was too much. Marthe pulled out a handkerchief and blew her nose fiercely.

Isobel laid a comforting hand on her loyal servant's shoulder. No one could have been more devoted to the de Montargises than Marthe, who had been her nursemaid when the revolution broke out. Of all the servants, Marthe had stuck by the family the longest as they wandered across Europe seeking out a safe haven. At first she had been solely responsible for looking after the baby Isobel, but as time went by she took on a variety of tasks, acting as lady's maid to the duchesse and nursing her in her final illness. Now she was cook, housekeeper, confidante, and surrogate mother to her former charge.

Even though Isobel had been her duty, Auguste was her pride. To her, he was the embodiment of all the noble characteristics of the de Montargises, with his burning love for France and his devotion to the chivalric ideals that were his heritage. Ever since he had been a child he had played at being a soldier, making wooden swords and strutting grandly around the chateau giving orders to imaginary armies. He had been an impressionable ten-year-old when they had escaped from France, old enough to have some idea of the state of affairs and young enough to believe that if he had been but a few years older he could have put himself at the head of a group of loyalists from the surrounding countryside and rescued Paris from the bloodthirsty mob.

After their arrival in England, Auguste had begged his parents to let him attend the school in Kensington run by the son of the Marshal Duc de Broglie, where the pupils sported military-looking blue tunics with gilded buttons, but the fee was beyond the resources of the de Montargises and he was sent instead to Stonyhurst in Lancashire, where he and his friend, the Vicomte Walsh de Serrant, resigned themselves to accepting their education at the hands of Jesuits from Liège instead of the military training for which they longed.

Burning to avenge the wrongs of his family, Auguste had begged to be allowed to join the Prince de Condé and his army in Europe and had objected strongly to reading Roman law under Monsieur de Barentin, but his father had been insistent. Since what little remained of the Condé's army was dwindling rapidly and as Walsh was to be a fellow pupil at Monsieur de Barentin's, he had accepted the inevitable.

While Napoleon's seizure of power and his subsequent military successes effectively spelled the end of Auguste's hopes to prove himself in the Condé's army, it had eventually offered him the opportunity to prove himself in another way by risking the return to France after peace was declared in order to try to win back some of the de Montargis property. As a would-be soldier, Auguste could not but be impressed on his arrival in France by the First Consul's military genius in spite of his loyalty to his family and friends and his dedication to the royalist cause. However, no sooner had Auguste arrived than he had been identified as an educated and able young man and had been forced to join Napoleon's army, for there was a pressing need for men who could lead the swelling groups of raw recruits from the country.

At first he and the other recently returned émigrés had held themselves aloof from their fellow officers, but gradually, when faced by fire from an opposing army, even though that army was ostensibly supporting the royalist cause, he had been forced to depend on the men in his company for his own safety. From that dependency had come a grudging respect which he had communicated to his sister in his letters. *These men, some of them from the most humble of backgrounds, have worked diligently to become what they are and one cannot but be impressed by their energy and ambition. I cannot help but wonder if more of us had demonstrated the same energy and ambition instead of bemoaning our fate while sitting safely in England whether we might have prevailed against the revolutionaries. If we had, at least we should have been free from the scorn of the rest of the world.*

Isobel could still remember the terrible day they had received this letter. She had trembled as she had read it out loud to her father. His pale face had grown red with fury and he had gasped for breath. "He forgets himself in all his glorious adventures." The duc had choked on his words. "That a son of France should mingle with those . . . those . . . *sans culottes*! It is execrable. He betrays his heritage, the memory of his past, the king himself, by serving with them."

"But, Papa, he had no choice. He was made to join the army."

"Then he should have refused."

"But they would have executed him as a traitor; surely you would not have wanted that."

"Better death than dishonor. It is the way of the de Montargises," the old man had replied with haughty grandeur.

His daughter had remained silent. It was not the moment to point out that he himself was alive while many of his fellow émigrés who had gone off to fight had lost their lives at Valmy or during the disastrous Quiberon expedition.

When the next letter arrived many months later the duc had declared that unless it contained news of Auguste's return to what remained of the French court in England or of his death then he did not wish to hear it, nor did he ever wish to see his son again except as a member of the French court or an officer in one of the armies of the Allies. Isobel had obeyed her father's injunctions and there was no more reading aloud of letters from Auguste. In fact, she and Marthe had agreed that it was best for the health of Isobel's father and the pace of the household if all further communications from his son were kept secret, hence the sharing of the latest news in the kitchen.

There were parts of the letter that Isobel kept even from Marthe for she, loyal though she was to Auguste, would not have understood some of the sentiments expressed. *It is incredible to me, dear sister, how for so many years I could have believed that birth alone made me superior to my fellow man. How foolish and dangerous a notion that is, for it allows one to become complacent and weak and it deprives one of the companionship of some incredible fellows. What Napoleon has done to restore the glory of France by using the talents of men from all stations in life is nothing short of brilliant. I could not be a loyal Frenchman and not admire his enormous contributions. You say that Papa calls me a traitor to my country, but what is my country? Is it an aging king and a foolish court who impoverished it for so many years before the revolution and have learned nothing from all this upheaval? Or, is it the land where I was born, the people who defend it, the artisans and lawyers, the merchants and farmers who are all working to restore it to its former glory?*

Isobel smiled secretly as she folded the letter and tucked it into the pocket of her dress. Auguste might sound dangerously Republican, but he was still the Auguste she remembered from her childhood: passionate, idealistic, and fiery in his devotion to his country. She lifted her apron from its hook and put it on, thinking as she did so, how long it had been since she had last seen her brother and how much she missed him.

Chapter 4

The Duke of Warminster, seated in his imposing mahogany library listening to his own brother's account of his experiences in the Peninsula, was thinking much the same thing—a long time had passed since he had last seen Christian and the intervening years had changed him, or had they?

There were lines of maturity, etched by hardship, in the tan face, and from time to time there was a hint of sorrow in the eyes that were set deep under dark brows. His expression was one of gravity that almost seemed to border on sadness, but it was the same old Christian who spoke, passionate to a fault and no more responsible, it seemed. "No, Albert, I have *not* come to my senses and sold out, nor will I, as I told Scunthorpe two years ago when you sent the poor devil all the way to Salamanca to remonstrate with me. I understand that Lavinia cannot bear any more children, but I do *not* understand that this situation makes it imperative for me to quit the army. Should something happen to me there is always Cedric. He would make just as good a duke as I would and I do not feel that it is my duty to save my own skin and desert my fellow officers to kick my heels in the drawing rooms of London on the unlikely possibility that you might stick your spoon in the wall."

"Cedric!" Albert snorted. "Really, Christian, have you no sense of family pride? Cedric is not a pure Hatherleigh. Surely you would not have someone who is not a pure Hatherleigh as head of the family. You cannot be serious."

"Never more serious in my life, old fellow. Ceddie would make an admirable duke. Why he is almost as much of a stiff-rump as you are."

"Is there nothing that you do not consider a fit subject for levity? One would think that a war and very nearly getting yourself killed at Vitoria could have instilled some sense of honor in you, some . . ."

"Contrary to what you seem to believe, Albert, there is a great deal that I take very seriously—duty to my country, responsibility to my companions-in-arms. What I refuse to take seriously is the absurd notion that I should spend my life as understudy to a man who is the picture of health simply because the blood runs purer in my veins than in those of someone who is far more suited to the position than I."

Albert stared at his brother aghast. Since boyhood Christian had been an irreverent scapegrace and completely devoid of any respect for family or tradition. A certain amount of irresponsibility was expected in a younger son, but it was also expected that after a period of sowing wild oats that the younger son would either see the error of his ways and return to the path of respectability and decorum or completely disgrace himself and fade from polite society altogether. Christian had done neither. Instead he had taken it into his head to defend Europe against the depredations of that little Corsican upstart, leaving Albert in the uncomfortable position of being unable to approve of him and equally unable to disapprove.

"Hmph. Well, that is all very well for you to say, but some of us are not allowed the luxury of choice in our actions, being born to a role of responsibility and a sacred trust, and . . ."

"And no one could be better suited to it than you, Albert." Christian smiled disarmingly.

Caught entirely off guard, the duke shot a suspicious glance at his brother, who returned his gaze ingenuously. That was the worst of it; just when one was thoroughly annoyed with Christian's contrary nature, he would suddenly do an about-face, completely depriving one of the luxury of righteous indignation.

"But I have taken up too much of your valuable time, brother, I must go pay my respects to Lavinia." And flashing another impish grin, Christian was gone, leaving the duke to fume silently.

Damn him, why did his younger brother always make it seem as though he, Albert, was somehow being unreasonable when it was Christian who was always flying in the face of convention. Albert sighed heavily and returned to the mountain of correspondence on his desk. While he was glad that the heir to the dukedom was home safe and sound, he did find it personally more trying to be in close contact with his insouciant younger brother than it was having him an ocean away.

Though the Duke of Warminster might view Lord Christian's return with mixed emotions, the duchess suffered no such qualms.

She greeted her brother-in-law with delight when he was ushered into the drawing room. "Christian!" She held out her hands to him. "I could hardly credit my ears when Sophia and Augusta told me you were here." She peered at him anxiously. "And your wound? Are you completely recovered then?"

"Completely. It was only a ball in the shoulder. It went right through, a clean shot and quickly mended."

Indeed, a closer look at his tanned face and powerful shoulders assured her that he appeared to be in prime twig. "I am so glad. One hears such dreadful things of the conditions over there. Adrian Wargrave's mama says that he is still much weakened from the fever he contracted there and it has been an age since he was treated for a saber cut."

"It is true that the cure can sometimes be more fatal than the injury. But you are looking well and very modish, if I may say so."

"The war has not rid you of your flattering ways, I see." Lavinia sank gracefully on the canary-colored damask sofa and patted a space next to her invitingly. "Come tell me everything. You know the young women will flock around you the moment you appear. Heroes are all the rage right now." And it was a rare hero who was more attractive than her brother-in-law, Lavinia thought as she smiled up at him. La, but he was handsome with those penetrating gray-green eyes, the mobile mouth, and high cheekbones. Why, if she were not a married woman he could easily make her pulses quicken, and as it was, she was extremely conscious of what a fine-looking man he was.

Christian grinned. "Nor have you lost yours, Lavvy. But I am just a rough old soldier and I hear that young women these days demand nothing less than perfection, a veritable tulip of the *ton*, someone with a distinct air of fashion."

"Pooh. And you are not? You cannot fool me, Christian, for all your talk of rough soldiers. I'll wager your coat was made by Stultz himself."

"Naturally." He chuckled. "You cannot think that Wellington would have any of his officers dressed by an inferior tailor, but you still would never confuse me with one of the dandy set."

Lavinia shook her head, smiling. "No, there will be no mistaking you for that." No one who saw those broad shoulders, narrow waist, long legs, and the athletic grace with which he moved would ever think that Lord Christian Hatherleigh was anything but what he was, a man in peak condition, up to any physical challenge and a horseman of incredible skill. And therein lay his charm. He was so different from most of the men who filled London's ballrooms and drawing rooms. There was an energy, a forcefulness about him that set him apart and made him quite irresistible to the fairer sex. "But mark my words, you will be all the rage."

"Anything or anyone new is all the rage. Even I have not been away from the *ton* so long that I do not remember that. But any interest will be over in a fortnight or less when it is realized that not only am I a younger son, I am also not hanging out for a wife."

"Are you not, Christian, not even now after all the years of camp life? Surely you must long for someone to make you a comfortable home."

"I have Digby for that."

"Your batman? Come now, let us be serious for a moment."

"I *am* being serious. He made me extremely comfortable in the worst conditions with next to nothing. Think of what he could do with Farwell Abbey. With a little help from Hickling he should do very well indeed."

"But even a butler, no matter how good or devoted he is, cannot supply a woman's touch."

"Very well, Mrs. Reigate, then."

"You are impossible, Christian. You know very well what I mean and it is not a housekeeper."

"I do. And I have experienced enough of a, er, *woman's touch,* as you put it, to know that it means that I shall be required to dance attendance on her, to escort her to all the balls, soirees, routs, and musicales at which she wishes to be seen, and not to the more interesting places I wish to go, such as . . ."

"I should hope not!" Lavinia's cheeks flushed a deep pink and her delicate brows rose in horror.

"Such as the theater and the opera," Christian finished smoothly.

"Oh, you, you . . . And who is to say that women do not enjoy the theater and the opera?"

"Oh they enjoy it well enough, if there is a sufficiently large crowd to admire them, but they would rather be at a ball where they can hear all the compliments from their admirers without interruption from the actors and actresses or the singers."

"You are as dreadful as ever. Not all women are like that. There are some serious sensible ones as well."

"I have yet to meet one besides you, my dear, and you *know* how vast my experience is." But even as he said this Christian realized that what had been true for so many years might no longer be accurate. He just might, in fact, have encountered his first serious woman, and here in this very house. Recalling the blue eyes flashing in annoyance at his intrusion into the music room, he was not entirely successful in stifling a grin. Yes, perhaps he had actually met a serious woman after all. But even if he was mistaken, he was going to enjoy himself learning more about her. He would have to be careful, however, for even now his sister-in-law was regarding him suspiciously. "Just remembering some of my past experiences," he explained.

"Oooh! You are the most provoking man!"

"There, you see, Lavvy, you should not be in such a hurry to inflict me on some poor unsuspecting female. For if *you* find me provoking, and you have the patience of a saint—anyone married to Albert qualifies for sainthood in my book—why no other woman would wish to have a thing to do with me."

The duchess was not about to let her brother-in-law escape so easily. As a self-respecting female, she knew it was her duty to make sure that such an attractive and eligible man was put in the way of single females. Certainly her husband had made it clear enough that she was responsible for finding his brother a wife who would make him settle down and take up the responsibilities he had so successfully avoided all these years. And besides, it would be so much more amusing to attend the *ton* events with Christian at her side. He could always be counted upon as a dancing partner while Albert loathed dancing, and Christian's cynical commentary on the foibles and presumptions of the Upper Ten Thousand was always wickedly humorous and often enlightening.

Yes, he would definitely make a much more satisfactory escort than her husband, who always made straight for the card room at any fashionable gathering or stood in a corner prosing on about politics with other like-minded and equally dull husbands. Now that Christian was home, Lavinia was going to enjoy the Season more than usual. "There is no escaping it, sirrah, I should be shunned by all of the most important fashionable hostesses if it were to become known that you were in town and I had not made a push to get you out and about," she declared firmly. "We shall begin with tonight. It is Lady Boroughbridge's rout and it is sure to be brilliant for it is so early in the Season that no one has yet tired of such things. I will not take *no* for an answer. Now I must run along and see to it that Cook knows we are dining in tonight before going to Lady Boroughbridge's.

Chapter 5

It certainly did seem, if one were to judge by the press of carriages in front of Lady Boroughbridge's imposing mansion in Berkeley Square, as though the entire fashionable world was beating a path to her brilliantly lit doorstep. To Christian, who was one of the throng of elegantly attired guests moving slowly upstairs to be greeted by the hostess, it felt like nothing so much as an army massing for a charge. Certainly Lavinia looked prepared to do battle. Cheeks flushed and eyes bright with anticipation, she eagerly scanned the crowd ahead of her, reconnoitering for elegant females.

"There"—she took her brother-in-law's arm in a firm grip—"that stately blonde ahead of us with the wreath of roses in her hair is the latest incomparable. All of London is at her feet, but I am sure there is no one as dashing as you paying court to her. She is the youngest daughter of the Earl of Rochfort."

"Who is one of the warmest men in the country and a fine old family. You won't go wrong there. Her mother was a Delaville and a great heiress. She herself must have at least twenty thousand a year," Albert supplied helpfully.

"Ah." Christian's eyes swept past the blond head to a lively-looking dark-haired young matron behind her, who, turning to speak to her companion, had caught his eyes and was now surveying him speculatively under coyly lowered lashes. From what he could remember of *ton* functions before his sojourn on the Peninsula, it was not the young misses, but their married sisters who offered far more amusement and many more possibilities to the attentive gentleman.

"Yes, and there is Lady Clarissa Harleston over there. This is her second Season. She took the *ton* by storm last year, but it is said that she is so extremely nice in her taste that not even Lord Fotheringay could convince her to accept his hand and he is a most unexceptionable young man." Lavinia prattled on, happily unaware of the glazed look in her brother-in-law's eyes.

Why had he allowed himself to be dragged here? Five years away and nothing had changed. The well-bred faces looked just as bored as they had at the rout he had attended with Lavinia the night before he had sailed to Lisbon. Albert now had a touch of gray at his temples and Lavinia's slender waist had thickened, but aside from that, they had not changed a jot. As Christian surveyed the extravagantly turbaned heads of the dowagers nodding to one another, the graying locks of their escorts carefully arranged *à la Brutus* or the more daring *coup de vent,* he surmised that the rest of their peers had undergone a similar lack of transformation.

It was incredible to Christian, though he knew he should have expected it, that they looked as untouched by the conflict that raged across Europe as if it had never occurred, as if Bonaparte and his Continental system, his code of laws, his conquering armies, did not even exist, had never existed. He could not help wondering, as he surveyed the bejeweled crowd, what Isobel would say to it all.

Surely her parents had attended similar parties in Paris or at Versailles. Had they been equally unconcerned about the world outside of the ballroom as the people chatting around him at the moment? In 1788 had they expected their crowd and their surroundings to remain as unchanged by 1793 as this scene was for him five years later?

". . . and I would like you to make the acquaintance of . . ." Lavinia's voice in his ear broke into Christian's reverie.

"I beg your pardon, I was not . . . I did not hear you and . . ."

"You were not attending." A dimple hovered at the corner of Lavinia's mouth. "I could see that you were somewhere else entirely so I thought I had better bring you back to the moment before you were presented to our hostess."

By now they were close enough to see the plumes in Lady Boroughbridge's headdress nodding as she greeted her guests. "And this is the hero returned triumphant," their hostess exclaimed theatrically when they had drawn close enough for her ladyship's slightly protuberant blue eyes to sweep appreciatively over Christian's well-knit frame, imposing in its severely cut coat and satin knee breeches. The simply tied cravat did not begin to compare with the ornate arrangements and absurdly high points of the dandy who had just been dismissed by Lady Boroughridge, but the contrast between the linen and the deeply tanned skin was all the more striking for the simplicity of his attire. "I vow I do not abhor Boney so much if it means it produces men such as these." Lady Boroughbridge fluttered her charcoal-darkened eyelashes at Christian as she extended a plump hand. "Lavinia, I had no idea that your brother-in-law was so well . . . I mean I had not seen him in such an age. He is nothing like Albert who . . . ahem, tell me, sir, are you not overjoyed to exchange camp life for the ballrooms of London?"

"But how could such a lovely lady even pose such a question?" Christian countered, suavely bending over a gloved hand so heavily covered with rings that it was a wonder she was able to lift it.

"He has not been away at the wars so long that he has forgotten how to charm a lady. It pains me to let such a gallant gentleman out of my sight, but you had best take him along, Lavinia, as there are scores of young ladies simply dying to welcome a poor soldier back to his native land." With a knowing wink and a chuckle, Lady Boroughbridge retrieved her hand and waved them toward the ballroom.

"There, you see, I told you that you would be all the rage. Albert, you need not glower so; naturally everyone is delighted to have your brother back where he belongs. Now run along to the card room for I simply will not have you standing around looking uncomfortable when I know you would much rather be playing cards and I would much rather be dancing with Christian. My feet are a good deal safer with him as my partner than with you."

"He is a dear to come with us," she whispered in Christian's ear as Albert, sighing with relief, turned toward the card room, "but he is miserable at these things. He simply can not move to the music and stomps around like a great ungainly bear. One must be exceedingly nimble to avoid being trod upon and my friends simply dread his asking them to dance. It is a great deal better for everyone if he joins his cronies in the card room and settles down to a comfortable game of whist. Now, let me see, to whom do I particularly wish to introduce you? Ah, there is Lady Meldon and her daughter Amelia. I expect that Meldon has already fled to the card room. Albert says he is a very fine whist player and related to all the best families. His sister is the Countess of Halford and there have been Meldons at Meldon Hall since before the Conqueror."

Lavinia urged Christian forward within earshot of a hatchet-faced woman in a purple turban who was expounding emphatically to a shy-looking young woman with a wreath of pink roses in her dark curls. "My dear Lady Meldon, how delightful to see you here and, Amelia, how charming you look. How fortunate that we should find you in such a crush for I am longing to present my brother-in-law, Lord Christian Hatherleigh to you. Perhaps you recall that I once mentioned to you that he has been away fighting in the Peninsula.

Christian barely had a chance to establish the color of the young lady's eyes, which were hastily lowered as she gulped and nodded at him, but her mother had no such qualms. He found himself subject to a steely stare before she nodded abruptly. "Very well, you may lead Amelia to the floor in the quadrille."

He did not know whether to feel flattered or insulted. Was being a veteran of the Peninsula or brother-in-law to Lavinia enough of a recommendation that someone would hand over her daughter to him without even bothering to ask if he wanted that daughter, or without conversing with him enough to assure herself of his suitability? However, there was no mistaking the tone of command in her voice. Bowing dutifully, he meekly offered his arm to Amelia and led her to the dance floor.

Apparently none of the Meldons had any conversation, for Amelia said nothing during the entire set. And while it was true that the quadrille did not lend itself to discourse, Amelia did not even have the temerity to mention the weather; in fact, she never truly did look him in the eye. The only indication that she was aware of Christian's presence at all was the flush that rose in her cheeks every time the dance brought them together. With a dragon for a mother, she was entitled to a certain amount of reticence, but when Christian's perfectly unexceptionable attempts at eliciting some response from her failed to win more than a nod, he gave up and finished the set in silence.

After such an experience with Amelia, he might have been pardoned for wondering if five years away from polite society had turned him into such a boor that no gently brought-up young woman would have anything to do with him. This notion, however, was quickly dispelled by his next partner.

Lady Selina Atwood, youngest daughter of one of Albert's rabid Tory acquaintances from Parliament, was thoroughly enjoying her first Season. "For at last Papa has allowed me to come to town. I truly thought that I should go mad if he did not, for there is absolutely nothing to do in the country, especially when everybody who is anybody is come to town, and how he could expect me to contract any sort of eligible alliance, buried as I was in the wilds of Oxfordshire, I have no idea. He was of the mind that I had no need of a Season, that he would choose a husband for me without my ever having to leave Atwood Park. Have you ever heard of anything so perfectly Gothic? But Mama would have none of it. 'Just because Maria married someone she has known this age in Oxfordshire does not man that Selina will do the same,' she told Papa. And she was entirely in the right of it. Why I would no more be the wife of a rustic like John than I would ride a cow, ha, ha. No, I want a proper Season with proper gentlemen paying court to me in the proper way."

At last she stopped to draw a breath and Christian, who was beginning to worry that she might continue until she turned blue in the face, would have been relieved except for the alarmingly coquettish glance she directed at him. He felt like nothing so much as a poor rabbit transfixed by a predator's glare.

It was with a great sense of having escaped a fate worse than any that had awaited him on any battlefield that he restored Lady Selina to her mama, and he was just beginning to congratulate himself on this when a silvery voice at his shoulder promptly dispelled any hopes he might have had for a few moments of peaceful reflection.

"Christian, how positively thrilling to see you! I had no notion you were in London. Naughty man! How long have you been here without telling me?"

He turned to look into the laughing eyes of Lady Jersey. "Sally! Had I known you were that *desperate* for the sight of me, I should have stopped at Osterly en route from Plymouth before calling in Grosvenor Square."

"Silly man. Now you are being absurd." She tapped him lightly on the shoulder with her fan. "But you may waltz with me by way of an apology."

There was no lack of conversation here either, but it was far wittier than Lady Selina's and Sally soon won a reluctant chuckle from him with her wicked description of Lady Meldon. "What you have done to win that harridan's approval, I can not fathom, for she is so high in the instep that she almost dares to give me the cut direct when I approach her. My guess is that the browbeaten Amelia is so cowed in spirit that even those men who are looking for a biddable girl as a wife are scared off. Lady Meldon must be desperate if she is considering a younger son; either that, or your brother must be beating Meldon regularly at cards. But as far as the girl goes, la, one might as well be married to a corpse—a very rich corpse to be sure, but a corpse, nevertheless. We must find you someone more lively."

"But perhaps I do not wish for a wife, biddable or otherwise," Christian protested when at last he was allowed to get a word in.

"Of course you want a wife! One can not really begin to enjoy oneself until one is married, you know." She smiled meaningfully at him and rubbed the thumb of the hand that was resting on his shoulder back and forth. It was the most discreet of caresses, but nonetheless it was provocative in the extreme for the very public nature of it and Christian was left with no doubt in his mind that the lady wanted him.

"A wife would keep you safe to enjoy yourself without having to worry about being caught in the parson's mousetrap."

"A fear that would be entirely justified since the scene you are imagining would presuppose that I was already caught in it."

"Well, yes, you would be, but if you were to choose for your wife a young woman who had no particular interest in you except as an excellent match, a young woman who had her own ah, er, *interests,* shall we say, then you should not truly be *caught in the parson's mousetrap* as much as you would be freed to do whatever you like." Again, there was the slight but unmistakable pressure of her thumb. "And with whomever," she finished huskily.

Fortunately, for Christian's peace of mind, his partner caught sight of Lady Clarissa Harleston dancing with Lord Eldridge at that particular moment and her attention was instantly diverted. "Why I do believe that this is the second time she has stood up with Eldridge, and it is a waltz at that. I wonder if they are to make a match of if. He is older than her father, how very *intrigant.*"

By the time Christian rejoined Lavinia, who had also been whirling around the room on the arm of her cousin Lord Stratford, he was desperate for a moment's peace and seeing her flushed cheeks, he offered to fetch her a glass of ratafia. She accepted gracefully, allowing herself to be escorted to a chair by the pillars at one end of the ballroom while her brother-in-law went in search of refreshment.

When he returned she took the glass and sipped it eagerly. "Why thank you, Christian. How lovely it is to be so pampered. You will make someone . . ."

"I warn you, Lavvy, if you refer to me once again in terms of the matrimonial state, I shall most assuredly do you a mischief."

Instantly she looked so contrite that he could not help laughing. "Perhaps I shall not go to such an extreme, but as everyone else in this room is bent on doing the same thing that you are, I do rather feel like a fox run to earth or a pig at the market. Let us talk of something else—your daughters, for example. Sophia and Augusta have grown prodigiously. I know that it is five years since I last set eyes on them, but still I was not prepared for them to be such young ladies. Certainly I would not have recognized the grass-stained hoydens who were forever climbing trees in the two young misses who welcomed me to London and offered me refreshment in the most grown-up manner."

Lavinia sighed. "It is the merest veneer, I assure you. Give them the countryside and they will revert immediately to their hoydenish state you recall so well."

"Perhaps their music teacher can contrive to teach them the proper airs and graces. She is a most rigidly proper young lady indeed, and frighteningly elegant."

"Oh, Mademoiselle Isobel. She is a treasure indeed and, yes, she does have the French talent for fashion which gives her an air of elegance no matter what she is dressed in. As far as being rigid, I cannot say. Certainly the girls adore her. Perhaps you put her off." Lavinia quirked a teasing eyebrow at him. "You can be rather bold you know."

"I? Bold? I am shocked, Lavvy. I am as well brought up as the next gentleman. Albert did not get all the respectability in the family, you know. I would never be so disrespectful to a young lady as to be bold."

"*Bold* may not be precisely correct, *direct,* might be more accurate, or *forthright.* She is French, you know, and accustomed to French conversation. The French quite abhor our plain way of speaking."

"Then I shall make a mental note of it to be less direct, more gallant, the next time I see her."

"Ah," was all Lavinia replied, but her dark eyes took in a great deal more than her brother-in-law suspected. So he had been intrigued by Isobel. Lavinia had rather thought he might be, but then, Christian was intrigued by any beautiful face. A far more interesting question was how Isobel had reacted to him.

Chapter 6

At the moment, the young woman in question was surrounded by the brilliant conversation to which Lavinia had alluded. Isobel had accompanied her father to one of Madame de Sallanches's salons, though she would have infinitely preferred to remain at home in order to read through some music she had just purchased and prepare for the lesson she planned for tomorrow; however, the duc would not hear of it.

"You cannot refuse an invitation from Madame de Sallanches, *ma fille*. Only the most distinguished are invited to her salons and it would be an *impolitesse* of the worst kind to ignore such an invitation. Now, do not forget the candles; you know she has so little to live on that she is most appreciative of anyone who brings some extra light. Let us, at least for this evening, help her to have rooms as brightly lit as those she used to grace."

"Very well, Papa." Isobel had meekly gathered up a few extra candles and accompanied him as he made his slow progress toward the door.

As always, there was a crowd at Madame de Sallanches's but upon their arrival, their hostess immediately broke away from the group surrounding her and came over to greet them, her hands outstretched. "*Mes amis, que je suis enchantée de vous voir!* Isobel, *ma chère,* you are more beautiful than ever. I do hope that you will be so kind as to charm us with your singing, that is, if your papa will permit it. Have you seen the new arrangement of our favorite old song "Ah vous dirai-je Maman?" According to Madame de la Tour du Pin, it is reviewed in *Ackermann's Repository* this month. She saw it at her aunt, Lady Jerningham's, house. But come"—she took the duc's arm—"my cousin is here and is longing to talk to you. She arrived from Hamburg a few days ago with news of the Comtesse de Neuilly and many of the others. She is over there talking with *Maman* about the old days." Madame de Sallanches led them over to the corner where

Madame Foudron was deep in conversation with Madame de Sallanches's aunt, Madame de Saint Veran.

Seeing that her father was occupied, Isobel made her way to the fireplace, where she lit her candles and placed them next to the others brought by appreciative guests. Before she could rejoin the duc she was accosted by a slender young man with an elaborately tied cravat and shirt points so high he could barely turn his head. "Isobel, my goddess," he exclaimed, bending low over her hand. "I hope you will complete my joy at seeing you by allowing me to accompany your singing with my flute. Of course I could not hope to do justice to your exquisite talent, but I would die for the honor of making music with you."

Before Isobel could draw the breath to reply he had launched into a recital of the Duc de Berri's latest efforts to secure a suitable wife. "It is of course difficult to find someone worthy to be allied with royal blood, and so many of those whose birth and upbringing make them a proper match are Protestant. Ah, mademoiselle, you have no idea how he suffers."

Isobel, whose only true luxury was attending the opera whenever some kindhearted soul invited her, had witnessed the Duc de Berri falling under the spell of the actress, Amy Brown. She said nothing, but in spite of her effort to remain impassive, her expression betrayed her incredulity.

"*Non,* mademoiselle, I know what you will say, but the duc has a warm heart. It is his passionate nature that often makes difficulties for him, but if he were to be assured of the love of a wife, why all would be well. It is so difficult these days. He is a man born for court, a man whose wit and charm are wasted now, as are yours. It is a crime that such beauty and grace is confined to these humble walls when you should be adorning the ballrooms of Versailles or the Tuileries."

Isobel glanced desperately around her looking for someone, anyone, to stem the tide of her companion's conversation. The Comte de Pontarlier was a nice enough young man, always impeccably attired and endlessly gallant, but his entire life was so wrapped up in his tailor, the Duc de Berri, the Comte d'Artois, and their entourages that he could speak of nothing else, nor could he imagine that everyone was not as fascinated as he by every nuance of the royal family's existence.

Help, of a minimal kind, arrived in the form of Madame de Colignac, who laughing gaily, broke in on the comte. "What, Hippolyte, you have not found a bride yet for your royal master?

Shame on you. For a man whose diplomacy and courtliness are known far and wide, you have been strangely lacking in success. Did you not find someone suitable when you visited at the court of King Gustave? Truly you are most unlucky."

"But Madame knows that there are so few Catholic ladies of a lineage noble enough for the duc that it is most difficult to find a suitable wife for him. Truly it has been a task *fort exigeant,* madame."

"Ah, Hippolyte, for a man of your *politesse,* the task should be simplicity itself."

"But these days even the most revered titles of France do not command the homage and respect they once did, madame, as you well know." The comte sighed sadly and shook his head. "That the flower of the French monarchy should be reduced to searching for a wife; it is too distressing."

"Mon ami." Madame laid a comforting hand on the young man's shoulder and Isobel took advantage of the moment to slip away. She had heard it all so many times before, the commiseration, the mourning of lost glories, with no thought, no plans for the future. It was all so pointless that from time to time she found herself wanting to scream at them, *Forget the past!* But for her father's sake, she contained her frustration as best she could. He was too old to change and his health was not so good as it once had been. With his wife dead and his son just as good as dead to him, he had very little to live for except his memories and the friends who kept those memories alive for him.

"Isobel, *ma chère."* Madame de Sallanches touched her on the shoulder. "Would you be so good as to delight us with your music? We should be most honored if you would." Saved from further mindless conversation, Isobel hastened to comply. As always, she was able to lose herself quickly in her singing and push everything from her mind but the music as she tried to share its beauty with her listeners. Knowing her audience, she chose the tunes they had known and loved before their enforced exile, even the tunes that had been sung to them in the nursery such as "Si le roi m'avait donné," and she was rewarded by the rapt silence around her, the tears trickling down faded cheeks or welling up in the eyes of those too young to remember much more than attic rooms in Soho and Marylebone.

"Thank you, *ma chère,"* her hostess whispered in a choked voice after she had finished her last song. "Your singing brings us all so much joy."

Looking at the tearstained faces in front of her, Isobel was inclined to dispute that, but she said nothing. If they enjoyed recalling what was lost forever and could never be again, then, yes, she had brought them some measure of happiness. But it was easy enough to move those who were disposed to be moved. How well could she reach a real audience? Would she be able to touch the hearts of perfect strangers? That would be the true test of her skill and oh, how she longed for the opportunity to try.

Accompanying her father on their slow walk home, Isobel wondered if she would ever have the chance to try her talents anywhere else. In her most despairing moments, tired out by the lessons and the household chores, she sometimes feared that life would never change and that she would spend her days in the dwellings in and around Manchester Square listening to the same old stories, condemned to live among people who only existed in the past. It was not that she did not care for them; indeed she loved the poor, brave hardworking Madame de Sallanches dearly, and she admired the energy and tenacity with which she supported her family and the determination with which she entertained her friends, but Isobel still could not help feeling stifled by the tight little circle of friends who clung so desperately to one another for support. She longed to move among people with ideas, with plans for the future, with interests that extended beyond the search for a bride for the Duc de Berri.

"I saw you speaking with the Comte de Pontarlier," her father's voice broke into her thoughts. "He is a fine young man, such an ancient and illustrious family. An alliance with the de Pontarliers would be a most excellent thing."

"And why is that, Papa?" Isobel did not bother to hide the exasperation in her voice.

"Because, my child, there are few families left who are suitable matches for ours, and even fewer have sons of marriageable age."

"Papa, there is no *need* for me to be married."

"No need? Who is talking of need? I am speaking of what is right and proper." The Duc de Montargis paused, and then with an expression of distaste, as though he had bitten into a lemon, continued, " And, naturally, though I do not regard these things, he would bring the addition of another pension to the family."

Isobel snorted. "A pension that is spent entirely on his tailor, which is to say, no pension at all."

"That is the response of a *bourgeoise*, not the daughter of a de Montargis."

Isobel bit her lip. "I am sorry, Papa." She tried unsuccessfully to sound meek. "But I *am* a *bourgeoise*. I do earn my living, after all."

The duc was too overwhelmed with it all to reply. He shook his head sadly and trudged along in silence for some time. "It is being a *gouvernante* and going among *les Anglais* that has made you this way. If only you could do the needlework your mother did, you would still be able to, ah, *sustain* yourself, but you would be able to join Madame de Sallanches and the others in their atelier. At least then you would spend your days among your own kind, people of gentility and culture."

"The Duke and Duchess of Warminster are hardly barbarians, Papa."

Her father did not bother to dignify this piece of nonsense with a reply. Everyone knew the English had no culture. One had only to taste their food—dreadful overcooked mush—to know that. The mere fact that they continued to make their home on this fog-bound island was enough to convince anyone that the Duke and Duchess of Warminster had no taste, and it was almost certain they had no conversation; none of the English did. If they talked of anything at all, it was of their horses and dogs. How was his daughter going to be protected from losing her gallic *espièglerie* and charm if she were forced to spend her days among such people?

Truly, the only thing to do was to find her a husband, but it was becoming increasingly difficult to do these days. So many young men had gone to join the armies of the Allies fighting Bonaparte and others had returned to France to reclaim their heritage, so that there was hardly anyone left that was a suitable candidate. Something had to be done, but what? The duc resolved to call on the Comte d'Artois the very next day and ask for a private audience. Surely he might have some suggestion. Monsieur was nothing if not a man of exquisite taste and refinement and he would sympathize with a father's worries. Though the Comte de Pontarlier was obviously not to Isobel's taste, there might be someone known to Monsieur who would be suitable, someone that he himself might have overlooked or forgotten.

Comforted by this thought, the duc mounted the stairs to his own drawing room and accepted his usual nightly glass of milk from Marthe in a happier frame of mind. The evening at Madame de Sallanches's had not been entirely disappointing. It had been good to see Madame Foudron again and to learn that many old friends were still alive and well in Hamburg.

Chapter 7

The duc would not have been quite so optimistic perhaps if he had known that his daughter, in preparing for her lesson the next day, wondered more than once if she would encounter the unsettling Lord Christian Hatherleigh again. It hardly seemed likely, she reassured herself, for her presence in Grosvenor Square was confined to the music room, a place he probably had little reason to visit. No sooner had Isobel arrived at this conclusion than she found herself feeling just the slightest bit disappointed. True, he had been both rude and provocative, but his appearance had brought a momentary dose of energy and adventure into her otherwise confined existence.

Resolutely thrusting Lord Christian from her mind, she blew out the candle and climbed into bed, but she lay awake for quite some time staring up at the ceiling in the darkness. This evening at Madame de Sallanches's had forced her to confront much of her life which she managed to keep at bay during her lessons and her practice. Now it all came crashing back around her. Would she be forever condemned to seeing the same people time after time, to discussing the same past glories and lost way of life until she thought she would go mad? Isobel felt the panic rising within her as she thought of her father's determination to find her a suitable match, a match that would place her more firmly than ever in that shadowy world where the past was more real than the present. Her brother, at least, had escaped. Lucky Auguste. Even long marches and night after night in an uncomfortable tent would be preferable to the monotony she was forced to endure. At least he must feel alive, no matter how uncomfortable.

I will escape, she muttered to herself. Closing her eyes resolutely, she pictured herself on a brilliantly lit stage acknowledging the tributes of an audience gone wild with enthusiasm. This vision never failed to calm her, to give her hope. She knew she had talent; all she lacked was the opportunity, but that would come. She would make it come.

Inspired by this dream, Isobel practiced even harder the next morning in Grosvenor Square after giving her lesson. Alone in the Duke of Warminster's elegant music room, she went over her scales again and again, throwing herself into the songs that stretched her range and challenged her vocal agility. She even returned to the music room in the early afternoon after having given the girls their French lessons to practice some more. At last she could sing no longer. Her voice was beginning to weaken and her fingers were becoming cramped over the keys of the pianoforte. It was not until she rose, indulging in a most unladylike stretch, that she caught sight of the top of an auburn head leaning back against the sofa that faced the French doors overlooking the garden.

Shutting the cover of the pianoforte with a bang, Isobel was opening her mouth to demand an explanation from the clandestine listener when he rose, forestalling her. "Thank you, mademoiselle." Lord Christian bowed ever so slightly. "I cannot tell you how much this has meant to me. It has been a long time since I have been able to enjoy such a moment of peace and beauty."

Isobel shot him a suspicious glance, but there was not a trace of guile in his face. The gray-green eyes looking down into hers were serious, in fact, his entire expression was one of great gravity. "I see that you do not believe me, most understandable after our introduction, but you are . . . you . . ." He broke off in frustration. "There is no excuse for our first introduction. I behaved badly, and, with your permission, mademoiselle, I should like to wipe the memory of our first meeting from our minds and begin again. Allow me to present myself. I am Lord Christian Hatherleigh, Lieutenant Colonel in the Kings Own Third Dragoons, lately arrived from the Peninsula—a barbaric soldier, perhaps, but one who appreciates music of any sort, particularly when it is so exquisitely performed. Again I see that you are skeptical, for what could a man of war know about opera? I will have you know that I have attended more of Madame Catalani's performances than most people, for I first saw her in Lisbon before she made her debut in London. I know whereof I speak and I say that you are on your way to being a serious rival. You do not yet have her control, but your taste is infinitely better than hers and your interpretation adds to the impressiveness of your performance. Control can always be learned; taste, however, is a different matter altogether. In time I believe you could surpass her, certainly in tragic roles, which are not her forte."

The astonishment that succeeded the initial blank look on Isobel's face told Christian that the young lady now considered him a perfect idiot as well as a barbarian. Damnation! He had been babbling like a schoolboy. What had come over him? Christian had never before been at a loss for words with a lady. Even before going to university he had been famed for his address. Be it barmaid or dowager, he had been able to capture them all with his ready smile, quick wit, and bold assumption that women were as interested in him as he was in them.

But this girl with the serious eyes was different. She practiced with an intensity of purpose that made such things as coquetry and flirtation seem almost sacrilegious. Her obvious dedication to her art commanded a respect from him that he felt for very few men, much less women. He wanted, in the space of a sentence, to assure her of this, to let her know he appreciated the drive and determination that kept her going over the same notes again and again. He wanted to prove to her that he was knowledgeable enough to recognize her skill and that his words were no idle flattery. And he wanted this so intensely that he had babbled on like a witless fool. Christian ran a hand distractedly through the thick auburn hair. "Forgive me, mademoiselle, for rattling on. I just wanted you to know, I mean, I, well, thank you."

Her face remained frozen in an expression of polite astonishment, one delicate dark brow raised ever so slightly. Chagrined, he turned to leave the room with what little dignity he had left when he caught a glimpse of an enchanting dimple quivering in the corner of her mouth. His own eyebrows rose questioningly. "Mademoiselle?"

Isobel could not help it; she broke into laughter. "Monsieur, you look so funny, as though I were going to shout at you or scold you." In truth, she had been ready to scold him and then sweep from the room in an offended hauteur, but his awkwardness had been totally disarming. She could see that he was a man accustomed to charming women. His very presence in the music room was proof enough of that, for he would have known from their previous encounter that she would be annoyed to find him there. Quite obviously he had counted on being able to talk her out of that annoyance and had begun the conversation with a most flattering apology. When she had resisted him by refusing to accept it readily he had faltered in some confusion and proceeded with an awkward earnestness that was rather enchanting. Indeed, she liked him better for it. There had been a touch of the pedantic in this speech about Catalani that seemed out of place in a dashing war hero, but that had made it all the more intriguing and had convinced her of his genuine appreciation.

Christian grinned. "Well, you were frowning like a thundercloud, and in someone as intensely serious as you, a frown is a fearsome sight."

"Now you are funning." Isobel smiled. "But have you truly seen Catalani? I never have, but I long to. One day I . . ." Isobel stopped. Whatever was she doing confiding her most cherished dream to someone who was practically a stranger, someone who, if half the tales his nieces told about him were true, was never serious about anything except his thirst for adventure and excitement.

"One day you . . ."

"Ah, one day I hope to see her perform," she finished lamely.

But Christian was not going to let her get away with it that easily. He had observed the delicate wave of color wash over her cheeks, had seen the momentary confusion in the deep blue eyes and knew that there was more to it than that. "No, you can not fob me off so easily, mademoiselle. You were about to say something else. I am more than seven, you know. What were you about to tell me before you thought better of it?"

He was quick, there was no denying that, and there was also no denying the accuracy of his assessment. His eyes were fixed on her with an intensity that made dissembling impossible; in fact, it almost felt as though there were no need to speak at all, so well could he read her thoughts. Isobel's chin rose defiantly and she drew a deep breath. "I was going to say that one day I plan to be another Madame Catalani." There, she had said it. She gazed out at the garden and waited for the derisive laughter. Anyone else would have been horrified by such a revelation from a gently brought-up young lady.

"Bravo." Though his expression was amused, his voice was serious and warm with approbation.

Isobel looked at him in surprise. While she had not expected outright disapproval from a man who seemed to lead a somewhat unconventional existence himself, she had not expected support of her crazy dream.

"And how do you propose to accomplish this feat? And it *will* be a feat if you succeed even in competing with the divine Angelica, much less rivaling her."

A faint flush tinged Isobel's cheeks. He did not express horror at her aspirations as being the road to social ruin, but clearly he was not entirely convinced of her ability to succeed, in spite of his previous flattering remarks. To be sure, she *had* sounded rather arrogant, as if becoming the equal of the world's greatest singer was nearly a *fait accompli*. "I shall work very hard." Isobel's chin rose a fraction of an inch higher.

A slow, appreciative grin swept over Christian's face. "I am sure you will, but it will take more than hard work, you know, to bring you to the notice of the world. We must find you a sponsor, a patron, someone who can give you the opportunity to demonstrate your undeniable talent."

"We?" Isobel's voice was frigid. Though she was grateful that he had not dismissed her dream with well-bred dismay or, worse yet, laughed at it, she certainly did not appreciate his appropriating it. Part of the happiness she derived from her dream was that it belonged to her alone and to nobody else. She certainly did not want some brash soldier thinking he could be more effective in making it come true than she could. He might have more worldly experience than she did and he might be a man, but she knew music and singing and she could manage very well without him.

"Yes, *we*. I can help you find such a sponsor." Christian spoke with quiet assurance, but he was casting about frantically in his mind for the right person to help her achieve her goal.

"That is most generous of you, and though I naturally appreciate your kindness, I believe that your brother, who values my talent and skill enough to offer me employment, is eminently qualified to help me himself."

"Albert? Qualified?" Christian almost hooted with laughter. "Albert does not know the difference between a soprano and a baritone and has even less interest. Why I should be surprised if he had ever sat in the family's box at the opera. Certainly *I* can not remember his ever being there and I go whenever I am in London."

"Nevertheless, it would be most improper of me to accept . . ."

"Improper? A young woman who wishes to become an opera singer, even the première opera singer in the world, lectures me on propriety? No, mademoiselle, that is doing it much too brown." Christian shot a keen glance at her. Isobel's fingers knotted and unknotted the short sash of lilac sarcenet that tied the front of her morning dress, accenting the gentle curves under the striped muslin. The flush tingeing her pale complexion deepened.

He was in the right of it. To announce boldly that one aspired to a career that no true lady would even remotely consider and then refuse help on the grounds of propriety was quibbling indeed. Isobel had no ready response. She stood there fiddling with the strip of lavender in her hands, wishing desperately that he would go away and leave her alone.

But Christian was not about to leave the young lady to her own devices. He had been thinking about her far too much since their last encounter, had laid his plans to be in the music room when she finished her lessons with his nieces far too carefully to give up so easily. In order to establish these plans, he had been forced to be extremely circumspect, enlisting the aid of his own family's most trusted retainer in order to obtain an accurate picture of Mademoiselle de Montargis's routine. Grinstead had known Christian since he had been in short coats and any obvious questions about Sophia and Augusta's lovely instructress would have immediately aroused the butler's suspicions. Therefore, it had taken several seemingly casual questions about the household in general and a good deal of listening to Grinstead's lament about the recent decline in the quality of servants in particular before Christian had been able to establish the hours that Mademoiselle Isobel was most likely to frequent the Duke of Warminster's music room.

"Forgive me, mademoiselle, for teasing you, but it was irresistible, you know."

"*Non*, monsieur, you are absolutely correct to say such a thing. I know that I must accustom myself to such remarks, but indeed, I have no need of assistance." Unconsciously Isobel straightened proudly and squared her shoulders.

Christian's eyes twinkled. So it was not the impropriety that upset her, but his interference that she feared. Very well. As someone who prized his own independence above all else except perhaps his honor and his country, he respected that, but he was also well enough versed in the ways of the world to know that success in anything depended as much, if not more, on influence than it did on talent. The challenge was to provide her with that influence without undermining her fierce pride. Having decided that he was going to help Mademoiselle Isobel de Montargis become as widely acclaimed as Angelica Catalani, Christian was not about to be hindered by such trivial details as Mademoiselle's own resistance to the idea.

"I would never be so bold as to suggest that you are in need of assistance, mademoiselle. I merely wish to assure you that you may command mine at any time. I am a soldier, as you know, and I am therefore accustomed to fighting for a cause when I see one. If I have overstepped the bounds, I beg your pardon, but I assure you it was only meant as a compliment to your considerable talent and to your ambition."

Isobel eyed him cautiously, but there was no hint of dissembling in his expression. She was inured to elegant speeches filled with fulsome praise and no action; in fact, she had spent a lifetime listening to them, but this man seemed to be in deadly earnest. The eyes fixed steadily on her never wavered. Instead, they seemed to gaze deep into her heart, honoring what he saw there. It was an entirely new experience for her to be taken seriously, somewhat unsettling at first, but Isobel found that all in all, she rather liked it. "Thank you, my lord. I did not mean to sound ungrateful, but . . ."

"But our dreams belong more to us if we can achieve them on our own than if we are forced to rely on the help of others. I understand, mademoiselle, believe me, I do, and I have no wish to deprive you of that. Now tell me how it is that you have conjured up this dream of yours? Surely as a noble daughter of France you are not being encouraged in such a pursuit by your family or your friends. I would expect that it is quite the opposite case. And if I were to hazard a guess, I should say that even acting as an instructress to the daughters of the Duke of Warminster is rather frowned upon and that marriage to some young man of ancient and illustrious lineage is being urged on you." The sardonic expression on his face and the raising of one mobile dark brow conveyed a rueful sympathy and understanding that gave Isobel the oddest feeling that she had found an unexpected and unlooked-for ally in this irreverent intruder. No wonder the rigidly proper Duke of Warminster had looked uncomfortable at the mention of his brother's name the other day, for Lord Christian Hatherleigh seemed to have a cynical attitude toward all that was constraining and confining in a system to which his brother unquestioningly and rigorously adhered.

"You could be correct in that guess, monsieur, but fortunately for me, the financial aspects of the situation work to my advan-

tage. Though Papa receives a small pension so generously donated by your government as well as the occasional token of appreciation from Monsieur, I mean, the Comte d'Artois, he does
not have enough to support our household, nor does the *young
man of ancient and illustrious lineage* and therefore, I am com-
pelled to do what I can to contribute to our welfare."

Christian chuckled. Mademoiselle Isobel, her eyes dark with
anger or flashing with conviction, was certainly lovely enough to
make a man catch his breath, but with a mischievous smile on her
face and a naughty twinkle in those eyes, she was utterly enchanting. "You are fortunate indeed to be so poverty-stricken as to be
forced to 'sing for your supper,' as we English say."

Again he seemed to understand something about her that no
one else she had ever encountered had been capable of recognizing, much less comprehending. Unwillingly, Isobel found herself
warming to the man who kept interrupting her treasured moments
of solitude with the pianoforte and her music.

This moment of mutual appreciation was broken by the arrival
of the duchess, who swept into the music room clutching a cream-
colored note in one had. "Mademoiselle, I was wondering if . . .
oh, Christian, whatever are you, I mean, Grinstead did not inform
me that you were here. How remiss of him. I cannot think why he
would be so neglectful. It is most unlike him." Lavinia frowned
and shook her head slightly.

"Grinstead did not announce me as I expressly asked him not
to. I wished to listen to Mademoiselle Isobel's artistry without interruption from solicitous relatives." He smiled teasingly at his
sister-in-law, daring her to reply.

"Oh." Lavinia glanced from Christian to Isobel and back again.
There was a devilish gleam in her brother-in-law's eyes, while the
young lady remained cool and composed; however, Lavinia could
not help feeling that Isobel was resolutely avoiding his gaze.

"At any rate, mademoiselle, I was hoping you could alter the
time of tomorrow's lessons as Mama has written that she is recovered from the cough that was plaguing her and is most anxious to
see Sophia and Augusta."

"But of course, madame. I shall be happy to attend them at
your convenience. When would you like me to come?"

"Hmm. Perhaps an hour earlier and then . . . no, for Mama will
undoubtedly expect . . . er, let me think. Perhaps we should forego
tomorrow's lessons altogether. Yes, that is better I think."

"Very well, madame. Then I shall see them the next day at the usual time. Now, if you will forgive me, I must be going for Papa will be wondering what has become of me." Grateful for the duchess's interruption of a conversation that had become almost too intimate, Isobel hurried from the room before anyone could detain her.

Chapter 8

Isobel might have escaped further contact with Lord Christian the next day and even the day after that, but she was unable to avoid him for very long. No one who knew him would have expected Lord Christian Hatherleigh to ignore any lovely woman, but it would have been entirely impossible for him to resist seeking one out who was not only exquisitely beautiful, but who sang like an angel as well.

In fact, Isobel expected it herself, though she would not admit to herself whether or not she wished for him to do so. Thus it was that she was not at all surprised to see him when she entered the music room to practice two days later. However, this time he seemed less inclined to talk than to listen as he sat quietly, his chin resting in his hand gazing unseeingly out into the garden beyond. Even when she had finished running through all her exercises and had sung two arias to her satisfaction, he remained silent, lost in thought. A nod in her direction was the only indication that he was aware of her at all.

Isobel told herself that she was grateful for this forbearance as later she negotiated her way carefully through the press of traffic as she crossed Oxford Street, but in fact she was just the tiniest bit disappointed that he had not wanted to converse with her, even the slightest bit, not even a comment on the remarkably fine weather they had enjoyed for the past few days. He had been silent to the point of being taciturn, a marked contrast to the previous glib encounters. Again she was impressed by the sadness in him that she had sensed at their first meeting. What was it? Where did it come from? Not even among her fellow émigrés, even those who had lost husbands and wives to the revolution, had she felt the deep sorrow that she felt in this man, and it made her more curious than ever about him.

In spite of herself Isobel found herself wishing to know more. However, she was not prepared to discuss him with the duchess, nor was she acquainted with anyone else who knew him so there was nowhere to turn for information except the man himself. But how did she begin without seeming either brazenly forward or intrusively inquisitive?

Fortunately, Lord Christian provided her with just such an opportunity several days later. Isobel had just finished working on Iphigenia's hymn to Diana from Gluck's *Iphigènea en Tauride* when Christian, who had again been staring silently at the garden, spoke, as if in an afterthought. "That has always been one of my favorite operas, Mark's as well."

"Mark?"

"Yes, Lord Calvert. He was a splendid fellow, up for anything, and ready to stand by one though the worst of it without a murmur."

"And?" Isobel held her breath, hardly daring to ask, but wanting to know. "What happened?"

"A ball in the chest at Vitoria. We were the terrors of our regiment, like Gluck's Orestes and Pylades."

Isobel, who had risen from the pianoforte, walked slowly over to the sofa and sank down on it opposite him. "Tell me about him."

"We met the day I joined the regiment and though he was younger than I, having bought his commission right out of Eton while I joined after university, we became friends. Everyone loved Mark. He had a talent for amusing that I have never seen equaled. Even in the most uncomfortable of situations he could bring a smile to men's faces with his stories, yet he was the bravest of the brave, always out in front leading everyone on. He was always saying 'Come on lads, it is not so bad as you think.' And naturally, once he had said that, it was not. He was doing just that in the thick of the fray at Vitoria when his luck ran out. I grabbed his horse as soon as he was hit and pulled them out from the first charge, but he would have none of it, told me if I insisted on taking him back to safety he would finish himself off with his own pistol. So I took his place. I told one of the other lads to look after him, but it was too late. Another thing he always said was 'That's the way I want to go, Chris, at the head of a charge, none of this becoming an old stick hanging around the clubs boring young men with stories of my youth. I want to be the one they tell the stories about.' And we do, we do." Christian's voice trailed off. He remained for some time staring at the floor, chin in his hands, the dark brows drawn together in a frown of such intensity that Isobel knew that what he was seeing in front of him was not the pattern of the Aubusson carpet, but the smoke and carnage of battle.

Now she understood where the sorrow came from; it came from the horrors of war and the loss of beloved friends. She wanted to offer comfort, but what comfort was there for memories like his, and what could she, a woman who lived the most circumscribed of lives, say that could possibly be of any solace? "I . . ." Isobel hesitated. Perhaps it was best not to intrude, not to say anything at all. But on the other hand, she could not bear the bleakness in his face. "I . . . I wish I could help you to . . . to forget it, or to . . ."

He turned to look at her now, the gray-green eyes focusing on her with an intensity that was almost more uncomfortable than his profound silence had been. "Oh, but you have. To hear your voice, to lose myself in the music, even for a little while, proves to me that there is still beauty left in the world, there is still life . . ." Christian paused and drew a deep, steadying breath. "I apologize. It is the height of rudeness to intrude on someone's private time as I have intruded on your practice sessions. To then burden them with one's problems is adding insult to injury. I have no excuse for it except that your music wipes away some of the darkness of it all. Lavinia is right; I have no notion how to behave in polite society anymore." He rose to go.

"No, please, sit down. I do not mind in the least. It is just that I have so little knowledge of these things that I can offer nothing except my deepest sympathy, but that seems so trivial in the face of what you have experienced. I cannot conceive of what it must be like to endure what you must have endured. I cannot imagine how one finds the courage to face such things."

Christian smiled grimly. "One arrives at such things by degrees, beginning as I began, with a noble idea, the idea that by joining up I could do something to stop the French from conquering all of Europe, that I could stop Napoleon and the war he was bringing to much of the world and help bring back prosperity to England and the Continent. Then, too, it is a very fine thing to join a bunch of lively, adventurous fellows who share the same sentiments. And there is the challenge of testing one's skills against the enemy. There is even the excitement of the charge, of men and horses risking all and plunging into battle. It is only afterwards, after a dozen charges and countless dead and wounded that the doubts set in. At first the anger against those who have killed one's friends and comrades is enough to keep one going, but sooner or later, there is just the resignation and the sorrow of it all for everyone, friend and foe alike."

"But you did not give up."

"No, I did not give up because by then I truly understood why I was fighting. It was not to stop the French or Napoleon, but to stop the battles and skirmishes, to stop the war, to bring peace to us all, to let the farmers in Spain and elsewhere rebuild their ruined villages and to return to their peaceful existences."

"And you did," she replied softly.

Christian looked at her in some surprise. The blue eyes that gazed steadily back at him were filled with compassion and understanding. Somehow, talking to her had helped him put it all into perspective. All those lives were lost, but they had not been wasted. He felt as though the wounds that were his memories of battle were beginning to heal at last. They were still painful, but they were not the raw, open wounds that had been, now they were more like a dull ache. "And I did," he reiterated slowly. He looked at her intently for a moment, then nodded slowly. "Thank you."

"For what?" It was Isobel's turn to look surprised.

"For listening. Most people simply dismiss such things. They want their heroes, but they do not want to hear what made them heroes. War simply is not a topic for polite conversation." His lips twisted into a bitter smile. "But then, I have never been one to confine myself to topics of polite conversation."

"I find polite conversation rather dull myself. One never learns anything of interest from polite conversation."

"How very true. You are most wise, mademoiselle."

"Perhaps it is because I have had a surfeit of conversations myself. I am tired of listening to people who discuss anything but the problems that are truly troubling them, people who talk in order to forget or to avoid confronting things too painful to confront."

Her stormy expression and the passion throbbing in Isobel's voice were as eloquent as words. So she did understand a great deal of what he was feeling. "Then I must be a refreshing change for you, mademoiselle." The teasing note had crept back into Christian's voice.

"Well, a *change*, at any rate." The dimple flashed again at the corner of her mouth. She was about to continue when the sound of the duchess's voice in the hallway made her glance at the clock on the mantel. "Gracious, look at the time. I must be going."

Before Christian could reply, she had gathered up her music from the pianoforte, snatched up her bonnet and pelisse, and hastily put them on. "I have tarried here far too long. Papa will be wondering what has become of me," she explained as she forced the ribbons of her bonnet into a rather bedraggled-looking bow. She gave it a final tug and whisked out door, but not before Lavinia saw her and paused in her conversation with Grinstead to ask after her daughter's progress. Isobel responded favorably enough, but her answer was uncharacteristically brusque and she seemed so preoccupied as to make the duchess wonder what had occurred to ruffle the young lady's coolly elegant air.

Lavinia peeked through the door of the music room. "Christian?" She fixed her brother-in-law with a suspicious frown. "You have not been plaguing Mademoiselle Isobel, have you?"

"*I*, plague someone?" He raised one eyebrow in mock dismay. "How can you be so unkind? I never try to plague people; it is far too fatiguing."

"Christian!" Lavinia's tone descended from suspicious to threatening. "I will not have you vexing Mademoiselle Isobel. She is far too quiet and self-effacing as it is without your alarming her."

"Mademoiselle Isobel, quiet? Surely we are not talking of the same person. Why, she very nearly took my head off for being a barbaric intruder the first time we met. And she very nearly did this time as well."

The grin that accompanied this speech was so disarming that Lavinia chuckled in spite of herself. "It is too bad of you, Christian. Must you pursue every young woman that crosses your path? Isobel's life is difficult enough without adding you to its complications."

"*I*? A complication? You are being most unfair, Lavvy, when you *know* I always do my best to help people with problems in their lives, especially the pretty ones."

"You are incorrigible, Christian, and yes, that is what I am afraid of," she responded darkly. "Now, be off with you, you scamp. I must see how the girls are doing with the rest of their lessons." And shaking her head over him, Lavinia gathered up her skirts and headed up the stairs toward the schoolroom. On the first landing, and out of sight of her brother-in-law's sharp eyes, she paused, allowing herself to indulge in the tiniest smile. So that was the way the wind blew, was it? Christian truly was interested in the beautiful young Frenchwoman, for he never would have run the risk of encountering his elder brother without some strong inducement.

While it was true that at this particular moment Albert was most likely to be found deep in political discussion with his cronies at White's, one could never be certain when he would return home and Lavinia was familiar enough with the inevitable friction between the two brothers to know that Christian tried to keep his contact with Albert to a minimum. With the best of intentions, her husband never failed to rub his younger brother the wrong way by prosing on, as he insisted on doing whenever Christian made his appearance, about family history and family duty in a way that was bound to set his adventurous sibling's back up. Lavinia had remonstrated with her husband time and again, but to no avail for the inevitable response was *No harm in the lad? Hmmph. No harm in someone who indulges in every adventurous whim without a thought for anyone but himself. Someone who risks his neck without the least consideration for the noble lineage he is risking along with it. No Lavinia, you are too soft on the lad. Someone must make him see his duty and apparently I am the only one around here who understands what that duty is.*

It was in vain that Lavvy pointed out that a thirty-year-old man who had spent the last five years commanding a cavalry regiment in the Peninsula was hardly a *lad* and that he was equally unlikely to listen to a civilian two years his senior who prosed on about duty and responsibility. Eventually she simply held her tongue and did her best to insert herself between the two of them at family gatherings and tried to keep any conversation to unexceptionable topics whenever they were together.

At any rate, it did appear, from her discovering him twice in the music room at Warminster House, that Christian was taking an interest in Mademoiselle Isobel. While it was true, as Lavinia had accused him, that he was always attracted by a pretty face and often inclined to flirt with one, he was equally protective of his bachelor status and therefore, rarely, if ever, exhibited any serious interest in any particular young woman for fear of having his name linked with hers. Christian's apparent seeking out of Mademoiselle Isobel was quite a departure from his usual behavior, which was to involve himself in conversation with a young lady once and ignore her completely the next time he encountered her. Lavinia's curiosity was thoroughly piqued and she resolved to pass by the music room rather more frequently now that she knew he was a regular visitor.

Chapter 9

However, Christian, veteran campaigner that he was, had not missed the speculative gleam in his sister-in-law's eye as she had chided him for plaguing Mademoiselle Isobel, and he was not about to furnish her with further reasons for conjecture. He was remarkably circumspect in his movements for the next few days and though he was longing to continue his conversations with the lovely instructress, he confined his visits to Grosvenor Square to a time when he was sure she would not be there, such as the early hours in the morning when his nieces could be found mounted on their ponies and heading toward the park for their daily riding lessons.

"Uncle Christian, Uncle Christian!" Gussie had shouted at him with unladylike glee the first morning he had appeared just as the groom was bringing around their ponies. "Come ride with us in the park. You will not believe how well I can make Prince mind me."

"Gussie, you must not screech like some heathen and it is not at all ladylike to boast about how well you ride. You sound like a common braggart," her sister chided.

"But it is true. I do make Prince mind me, better than you make Titania mind you," Gussie protested.

Sophia did not deign to reply to such an unworthy remark, turning instead to smile graciously at the groom as he helped her mount.

Christian winked at the infuriated Gussie. "Never mind, my girl. Come along, then and let us see if you can live up to your claims."

"I can. I can." Gussie muttered under her breath as, casting a defiant look at her elder sister, she scrambled onto her pony's back without any assistance.

She was as good as her word, and when they had reached the park, she put Prince through his paces with the skill of a natural-born horsewoman.

"Very good, Gussie, most impressive, but do not become so confident that you are careless. A horse can sense inattention in an instant and you could find yourself on the ground before you knew what happened."

"Oh Prince would never do such a thing. He is so tame he would not hurt a fly."

"Prince might not, but you are not going to be riding Prince all your life. From what I have seen of you, young lady, you will be wanting to test yourself soon enough on some prime bit of blood with a temper to match."

"Like your Ajax?" The little girl glanced at him provocatively.

Christian chuckled. "I am too anxious to keep Ajax on his best behavior to hand him over to a neck-or-nothing rider like you. Ajax has lived a long and exhausting life and he deserves a peaceful old age. But perhaps we can find another horse for you to try."

"Will you? Will you? Promise?"

"Yes, but only if you apply yourself to your other lessons with as much diligence as you do to horseback riding. I hope you listen to all that Mademoiselle Isobel tells you and that you practice faithfully."

Gussie fell silent, chewing self-consciously on a wisp of blond hair that had escaped from her bonnet.

"No she does not. She would rather ask Mademoiselle about the revolution than learn French or music," Gussie's older sister volunteered as she trotted up sedately to join them.

"You must not plague Mademoiselle Isobel," Christian added. "Undoubtedly her life is difficult enough without a recalcitrant pupil to worry or to beg tales from her that might upset her."

"But she knows ever so many people who have such stories to tell. She is friendly with Monsieur who is brother to the king who was put to death on the guillotine. When I asked her 'Monsieur who?' She told me that he is simply called Monsieur. He used to be called the Comte d'Artois, but when his brother the king was killed, the king's other brother, the Comte de Provence who used to be called Monsieur, became king and now the Comte d'Atrois is called Monsieur. It is all very complicated. I asked her if she knew Marie Antoinette, but she said no, she had been too young. She had seen her once but that is all and she does not remember anything more about her except that she was pretty and laughed a lot. She did not even know who she was, but her mother told her it was the queen."

"Gussie, you must not ask her about King Louis XVI and Marie Antoinette." Sophia was aghast.

"Why not? I think it is very interesting that they were put in prison and that they had their heads chopped off by the guillotine."

"But I am sure that Mademoiselle Isobel does not, and I am sure it makes her very sad to have lost all her friends," Sophia protested.

"But she has not lost all her friends. Lots of them are still alive and they live here in London. She often complains about all the parties she must attend with her papa." Gussie shot a triumphant look at her sister.

"Then she must live rather near these friends if she sees them so often," Christian probed ever so delicately.

"I think that she lives near Monsieur for she mentioned her father's calling on him and I know that they do not keep a carriage so he must have walked and, since I know her father is an old man, he must not have had to walk far." Gussie, secure in her superior knowledge, directed a condescending smirk at Sophia.

"Ah, near Baker Street, then?"

But the name meant nothing to Gussie.

"And she said they also moved from the country to their house in London when her mother died so they could be near her father's friends and near their church." Sophia was not about to be outdone by her younger sister.

Christian racked his brains trying to think of churches serving those of the Catholic faith that were to be found in London, but could come up with none except the chapels attached to embassies of the foreign powers—the Sardinian in Lincoln's Inn Fields, and the Spanish in Manchester Square. He had heard that the Duc de Berri lived in Manchester Street and it seemed likely enough that other émigrés must live near someone so central to the court as the Duc de Berri, and, if Gussie was correct, the Comte d'Artois was not far away in Baker Street.

A sly smile hovered around Christian's mouth. Manchester Square and Manchester Street were not in his daily routine, which began with a ride in the park usually followed by a peek in at Tattersall's to see the latest in horseflesh that was for sale, regular sparring at Gentleman Jackson's, shooting at Manton's, or the occasional visit to Signor Angelo's for a little swordplay, and finishing up with a congenial bottle or two with acquaintances at Brooks's or an evening at the opera. However, he did have friends now stationed in the Portman Square barracks that he had not seen in some time. He might look in on them and saunter home with a little detour by way of Baker Street and Manchester Square, some time in the early afternoon when he might catch a glimpse of a tall, slender woman with music under her arm.

The first morning riding with his nieces had proven to be so instructive that Christian often joined them as they were setting off from Warminster House. And equally often he accompanied them home again, stopping to exchange a few words with their mother as she returned from visiting her favorite Bond Street establishments.

In fact, he was a frequent-enough visitor that his brother, never one to notice anything that was not directly under his nose, remarked on it one evening as he and his wife were driving back from Lady Daventry's soiree. Albert had allowed himself to be dragged along because Lord Daventry, aside from being the owner of several hugely prosperous coal mines was a man of some political influence in the north who had not yet allied himself with any particular faction in Parliament. Albert, having spoken at great length with his lordship that evening, had gotten him to agree to meet the next day with his closest political cronies. Encouraged by this success, and having downed more than his usual quantity of port, he was in an expansive mood as they rolled along toward Grosvenor Square. "Grinstead tells me that Christian is a frequent visitor lately, not that *I* have seen him."

Lavinia smiled in the darkness at the pettish note in her husband's voice. Different though the brothers were and critical though he might be of Christian, he still longed to be sought out and consulted by him. "But, my dear, you are so often from home that it is unlikely that anyone who calls on you there would find you."

Albert considered this a minute before replying. "What you say is true. Perhaps he has come to his senses at last and is seeing the responsibilities that lie before him. I had almost given up believing that he would come round, but he is a Hatherleigh after all, even if he has not acted like one until now. It is too bad that he has missed me. I shall make it a point to be there more often so that I may offer him some direction."

"But, Albert, I do not think that you are necessarily the reason for his visits," Lavinia ventured gently.

"Nonsense. Why else would he call at Warminster House?"

"Well, he has been riding a good deal with Sophia and Gussie."

"Hmph. Child's play. A man who is as fine a horseman as Christian does not ride with children by choice. Mark my words he has something else on his mind."

"I quite agree with you there, dear."

"Any idiot can see that, Lavinia. He has other interests on his mind besides two nieces who are more rambunctious than they should be. As I said, I shall make it a point to be around the next time."

"But, Albert, I do not think that you or the family is the object of that interest," Lavinia objected softly.

"Well, what else is there of interest?"

"Mademoiselle Isobel."

"Mademoiselle Isobel!" Albert's large jaw dropped, making his long face appear even blanker than usual. "Mademoiselle Isobel?"

"Yes, dear. You remember her, she teaches the girls their music and their French."

"A governess? Christian is interested in a governess? No, Lavinia, I may not be so nimble-witted about these things as some, but I know my brother would never be interested in a governess—an opera dancer perhaps, but never a governess."

"Mademoiselle Isobel de Montargis is not just any governess, my dear, she is a French émigré of impeccable background and prodigious talent who was highly recommended to me by Mama's friend Lady Barford with whom she and her family lived for many years after the de Montargis escaped from France."

"I'll not have a Hatherleigh consorting with some damn Frog, Lavinia, and there's and end to it—a governess at that. I am astounded that Christian, who has spent so much time fighting those damn Frogs, will have anything to do with one, even if she *is* a female."

"But, Albert, he was fighting Napoleon. The French émigrés are on our side."

"She's French, ain't she? The exiles are no better—a pack of papists living off pensions from our government with no more gratitude for what we have done to save their lives than . . . Bah! they carry on their little court and make merry in their salons as though the death of their king and queen had never happened. I tell you, I have no patience with the French—royalists or otherwise."

After this tirade, Albert lapsed into gloomy silence while his wife strove mightily to think of some more salutary topic with which to distract him. "Grinstead tells me that the new footman is doing very well and he feels much encouraged at how quickly he has learned his duties."

A discouraging "Hmph" was the only reply, so she abandoned this effort and fell silent herself, hoping fervently that her husband would soon forget that she had ever mentioned Mademoiselle Isobel's name in connection with his brother's.

But Albert did not forget and he brooded over the situation for several days. Christian had always been a problem where women were concerned. They were forever falling in love with him. From the chambermaid at Warminster Hall, who neglected her duties to pine over the handsome fifteen-year-old lad, to the actress in his university days, to some of society's more dashing matrons, he had always found himself in situations of a most sensitive nature. In all honesty, Albert had to admit that Christian had never been the one to initiate these situations, but in Albert's opinion, if his brother had exhibited the proper sense of what was due to his position in society instead of adopting the easy, friendly air that characterized his relations with the servants and all his social inferiors, these regrettable affairs might never have occurred.

Albert had been all for getting rid of the chambermaid, but somehow Christian had gotten wind of this and protested mightily. "You must not blame the girl for falling in love with me, Albie, she cannot help it." Christian had winked broadly at his brother, whose rigidly disapproving expression had not altered in the slightest. "Why not put her in the kitchen? At least there our paths will never cross and she will constantly be under Cook's eye. That would cure anyone of a grand passion."

"I wish you would not call me by that ridiculous name. It is entirely unsuitable," Albert had responded irritably, but he had followed his brother's suggestion and peace, along with some semblance of order, was once again restored. But the maid was only the first of many women who had been irresistibly drawn to his brother, all of them highly unsuitable. While it was true that as he got older more of the women were from his own class, they were always women with reputations that did not bear much looking into. Albert was thankful that none of the women whose names had been linked to Christian's were eligible young ladies of good family. His brother was too confirmed a bachelor to tempt them, and those who did happen to be attracted by the teasing smile, the rakish air, the wicked glint in the gray-green eyes, or the athletic physique, were quickly warned off by their watchful mamas. However, the fact that Christian preferred to be avoided by these well-bred young women only infuriated Albert all the more.

But this young woman was someone over whom the Duke of Warminster had some influence and he resolved to use that influence at the very first opportunity.

Chapter 10

While Albert deplored Christian's latest interest in the fair sex as being rather too close to home, he would certainly not have been reassured by his brother's appearance at a snug little house in Marlyebone the very next day. The owner of the house, however, felt quite differently and had welcomed Christian with open arms.

Blanche Desmoulins had been plain Blanche Miller, a rising star in a group of traveling players from Derbyshire until she had been discovered by Lord Ormesby, who had repaired to his country estate to recover from disastrous losses at the gaming table. He had been so pleased with the young lady that when he had recouped his finances sufficiently to return to London, he had taken her with him, set her up in a house in Marylebone, and, at the lady's request, introduced her to some influential people in the theatrical world.

Blanche, who possessed a fair degree of natural talent as a dancer, was even more distinguished by her willingness to work hard as well as an ability to get along with everybody, a trait that endeared her to managers accustomed to coping with a variety of artistic temperaments, all of them difficult. It was this reliability that had soon won her a permanent position in the *corps de ballet* at the Royal Opera House.

Lord Ormesby had again been forced to rusticate, but by this time, Blanche had won herself a score of admirers and was well on her way to becoming a permanent fixture among the theatrical set. It was at this point that Christian, home on leave from the Peninsula and already bored to tears by a few days of *ton* parties, had discovered her. Neither the lady nor the gentleman had expected anything but a brief, physically satisfying relationship from the affair that had ensued and they parted cordially, but without great regret, when Christian left to rejoin his regiment. However, he had visited Blanche on the rare times that he returned, finding her easy company and a refreshing change from the exacting expectations of her more fashionable sisters.

Blessed with many wealthy admirers and commanding a salary from the Royal Opera Company, Blanche could afford to enjoy Christian's visits purely for the sensual gratification they afforded her and therefore did not plague him to devote more time and effort to her than he wished to.

Over the course of the years they had become friends, each finding in the other's company an appreciation and an acceptance that they did not find elsewhere. Therefore, when Christian arrived at the decision to do all that he could to promote the career of Mademoiselle Isobel de Montargis, it was natural that he should turn to Blanche Desmoulins for her advice and guidance. It had taken him some time to realize that he wished to involve himself to such a degree in that young woman's life, but once he had, he had immediately sought out Blanche.

"Hmmm." The lady, reclining luxuriously on a red damask sofa, played with the magnificent rope of pearls cascading over her generous bosom, and stared meditatively at the pair of lovebirds in the gilt cage by the window. "No matter how talented you say the young lady is, she will need someone to sponsor her. Let me think now . . . Yes, that is it." The riotous mass of golden curls bounced vigorously as she nodded. "She must engage Signor Bartoli as a singing master, for without his recommendation she will never succeed anywhere. However, if she wins his approval, her career is made. He lives in Saint Martin's Street." The lady rose slowly, stretching languorously in a manner calculated to show every curve in her exquisite figure to its best advantage. She glided over to the escritoire by the window, which she opened and, pulling out a sheet of paper, scrawled a few lines, sanded it, folded it, and handed it to Christian.

"There, this should offer you some introduction. The signor is notoriously temperamental and very jealous of his time. He will not waste it on anyone, certainly not the mere brother of a duke or a hero of Vitoria, unless that person has some connection to the world of music. This, however"—she waved the note and glanced saucily at Christian—"should at least make him listen to you. After that, you are on your own and it is up to you to convince him of your protégée's merits. And I warn you, she must have a more than a beautiful face and elegant figure to recommend her."

"But"—Christian surveyed Blanche appreciatively from head to foot—"a beautiful face and elegant figure obviously help."

"Oh, make no mistake about it. While it is true that Signor Bartoli would not have had anything to do with me if I had not in some way been connected with the opera, our connection was . . . er . . . not a musical one."

"Ah." Christian grinned. "At least he possesses some human failings, then."

"Very few. It was quite a long time before he paid the least attention to me, and even longer before we were, ah, mmm, *intimately acquainted*."

"You worry me. This man sounds truly formidable."

The lady nodded slowly. "Indeed he is, which is why his recommendation is invaluable. It will be difficult to obtain, but if your singer is truly the talent you say that she is, and if she wins his approval, then she will need no other patron, believe me."

"My utmost thanks, Blanche." Christian reached over to clasp one dimpled hand and caress it with his lips. "And, now, what can I do for you?"

"Need you ask, my lord?" The lady pulled him to her and slowly entwined her arms about his neck, drawing his lips down to meet hers as she molded her body to his.

"It has been a long time." He sighed against her full red lips as she expertly undid his cravat.

"Too long," Blanche agreed, sinking back on the sofa still tugging gently on the cravat.

Christian gave himself up to the inevitable, not that he objected in the least, for Blanche was an even more talented lover than she was dancer and she took her partner's pleasure seriously. He never failed to enjoy himself with Blanche, and he never felt anything but completely satisfied and pleasantly exhausted when he left her. She never ruined a delightful interlude by demanding to know when she would see him again or by hinting at an inclination for expensive jewelry, a new carriage, or complaining of ruinous dressmakers' bills or household expenses.

It seemed such a simple, logical thing for a woman to enjoy a man the same way a man enjoyed a woman, but in all his years of loving them, Christian had never met a woman besides Blanche who did not demand something of him besides the pleasure of his company.

It was this thought that lay at the root of Christian's bachelorhood. It was not that he did not like women; he did—some people said that he liked them too much. It was not that he did not believe in love; he did. It was just that he had never met a woman who had convinced him that she loved his person better than she loved his title or his position. It was not even that he did not believe in marriage; he did, in theory. It was just that he had yet to encounter two people who had married simply because they enjoyed one another's company. Christian felt that he was being entirely reasonable in expecting that, if he were going to commit himself to one woman for the rest of his life, that she commit herself to him, Christian Hatherleigh—not Lord Christian, not brother to the Duke of Warminster, or the master of Farwell Abbey, not even Lieutenant Colonel Lord Christian Hatherleigh of the Third Dragoon Guards, though, for some reason, that would have been more acceptable than the others. But thus far, he had never met anyone who simply wanted Christian, the man, except Blanche. But then, Blanche wanted Charles, the man, and Gerald, the man, and a host of others. While Christian did not object to sharing such a delicious ladybird with other connoisseurs of female pulchritude, he did object to becoming serious about someone who enjoyed such a wide variety of male acquaintances.

Some hours later, he left the house in Marylebone, having shown his proper appreciation for its owner's advice, and promising to let her know if there was anything further she could do. Like everyone and everything else in London, Blanche Desmoulins had remained unchanged in Christian's absence, but unlike everyone and everything else, it heartened him to see that she had remained the same.

As the sky was already turning pink in the west, Christian decided that, despite his eagerness to advance Mademoiselle Isobel de Montargis's career, he would put off calling on Signor Bartoli until the next day, using his time instead to attend a vocal concert in the New Rooms, Hanover Square where Charles and William Knyvett were performing. Christian had purchased a subscription to the complete set of concerts after reading that Madame Catalani had been engaged for the entire Season, and there was no time like the present to familiarize himself with the players if he were going to help his protégée take her proper place in the concert world.

Indeed, as Christian sat through the vocal offerings of the Knyvetts, he spent a great deal more time envisioning Mademoiselle Isobel's graceful figure and expressive face before him in this particular setting than he did actually listening to the music. As he was leaving the concert, he did examine the crowd to see if perhaps he could discover someone who might be Signor Bartoli, but as the majority of the audience seemed to consist of stately dowagers accompanied by timid female companions, it seemed unlikely that the singing master was present.

The next day, however, Christian put his plan into motion, sending Digby to the house in Saint Martin's Street with a request for an audience with Signor Bartoli.

"He says you may call this afternoon, though he didn't look to be pleased about it," the batman reported later. "Said he does not take pupils no matter *who* their relatives might be. You will have to look sharp about you when you talk to him because it's my opinion that he knows a plumper when he hears one, and you can't win him over by offering him Spanish coin neither. He is going to mistrust anything you say about wanting to help a young woman because of her talent. This signor is a gentleman and has all his wits about him and then some, but he has agreed to see you because I said you were a true *connosewer*."

"Thank you, Digby. I shall endeavor to establish my credibility at the outset and do my best to live up to the reputation you have given me."

That afternoon Christian presented himself at the slender brick building in Saint Martin's Street. The door was opened by a young maidservant who was obviously taken aback by his appearance. Either the master of the house had few callers or they did not resemble Christian in the slightest. He was just beginning to wonder what type of callers did frequent the house when a querulous voice called, "Maria, *che fai? Vieni qui!*"

Taking his beaver, the maidservant led him up the slender staircase to the sitting room. Christian, who was noted far and wide for the elegant severity of his attire, had dressed with more care than usual that morning, arranging his cravat in the simplest of styles, and choosing the plainest of waistcoats to go with his dark blue coat and biscuit-colored pantaloons. Despite this lack of ostentation, however, he still could not help feeling, as the music master scrutinized him disdainfully from under shaggy brows, that to Signor Bartoli, he presented the picture of the veriest fop, a Bond Street fribble who was entirely beneath the gentleman's notice. It was a novel, if not unnerving, experience. Not even as the rawest of subalterns being reprimanded by the colonel of his regiment had Christian felt as lowly as he did at this moment.

"Well, sir, I hear that you insist on wasting my time begging me to listen to some acquaintance or some family member who thinks she can sing."

"If it were going to be waste of *your* time, signor, be assured that I would not waste *my* time," Christian replied somewhat sharply. He paused, took a deep breath, and began more calmly. "Narually you are suspicious, sir. However, the person is neither a relative nor some ladybird whom I wish to launch on a convenient career. In fact, the lady in question has not the least idea that I have taken this step. Undoubtedly she would be supremely annoyed if she knew the extent to which I am meddling in her life. Even if I can succeed in winning your permission to introduce her to you, I am not at all certain that I can convince her to be introduced, for she is someone who values her independence above all else and who is confident enough of her talent to believe that she has no need for the patronage or influence of anyone. It was Mademoiselle Desmoulins who insisted that I speak to you, and as the note from her delivered by my batman attests, she can vouch for my sincerity."

The music master subjected Christian to a piercing glance. "Very well, then." He pointed to a chair on the other side of the fireplace as he settled back into the chair opposite it. "And what makes you so certain that this, er, young person would be of interest to me."

"She is not a young person," Christian responded evenly enough, though the casual observer would have been able to see from his clenched jaw that he was exerting some effort to keep his temper in check. "She is Mademoiselle Isobel de Montargis, daughter of the Duc de Montargis, and she has been engaged as a music teacher to my nieces. It was at my brother's house that I overheard her singing *'Der Hölle Rache kocht in meinem Herzen'* with such clarity and precision that I was immediately struck by it. I have also been impressed by her exquisite rendition of *'Porgi amor,'* which, of course, does not show off her range as well as the other, but I once heard Catalani in the same role and did not think she performed it nearly so well as Mademoiselle de Montargis." Christian did not miss the significance of Signor Bartoli's skeptically raised eyebrow. "Naturally, I am the veriest amateur, but I have heard no one equal to Mademoiselle de Montargis, which is why I have come to you for only you can truly evaluate her potential."

"And why should I wish to do that?" The music master was only slightly mollified by this acknowledgment of his superiority.

"Mademoiselle Desmoulins tells me that everyone in the operatic world looks to you as the arbiter of taste and quality. When a new singer makes her debut upon the scene, and Mademoiselle de Montargis *will* make her debut, everyone will follow your lead in assessing her ability. I should think that you would wish to maintain your position as the leader of musical taste. Should someone besides you discover the next Catalani, people might begin to doubt your reputation as the leader of the musical world here in London. Popular acclaim can be so very fickle, you know, and it would be unfortunate if your leadership were superseded by someone who is your inferior." Christian spoke in the most conversational of accents, but here was no mistaking the steely undertone in his voice.

Though inclined to look askance at men-about-town who considered themselves to be musical connoisseurs, Signor Bartoli was astute enough to recognize a man who put considerable thought into whatever he said or did. There was an intensity of purpose in the eyes boring into his that was rare in anyone, particularly a member of the *ton* and, in Signor Bartoli's experience, this intensity shone only in the eyes of those who were extraordinarily gifted or extraordinarily dedicated. However, he had a reputation to maintain and he was not about to give in easily, no matter how noble the cause.

"Hmmm." The music master narrowed his eyes thoughtfully. "*Davvero*. What you say may be true, but if she does not become the next Catalani, then where is my reputation. *Finito!* You had better bring her to me. I shall listen to this young person and, believe me, with the first note I shall know if you have fooled me into listening to a crow instead of a nightingale. As you say, signor, I am the arbiter of quality, and if I find that there is nothing there, why there is not anything you could do to give this young person a career in the opera. *Capite?*"

"Understood. And I thank you, Signor Bartoli."

The old man rose and waved his hand dismissively as he headed toward the door. "*È niente.*"

The interview was obviously over. Christian rose and retrieved his hat from the hall table where Maria had placed it. Bowing with as much dignity as he could muster in the face of such a brazen dismissal, he thanked the music master again, descended the stairs, and stepped out into the busy street. He tossed a coin to the boy who had been holding his horse, mounted Ajax, and made his way slowly toward Piccadilly, puzzling on how to accomplish the next step in his plan, which was to convince Isobel to visit the music master. This step was likely to be as difficult, if not more so, than his dealings with Signor Bartoli.

Chapter 11

Christian received assistance with his stratagem from a most unexpected quarter in a most roundabout way.

Albert had been so outraged by his wife's suggestion that a Hatherleigh, even a Hatherleigh of such dubious reputation as his brother, should be evincing an interest in a servant in his household, and a French servant at that, that he took advantage of the first opportunity to speak to Mademoiselle Isobel. Just two days after Lady Daventry's soiree and his wife's revelations, he called his daughters' music teacher into the library.

Isobel, who had rarely seen the duke in all her visits to Grosvenor Square, was completely mystified by the summons to the library, however, one look at his grave expression told her that the interview was not going to be pleasant. She could not imagine that she had done anything to displease her employer, but he certainly looked far from happy. In fact, he appeared to be distinctly uneasy as he sat behind the enormous mahogany desk, fiddling with a silver letter opener.

"Ah, er, it has come to my attention, ah . . ." He paused uncomfortably. "Ahem. As you well know, we Hatherleighs have a proud heritage to, er, maintain and . . ."

Isobel could not help thinking how very different this square-faced ponderous man was from his glib, audacious brother and, for a moment, occupied with this interesting thought, she lost the thread of his argument, which had not actually progressed any further than the illustrious nature of the Hatherleigh name and his role as head of the Hatherleigh family and Duke of Warminster.

At last she could endure the hemming and hawing no longer. Obviously the gentleman was in need of some assistance, unless she wished to be stuck there the entire day while he made up his mind as to the best approach for addressing what was obviously a delicate subject. "Your Grace, if you have called me in to speak to me in private, there is clearly something troubling you that has to do with me. Pray tell me what it is and I shall endeavor to address whatever concern you might have."

Under the clear-eyed gaze of the self-possessed young woman sitting in front of him Albert felt horribly ill at ease, though nonetheless convinced of the rightness of his position. Damn it, she was a servant, and French. The idea that his brother should have any interest in her was preposterous, but her poise and her calmness were unnerving. It was unnatural for a servant called before her employer to be that calm. "Ah, well, Lord Christian, I mean it is most improper, though I suppose with the proximity . . . ahem, as head of the household I cannot allow you to continue seeing Lord Christian."

A cold fury washed over Isobel. How dare he even think that a daughter of the de Montargis's could possibly contemplate such dishonorable behavior! She gripped the arms of her chair and took a deep breath as she struggled to master her anger long enough to speak. When she was certain that her legs would support her, she rose to her full height and stared contemptuously down at the duke. "How dare you, sir, question the honor of a de Montargis? I should never behave so improperly as to have any personal connection with anyone in the house of my employer. And, if I were contemplating such a connection, I should certainly not allow the name of a de Montargis to be linked to that of an English parvenu. You need not trouble yourself to show me out. I shall bid Sophia and Augusta adieu before I go, for it would be unseemly to disappear without a word, but rest assured that I shall no longer have any contact with your family." And turning on her heel, Isobel marched from the room, leaving Albert to stare blankly after her.

He was still staring blankly at the books on the wall in front of him when his wife hurried in some twenty minutes later. "What in heaven's name has happened, my lord? I was conferring with Grinstead about the wine order when Sophia and Augusta came in crying to me that Mademoiselle Isobel had come to bid them good-bye. She offered no reason of her own for leaving and since I have been most pleased with the girls' progress I can only assume that you know something about this."

The duke shifted uneasily under his wife's accusing gaze, but he soon recovered himself. "Dammit, Lavinia, we cannot have Christian involved with a servant in his own household."

"Servant? Isobel de Montargis's birth is better than yours, my lord. Her ancestors were leading the Crusades while yours were still sturdy yeomen tilling the fields in Hampshire." Lavinia, whose own lineage was far more ancient than her husband's, could not entirely hide the triumphant note in her voice. Albert, who was extremely sensitive to the fact that his title had only been in existence since his ancestors had given aid and comfort to Charles II, flushed uncomfortably. "Perhaps, but that still does not change the fact that she is French and entirely unsuitable for Christian."

"Albert," Lavinia burst out in exasperation, "we are not talking about a match for Christian, but someone who teaches the girls. Your brother, who is far more likely to go to his grave a bachelor than the victim of an ruinous match, is eminently capable of watching out for himself. In the meantime, Sophia and Augusta have lost an excellent instructress and someone they truly admired and enjoyed. There was not the least need to speak to her, and even less need to give her notice."

"But I did not give her notice. *She* gave *me* her notice." Albert was beginning to feel very ill-used. All he had wished to do was to protect the honor of the family and his brother's good name and for doing this, for accepting the responsibility to which he had been born, he was being treated as though he were some sort of an ogre.

"And well she might after being so insulted. I should have too," Lavinia concluded severely as she swept from the room, leaving her beleaguered spouse to sift glumly through the pile of correspondence on his desk.

But Albert was not done with recriminations. The next morning he was again accosted in his library by an outraged family member. This time is was Christian who was furious and he was even more damning toward his brother's behavior than Lavinia had been. Still in his riding clothes, he strode into the library, his face dark with anger. "I should like to know, Albert, by what right you justify your intrusion into my affairs?" His voice was icily calm, but it took no special powers of intuition on his brother's part to see that he was seething.

Albert had never seen Christian so angry. The gray-green eyes glittered emerald in their intensity, and his face was white and taut with suppressed fury. If the truth were told, Albert was already a little in awe of his younger brother, who had always possessed a daring and savoir faire that Albert secretly envied and he lived his life with a passion that made the stately Albert acutely uncomfortable. "Well, I . . ." Albert struggled to regain control of the situation, but his session with Lavinia had already shattered his customary sense of righteous responsibility. He took a deep breath and rose to his full height, which, unfortunately, did not exceed his brother's six feet three inches. "As head of the family, it is my duty to see . . ."

"If you will recall, I reached my majority nearly a decade ago, and I have been risking my life for my country for some time. I think I have the right to live as I damn well please, and I certainly have the right to make an acquaintance without my elder brother's jumping to conclusions. As far as your responsibility goes, it is your responsibility to treat anyone and everyone in your employ with respect. Devoid of a sense of responsibility though I may be, even I know that. Now I am going to do *my* duty for the family by seeing to it that someone in its employ is not cast off without some means of support. And if you so much as think about stopping me, let me remind you that the family reputation is in my hands as well as yours." In truth, Christian had not the slightest idea what he would do to carry out this threat, but he knew that his brother, who worshiped the god of respectability, would never do anything to risk incurring the slightest blemish on the family's good name, so he felt reasonably assured that Albert, much as he might wish to, would not interfere in Christian's plans for the Duke of Warminster's former governess.

However, as Christian well knew, getting the young woman in question to accept those plans was another thing entirely. There was no time like the present and, driven by the energy of his angry interview with Albert, Christian made his way toward Manchester Square.

Having gleaned a rough idea of the location of Mademoiselle Isobel's lodgings from his nieces, Christian had had the forethought to send Digby to discover the precise number of the de Montargis residence in Manchester Street. The redoubtable servant had quickly struck up a nodding acquaintance with several of the domestics in that area and was able to furnish his master with the young lady's direction with his customary dispatch.

Assured of the address, Christian now grasped the shiny brass knocker and rapped imperiously. Even Grinstead, who could, when called upon, assume the haughtiest expression of any butler in London, could not have examined Lord Christian as critically as the servant who opened the door and conducted him up the dimly lit staircase to the sparsely furnished drawing room. Marthe was always fiercely protective of her family, but when the visitor was an unknown Englishman, she could be positively threatening. Her square figure was as solid as any man's and the arms, strengthened by years of rolling out her delicate pastries, were even bulkier than Digby's. The tiny dark eyes set close together over a snub nose in a broad face regarded him warily, nor did this expression change even when he gave her his name.

Faced by such a daunting figure, even Christian did not have the temerity to ask for Mademoiselle Isobel, but settled instead for requesting an audience with her father, hoping that the Duc de Montargis would be more approachable than his formidable servant.

"Milord Christian Hatherleigh," Marthe announced to the figure bent over a desk by the windows.

Thus interrupted, the Duc de Montargis rose and turned to receive his visitor with all the stately graciousness of a levée at Versailles, as though the worn blue carpet that Christian crossed was the finest Aubusson and the walls were hung with magnificent tapestries instead of a few prettily executed watercolors in the simplest of frames.

The duc took a chair on one side of the meager fire and waved his hand in the direction of a most uncomfortable sofa covered with faded blue damask and, inclining his head with an air of old-fashioned dignity, waited for his unexpected caller to state the purpose of his visit.

Fighting the urge to fidget under that calm, indifferent gaze, Christian began. "Your Grace, I made the acquaintance of your daughter at the home of my brother."

There was not the flicker of a response or recognition in the pale blue eyes surveying him.

Refusing to be daunted, Christian continued, "The Duke of Warminster. Mademoiselle Isobel is, er, instructing my nieces in music, I believe."

The duc remained infuriatingly impassive.

"At any rate, I was most impressed by her exquisite singing. She has a gift, a rare gift, and it is a great shame to have it wasted on my nieces, who can not possibly appreciate it."

The duc unbent enough to acknowledge this praise with the most infinitesimal of nods.

"And I should like." Christian paused. What precisely did he want? Actually, all he had hoped to accomplish by this visit was a chance to see Isobel again and perhaps to convince her to meet with Signor Bartoli, but how he was to accomplish this with her father treating him as though he were some vassal on the de Montargis's estates, Christian had no idea.

He cleared his throat. "I have an acquaintance, very influential in the musical world, to whom I would like to introduce her." Christian cursed himself for a fool. Lord, he had not sounded this awkward since he had been called upon to recite his first Greek translation at Eton.

"It is very kind of you to wish to encourage my daughter in her interests, but there is really no need. She is amply supported by our own friends and any further show of interest would undoubtedly make her uncomfortable. She has been most carefully brought up, monsieur, and is not accustomed to the freedom that your English young women have. I fear that she would find your concern, though kindly meant, most disconcerting. Her nature, like her mother's, is gentle and retiring, and the thought of encountering people outside of our world would undoubtedly prove distressing to her."

Christian had a brief vision of the duc's *gentle* and *retiring* daughter taking him to task for interrupting her private moment at the pianoforte. Carefully brought-up she might be, but Christian would never use the word *retiring* to characterize Mademoiselle Isobel. However, he could see that he would get nothing from her father. It was quite obvious that the duc considered Christian as unacceptable an acquaintance for his daughter as the Duke of Warminster considered Mademoiselle Isobel for his brother and it was equally obvious that Christian was not going to be allowed to see the young woman herself. Swallowing his frustration, he rose and, bowing slightly toward the duc, thanked him for his time. "And should you ever need the assistance of anyone beyond your circle of acquaintances, I do hope that you will not hesitate to call upon me."

The duc inclined his head slightly. "That is most kind of you, Lord Christian." His words and demeanor were gracious enough, but it was obvious to both the duc and his visitor that the Duc de Montargis would never need the assistance of Lord Christian Hatherleigh. And it was equally obvious that his daughter would never learn of Lord Christian's visit from her father.

As he left the drawing room, Christian nodded in a friendly fashion at Marthe who, knowing that no Englishman remained for any length of time with her master, was hovering in the hall ready to escort him to the door. He wondered briefly whether or not she was likely to inform her mistress of his visit, but he could read nothing in the shrewd black eyes or impassive face that gave the slightest clue as to the degree of closeness between her and Mademoiselle Isobel.

The door shut behind him and Christian stood rooted to the pavement as passersby on Manchester Street made their way on either side of him while he contemplated his next step. It was clear that he would have to arrange an encounter with Isobel somewhere else if he were hoping to speak to her, but as he had no idea of the pattern of her daily existence, this would be difficult, if not impossible. The only possible recourse he had was to frequent the neighborhood in Manchester Square, hoping that he might run into her as she called on friends. Surely the de Montargises had chosen to live in this area of the city in order to be close to their fellow émigrés.

When the second person who passed him glanced back over his shoulder at the man standing motionless in front of the de Montargis's door, Christian decided it was high time to leave. He could not very well just wait outside her door until Mademoiselle Isobel either entered or exited. Such behavior would undoubtedly raise the suspicions of the formidable servant, who had certainly looked brawny enough to toss him into the street if she took issue with his presence outside the family's residence.

Chapter 12

Though unsuccessful in his interview with Isobel's father, Christian was far more fortunate where the daughter was concerned. In fact, Isobel had not been home at the time of his visit, but worried about their livelihood now that she had left her position at the Duke of Warminster's, she had gone to call on the Comtesse de Sallanches at her atelier in Soho to offer her services for hemming and the cruder sewing that needed to be done on the embroidered dresses the comtesse had made so popular.

The atelier had been so dark and depressing and so drafty and cold that in spite of the comtesse's and everyone else's delight at seeing her, and in spite of their warm urging her to come join them, Isobel had left more discouraged than she could remember feeling since coming to London after her mother died.

While teaching French and music to the Duke of Warminster's lively but musically inept daughters had been nothing compared to her dream of mesmerizing an audience from the stage at Covent Garden, it had offered the advantage of the exquisite surroundings of the music room at Warminster House with its view of the peaceful garden, lovely even in the winter sunshine, the delicately drawn pictures of the muses that graced the walls, and the superbly efficient fireplace both in that room and the school-room two floors above it. And the girls, with their energy and exuberance, always looking forward to the next day and the future that lay before them offered a contrast to the undercurrent of sadness that constantly flowed through the gatherings of the émigrés. Isobel had rebelled against this gentle melancholy all her life, refusing to think in the past, but living in the present with as much energy and enjoyment as possible and working to build a future that was not simply a re-creation of what had been. Teaching in the Duke of Warminster's household had helped her to expand her horizons and keep this optimistic frame of mind, but she was not sure she could maintain it if she were forced to spend her days with people who conversed about nothing else but days gone by.

Trying not to think about the loss of the exquisite pianoforte and the opportunity for at least two hours of uninterrupted practice every day, Isobel trudged home dispiritedly from the comtesse's attic workshop. The weather, damp and gray, did nothing to life her spirits. It was on February days like this one that she most missed the country and her life in the dower house on the Barford estate. Weather there was no less cold and damp, but the air always smelled fresh, and even on the dampest days, brought with it the compensation of the rich aroma of newly turned earth or the tangy scent of cedar. Here in the city, the dampness only made one more aware of the stifling smoke from countless fireplaces.

At first Isobel had been delighted at the thought of moving to London, for their quiet life at Barford had been even quieter after Jane and Emily had left for their Seasons, and the dower house, deprived of Isobel's mother's presence, quiet though it had been, felt empty. In reality, London had turned out to be more confining than Buckinghamshire and her life, constricted as it was by the high degree of formality retained by the émigré community, actually offered less freedom and less opportunity to move about in the world than she had had in the country. If she had been a man, of course, it would have been different and there would have been endless opportunities, even for one who was not too plump in the pocket, to enjoy himself.

And now, in a fit of pride, she had narrowed her life even more by depriving herself of the daily escape to Grosvenor Square. Where had her much vaunted practical nature been when she needed it most? A truly practical person would have been properly distressed to hear that the Duke of Warminster could even think that she had noticed his brother, much less had designs on him, and she would have reassured him that his worries were groundless. Instead, Isobel had allowed the lamentable pride of the de Montargises to govern her actions. In doing this she was acting no better than her father, who clung to the reputation of past generations, living off their reflected glory instead of dealing with the more important issues of life.

She was justly punished now for acting so stupidly, for she had deprived herself of all the advantages of her connection to the Duke of Warminster's household. She had even put herself one step further away from her dream by distancing herself from someone who could have recommended her to powerful patrons, if not offering to sponsor her himself. Though Lord Christian Hatherleigh had scoffed at the idea of the Duke of Warminster's furthering any musical career, she might have been able to change all that, but no, she had been too furious at the very idea that someone could suspect her of being anything but completely honorable in her dealings with her employer and his family to think clearly about anything else but hanging on to her pride whatever the cost.

Isobel let out a gusty sigh as she rounded the corner from Duke Street into Manchester Street. She was so wrapped up in her own discouraging thoughts that she did not even notice the tall man making his way purposefully toward her.

"Mademoiselle Isobel."

With a start she realized that she was being addressed and looked up to see a broad chest encased in a many-caped greatcoat directly in front of her nose. Isobel gasped as she found herself being scrutinized by a pair of gray-green eyes glinting with amusement. "Milord, I did not expect to see you here in this part of town." She flushed and broke off hastily as she realized that her words made it sound as though she had been looking for him in other parts of town. The fact that she had made her blush even more.

The amusement in Christian's eyes deepened. "I occasionally have, ah, er, *interests* that bring me in this direction."

She glanced up at him suspiciously. "What sort of interests?"

Christian chuckled. The expression in the blue eyes examining him warily was one of patent disbelief. There was no doubt that Mademoiselle Isobel was as perceptive as she was talented. "Very well, since you are unbecomingly suspicious as it is, I shall risk your immediate censure and blurt it right out. I came to see you. However, once I had endured the disapproving scrutiny of the ogress at the door, I lost my nerve and requested an audience with your father."

There was a sharp intake of breath. One slim gloved hand rose to her lips. "Papa? You spoke to Papa about me. Ah, *mon Dieu*, what did you say?"

"I told him the truth, that you were extremely talented and I wished to introduce you to someone who could properly appreciate that talent."

Isobel slowly let out some of the breath she had been holding. "You did not tell him that . . ."

"That my impossibly overbearing and patronizing brother drove you from his employ? Certainly not. Much as I may deride the concepts of familial pride and duty, I do feel I owe it to our good name to keep such shameful behavior as secret as possible."

Isobel let out the rest of her breath. "But you spoke to Papa about my singing? What did he say?" The blue eyes were dark with apprehension.

"I did, but he was so intent upon dismissing me, in the most gracious way possible, of course, that the issue of your musical abilities was never properly addressed."

"Oh yes, Papa is very protective of me. He is rather old-fashioned and I am all that he has. Even now he must be wondering what is keeping me."

Isobel did not evince the slightest curiosity about the identity of the person he wished to introduce her to. In fact, she seemed purposely to avoid it, but Christian, once committed to a course of action, was not about to give it up easily. "I can understand that, but you are not the sort of person to sacrifice yourself or your ambitions to another's wishes."

Isobel was silent. The man was far too acute and she was not at all certain she liked having her character so easily understood.

"But it was not really your father whom I wished to see."

"Oh."

She still would not look at him, the minx, but he had known it would not be easy and was prepared for it. "I wanted to tell you that I spoke with Signor Bartoli about you and he is interested in meeting you." It was not precisely the truth—*interested* was not a particularly accurate description of the music master's reaction—but it was not precisely a lie.

"Signor Bartoli? That got her attention and she glanced up at him with some surprise. "How do you know . . . ?" Her eyes darkened as the implications of his words dawned on her. "But, my lord, I believe I told you that I did not require any assistance, that I, I . . ."

"Wished to fulfill your dreams on your own without anyone else's assistance or interference. I am quite aware of that and, believe me, you shall. Signor Bartoli has not promised to take you on as a pupil. He has merely agreed to listen to you. It took everything I had to convince him to do that. Now it is up to you to prove to him that I have not wasted his time as he claimed I had done."

"Ah." She looked thoughtful.

Christian quickly suppressed the smile that rose to his lips. She was weakening. It was just as he had thought it would be. She would never accept help from him, but if he put it to her as a challenge, she would not be able to resist. "I have told him that you will call on him at his house in Saint Martin's Street. If you do not, he will see it as a lack of resolve on your part and should you try to make a name for yourself after that without having consulted him, he will not take you seriously. And I have it on good authority that if one wishes to become well known in the musical circles to which you aspire, it is absolutely essential to win his good opinion."

Isobel nodded reluctantly. "Yes, I have heard that. What you say is true, but how did you discover that?"

It was Christian's turn to look slightly disconcerted. "An, er, ah, an acquaintance told me."

She looked sharply at him, but said nothing. The fact that he had a *chère amie* was less interesting to her than that he should be uncomfortable about admitting it. From what she had previously seen of the bold and provocative Lord Christian Hatherleigh, she would have thought that he would not scruple to acknowledge such a thing, even to her. "Very well, I shall call on this Signor Bartoli, but I will tolerate no further interference, my lord. Now I must be going." She proceeded past him and then stopped to look back. "Ah, thank you." It almost seemed as though the words were forced out of her rather than spoken.

"You are most welcome." Christian turned his head to hide the grin that he could not suppress. She was proud as the devil all right—equally proud, in her own way, as that haughty father of hers. The only difference between father and daughter was that his was the pride of birth while hers was the justifiable pride in her own independence and her accomplishments, with which Christian could certainly sympathize.

Christian began to make his way back along Duke Street. He was going to enjoy watching her progress. Once she began her lessons with Signor Bartoli he would know of at least one other place in London where he might encounter her and she was certainly likely to walk down Oxford Street on her way to her lessons. Yes, he would most definitely keep a close eye on Mademoiselle Isobel's progress. Christian chuckled as he turned into Oxford Street and headed toward Gentleman Jackson's. He could not remember when he had last enjoyed himself this much. A round or two with the pugilist was just what he needed to top off his morning. He wondered again as he sauntered down Oxford Street and turned into Bond Street if the Duc de Montargis would mention Christian's visit to his daughter. He rather thought not. While the nobleman had been polite enough, his expression, when speaking to Christian, had been that of a man who had just come across some rare species of insect; he had been more repelled than curious.

Chapter 13

Christian was entirely correct in his supposition. When Isobel stopped by the drawing room on her return from the Comtesse de Sallanches's, the duc inquired after her health and spoke of the progress he had made that morning on his memoirs, but he made not the slightest reference to a gentleman caller.

Marthe, on the other hand, was somewhat more forthcoming. "Oh, mademoiselle," she exclaimed as she took her mistress's pelisse, damp from the long walk in the fog, shook it and hung it to dry by the kitchen fire. "Such a handsome English milord who called upon Monsieur le Duc this morning!"

"An English gentleman calling upon Papa?" Isobel hoped her assumed innocence sounded convincing. Very little escaped the sharp eyes of Marthe, especially where her mistress was concerned. She had cared for Isobel, not to mention the rest of the family, since they had left France when Isobel had been a baby, and there were very few things about the de Montargis that Marthe did not know. "Whatever did the man want?"

"Who can say?" Marthe shrugged.

"Marthe?" Isobel shot her a suspicious glance. If there was very little about the de Montargises that Marthe did not know, there was also very little about Marthe that Isobel did not know, and she was well aware that curiosity was the loyal servant's besetting sin. Marthe would never have passed up the opportunity to listen at the keyhole, especially where an unexpected visit from a total stranger was concerned.

"Very well." Marthe did not bother to deny it. "He came to speak about you and one of his acquaintances who is influential in the music world."

"Did he now? Well I will have no gentleman interfering in *my* life, influential musical acquaintance or no influential musical acquaintance."

"But, mademoiselle, this gentleman had the air of an *homme du monde* and looked as though he knew what he was about."

"I am sure he did," Isobel responded dryly.

"Mademoiselle knows such a man?"

The faintest of blushes warmed Isobel's cheeks. "From what you say, I imagine it must be Lord Christian Hatherleigh, brother to the Duke of Warminster, whose daughters are my pupils."

Marthe's shrewd eyes brightened. Here was a situation indeed! She had not described the visitor so definitively that he could not be one of many Englishmen, but her mistress seemed to have no doubt in her mind as to the identity of the visitor, nor did she, in spite of her efforts to act noncommittal, seem as uninterested in this person as she tried to appear. There was a sparkle in her eyes, a consciousness in her expression that belied her claim that she would not allow any gentleman to involve himself in her life.

"Then Mademoiselle has met this gentleman before?"

The blush deepened. "I did encounter him once at Warminster House," Isobel admitted.

"Ah." Marthe's face and voice registered no expression as she turned to poke the fire into a brighter blaze, but her mind was working furiously. There was more to this business than met the eye. Handsome English milords did not stop by every day with offers of assistance of any sort, especially offers concerning the daughter of the house. To the best of her knowledge, Marthe could not remember Mademoiselle's ever having blushed at the thought of a man. If the truth were known, the trusted servant had worried over Mademoiselle's cool dismissal of the entire opposite sex.

While there were not many young men that the Duc de Montargis considered important enough to present to his daughter, there had been some—the Comte de Pontarlier, for one, and his friend the Chevalier d'Entremont, for another—that he deemed worthy of his daughter, but Isobel could not be bothered with either of them, dismissing them both with a disdainful sniff as she later confided to Marthe that she had no use for men who spent more time thinking of their tailors or clever repartee than they did trying to support themselves or their impoverished families. "They remind me of nothing so much as clever monkeys in a menagerie, relying on someone else to feed and clothe them merely because they are amusing and always well dressed," she had scoffed.

In fact, Marthe's mistress spent far more time in the company of men her father's age than she did with young men of hers.

After a particularly lengthy evening at the Comte d'Artois's establishment in Baker Street, Isobel had confided that "For the most part, Papa's friends speak of more sensible things. They do not devote their entire effort to impress me, but engage themselves in conversation that is worth my while. These others, bah, they act as though they wish to talk to me, but one can see they are far more interested in speaking of themselves than they are in what I might have to think about or say." Accustomed to this scornful attitude in her mistress, Marthe was all the more astounded then to see the conscious look in the hastily averted eyes as Isobel had toyed with the gloves she was still clutching. So she did not want Marthe to know what she was thinking about this English milord. This was interesting indeed! The entire situation would bear some watching.

For her part, Isobel was wondering if she should take Marthe into her confidence. On the one hand, she preferred to keep her singing aspirations as private as possible—even now she could not fathom why she had confided them to Lord Christian. On the other hand, she did need Marthe to take a message to the address that Lord Christian had given her for Signor Bartoli.

In the end, Isobel decided to entrust the errand to a likely looking young lad from a nearby stable whose master allowed him to run an occasional errand for the de Montargises. The very next day she gave the boy a note for Signor Bartoli, instructing him to wait for the answer, and then she went out to put her name in at several agencies that placed governesses in noble households. Not wishing to worry either Marthe or her father, she had not told either of them that she had left the Duke of Warminster's employ. Until she found another position she planned to leave the house at the time she had normally gone to Grosvenor Square and stay away doing errands or inquiring about positions until she could find employment.

Later that afternoon the lad came back with Signor Bartoli's reluctant invitation to call on him in Saint Martin's Street the next morning. Though she would rather have died than admit it to Lord Christian, Isobel was thrilled at the opportunity to test her ability before the noted musician. It was the opportunity she had been hoping for, waiting for, the chance to learn whether or not she had been deluding herself all these years in thinking that she could rise to the level of a Catalani, or even a Grassini.

Signor Bartoli's reception of her was not promising. He did not bother to rise from his seat at the pianoforte when she was ushered into the music room, but looked at her sharply. "Signorina, do you believe, *veramente* that you have the necessary skill to make me waste my time listening to you?"

Fighting to control her nervousness, Isobel slowly and deliberately removed her lemon, kid gloves. "Of course that is for you to judge, monsieur, but I am musician enough not to wish to subject *anyone* to bad music."

He was silent for a moment, then nodded begrudgingly. "Not a bad answer, signorina. Come, then, tell me what you wish to sing for me and I shall accompany you."

"There is no need for that, monsieur. I am perfectly capable of accompanying myself, which will give you a better opportunity to concentrate all your attention on evaluating my performance."

He rose and waved his hand toward the bench he had just vacated as he took his position in a chair close to the fire. "Very well. Your patron tells me that you do a creditable job of performing *'Der Hölle Rache kocht in meinem Herzen.'*"

"He is not my patron," Isobel stated flatly, settling her skirts around her as she took her place at the pianoforte. "But yes, he has heard me sing that."

The music master did not miss the dismissive tone of voice nor the defiant lifting of the chin. She had pride, this one, an honest pride, which was not a bad thing in a performer. "Very well. Begin." He watched the hands gliding over the keys as she played a few bars of introduction. They were long-fingered, capable hands that moved with assurance over the keys. There was no nervousness, no unnecessary flourish, nothing to distract the observer from the music itself. He was still thinking about her quiet poise when the first notes of the aria poured forth. Those first notes, clear, true, and perfectly modulated made him forget that he was there to advise and to criticize, but instead he found himself being swept away by the beauty of the song itself.

Isobel finished and glanced anxiously at him, but Signor Bartoli's face remained utterly impassive as he sat there, head back and eyes closed. She was not at all sure of what she should do next. Had he closed his eyes because it was so awful he could not bear to look at her? Should she tiptoe quietly out and forget that the entire scene had ever happened? She sat there for some moments staring at the hands she was twisting in her lap and trying to decide what to do next.

Slowly Signor Bartoli opened his eyes and, seeing his visitor's bowed head, took advantage of the opportunity to observe her

closely, the rich brown hair was pulled back smoothly and gathered in a cluster of curls at the back of her head, emphasizing the
exquisite oval of her face, the long slim neck, and the elegant
shoulders. At last she looked up, the sapphire eyes serious, but
unwavering under the delicately arched brows. She had courage
this one, the courage to look an irascible old man straight in the
eye and wait for an answer. His habitually stern expression softened, smoothing out the sharp lines that ran from the beak of a
nose to a surprisingly sensitive mouth. "Occasionally I forget
what a truly gifted composer Mozart was."

Isobel's heart plummeted to the toes of her jean half-boots. Her
singing must have been such a disappointment that he could not
even bear to comment upon it. She rose quietly, gathered her
gloves and pelisse. "I thank you for your time, monsieur."

The music master rose also and shuffled over to her. He laid a
fatherly hand on her arm. "You misunderstand me, signorina. I
am so familiar with Signor Mozart's work that only a true *artista*
can make it fresh and new again for me. And that you have, signorina, the soul of an *artista*. It flows through your fingers as well
as from your throat." He lifted his hands and raised his shoulders
in an expansive shrug. "The voice, it could use more power on the
high notes, more power from here"—he pounded his nonexistent
stomach—"but that is to be expected. You are young and we will
work on these things, but the soul, *that* a music teacher can do
nothing about—one either has it or one does not. La Catalani, I
tell you very frankly, she does not—drama yes, she has drama,
but *l'anima*, no."

"Does that mean . . ."

"That I will make you greater than Catalani? Possibly. That I
will make you one of the most sought-after singers in London?
Sicuramente . . ."

"Ah, monsieur." Isobel blinked back the tears that would well
up in spite of her best efforts.

"Now you run along, drink hot tea, eat well, not this dreadful
English food that has no taste, but some true French cooking and
come to me tomorrow. We will begin then, no?"

"Mais oui," Isobel breathed. She pulled on her pelisse and
gloves as if in a trance and turned toward the door. "But, monsieur, the fee . . ."

"Has been taken care of, signorina." The music master was
amused by the sparkle of anger in those magnificent eyes and the

proud lift of the head. Yes, she had pride, the little one did, and with any luck and some help from him, she would go far.

There was nothing to say, but Isobel resolved to pay back every penny of her lessons to Lord Christian Hatherleigh if it took a lifetime. It was bad enough that with one brief visit he was able to enlist the aid of one of the most powerful figures in London's musical world. She swallowed hard and made her way to the door. "Then thank you, monsieur. I shall look forward to seeing you tomorrow."

Signor Bartoli opened the door for her and followed her down the stairs. "And I shall too. Good day to you, signorina."

Once outside, Isobel heaved a sigh of relief and glanced around her before walking briskly toward Oxford Street. The gray winter clouds had lifted and here and there patches of blue were showing through. She wanted to shout with joy. It was true then and not just an empty dream born of her desperate wish to do something with her life. She wanted to turn back in and throw her arms around Signor Bartoli. She wanted to run to Grosvenor Square and tell Lord Christian.

The thought made her stop in her tracks. Tell Lord Christian? Why should he be the first person to pop into her mind? Resolutely she pushed the thought aside. There was no Lord Christian in her life now and she was glad of it. His regular appearance in Grosvenor Square had been disturbing enough and his showing up in Manchester Square had been disconcerting in the extreme, but now that his goal had been accomplished—he had apologized and made amends for his brother's behavior and made sure she was introduced to Signor Bartoli—there was no likelihood that he would ever intrude into her life again. Odd how this thought, which should have relieved her, left her feeling so empty.

Ruthlessly she shoved these reflections aside as she turned the corner into Oxford Street, concentrating on the scene around her so as not to be distracted again by such unwelcome thoughts. She was glad that she had not told Marthe about leaving the Duke of Warminster's because now she could proceed with her lessons, secure in the knowledge that everyone in Manchester Square would simply assume that she was going to Warminster House instead of to Signor Bartoli's.

By the time Isobel had reached Bond Street, she had completely cleared her mind of all thoughts of Lord Christian and was concentrating instead on the many questions she wished to pose to Signor Bartoli. There was so much she wanted to know and it had been so long since she had had anyone to help her with her music, not since she and her father had left Buckinghamshire and Barford Court six years ago.

On impulse she turned down Bond Street rather than heading straight home. She usually did not linger on the fashionable thoroughfare because she never purchased anything from any of the establishments there, but today she decided to allow herself the luxury of strolling along imagining what she would purchase if she could command the fabulous sums that Madame Catalani did.

She was wrapped in such a pleasant haze of speculation that at first she did not hear her name being called.

"Isobel! I vow you have gone deaf from all the noise in this town," said a voice at her shoulder.

Isobel jumped and turned around to discover two ladies dressed in the height of fashion draped in nearly identical dove-colored Austrian shawl cloaks trimmed with sable and wearing Circassian turbans, one a deep crimson and the other a rich olive velvet. "Emily! Jane!" she squeaked. "I had no idea you were in town. I thought you remained buried happily in the country from one year to the next."

The Countess of Mordiford and the Marchioness of Verwood looked at one another and laughed. "We do. That is, we did, until our offspring grew to be so obstreperous and unmanageable and our husbands so dull that nothing but a Season in town could alleviate the tedium of our lives," the taller of the two replied.

"We only arrived in town last week and have taken houses next to each other in Brook Street and as Jane's Edward is only a year older than my Charles and her Maria is just the same age as my George they are close enough in age they can tease each other rather than their parents. And now that they are of an age to enjoy the Tower and the menagerie there to ride their ponies in the park, we convinced Mordiford and Verwood to bring us to town. Of course, we had to assure them they could spend their days looking over the horseflesh at Tattersall's and their evenings with friends at White's and we had to promise them we would only attend the barest minimum of fashionable squeezes before they would consent to bring us."

"Your mother and your father?"

"Are still at Barford Court," Emily replied. "We might be able to lure our husbands away from the country, but never Mama and Papa. Papa nearly went mad fretting about his sheep and his prize bull when they came to town for my Season and vowed never again to leave Barford for such an extended period, though it was less than a day's journey and he had weekly reports from Mr. Watson. And how does your papa go on?"

Isobel regaled them with stories of the French community, hoping against hope that they would not ask about her pupils and the Duchess of Warminster. Though Jane and Emily were not likely to encounter her father, she did not want to run the risk of their revealing to him that she had left her position in the Duke of Warminster's household, a position that their mother had been instrumental in procuring for her.

Hoping to avoid questions along this line, Isobel soon excused herself on the pretext of her father's concern for her whereabouts.

"But you must come driving with us in the park. Now that we are established, we expect to see a great deal of you, and you must join us in our box in the opera, though I am sure any singing that you hear will be far inferior to yours." Jane smiled fondly at her.

"If it is a fine day tomorrow, we shall send the carriage around for you at half after four and then you can take the air with us and catch us up on all the news," her sister added.

Isobel was not entirely sure she wished to run the risk of further conversation, for at the moment there were too many things she wished to keep private, such as leaving the Duke of Warminster's household and her becoming Signor Bartoli's pupil, but they were so patently delighted to see her and so insistent that she would not refuse. She had missed them. After she and her father had left Barford Court there had been a regular, if infrequent exchange of letters, but Emily and Jane had become so involved in their own lives that these communications had been brief at best, and nothing could quite take the place of conversation. Isobel looked forward to the next day with happy anticipation, for not only was there the drive and conversation with Jane and Emily to look forward to, but there was her first lesson with Signor Bartoli.

Chapter 14

The next morning Isobel presented herself at the house in Saint Martin's Street promptly at ten and found Signor Bartoli awaiting her with some impatience. The clock on the mantel was just striking the hour as she handed her pelisse to the servant girl who had led her to the music room.

"Ah, signorina, just on time," he greeted her approvingly from the bench of the pianoforte. "That is the mark of a professional. It is only those who pretend to be *artistas* who keep everyone waiting. Now"—he ran his fingers over the keys—"let us begin with some scales. I know that you are accustomed to accompanying herself, but you will concentrate better on the voice if I concentrate on the pianoforte, no?"

The time flew by as Isobel went over exercise after exercise, reaching higher and higher for the notes he played, but striving at the same time to gain them with the strength and control he demanded. "No, signorina, the music comes from here"—he patted his diaphragm—"not from here." The music teacher encircled his scrawny neck with long, bony fingers. "If you bring forth the music from the throat only and then try to project it and give it power you will produce only a screech of the most horrible kind. Now, try again, this time from deep inside you, or if it is easier for you to think of it, the heart. All music comes from the heart and you must dig deeply into yours to bring it forth. Yes"—he thumped vigorously on the pianoforte—"that is it. *Brava*, signorina. Now, once again." He played the rippling scale, but half a step higher. "Ah, yes. *Brava, brava.* Now perhaps you would like to try some songs." He sorted through the music in front of him, pulled out a sheet, and handed it to her.

Isobel was so exhausted from concentrating on her breathing and in following his instructions that she very much doubted she had the strength to sing another note, but oddly enough, once she began, the notes flowed effortlessly and with more power and assurance than she could ever remember experiencing before.

"Here are some new arrangements by Parke and Mazzinghi that might be suitable for the Countess of Morehampton's musicale."

"The Countess of Morehampton's musicale?" Isobel looked blankly at her instructor.

"Why yes, the countess sent me a note yesterday saying that she would dearly love to give a musicale if I could but suggest someone who could be counted upon to charm an audience. I wrote back that in fact I knew of such a person, an unknown, which of course delighted the dear lady even more for there is nothing she likes better than being the first to discover a new talent. There will be a quartet and a performer on the pianoforte, but she wished to have a special vocalist to offer to her guests. She takes great pride in her reputation for introducing new performers to the fashionable world."

"Oh, *mon Dieu*, but I do not know if I could . . ."

"Signorina, either you wish to become a great singer, or you do not. If you do not, then I wash my hands of you, for my time is too valuable to waste on someone who trembles at the thought of singing for an audience."

Isobel swallowed hard. "*Non*, monsieur, I am not afraid of singing for people. It is just that I do not know if I am a worthy . . ."

"Signorina, I am listening to you. If I, Guilio Bartoli, spare my time to listen to you, *credimi*, you are more than worthy to appear before a roomful of people who will be paying more attention to who is flirting with whom and what this one is wearing than to your music or your singing."

Isobel could not help chuckling at the accuracy of this statement. Though she did not frequent *ton* gatherings, she knew enough about human nature, and had observed enough among her own acquaintances to know that the music master was correct.

"Besides"—Signor Bartoli's eyes gleamed slyly—"the countess has already sent me a handsome sum to give the artist of my choice as an enticement, and I am prepared to give it to you to use as you, er, see fit."

Having witnessed his new pupil's reaction to the news that her lessons were already taken care of, the music master felt reasonably certain that she would insist on repaying her benefactor immediately and it amused him to picture it. The Italian had come to his own conclusion about Lord Christian Hatherleigh's reasons for taking an interest in Isobel de Montargis's career and they included more than sheer musical talent, though the young lady did possess that in abundance.

"That is most kind of her, and of you." Isobel hoped she did not sound too eager. Ordinarily she would not have given the money a second thought—it was the chance to sing and the confidence that Signor Bartoli seemed to have in her ability that were important—however, the thought of being able to march straight up to Lord Christian Hatherleigh and promptly dispose of her debt to him was extremely gratifying.

It was Signor Bartoli's turn to chuckle, for his pupil's expression reflected her thoughts as clearly as if she had spoken them, and he was willing to bet his pianoforte, his violin, and the cello leaning over in the corner that even before she returned home, she would call on Lord Christian to repay him for this lesson and to inform him that in the future she would take responsibility for all remunerations owed to her teacher.

The music master drew a heavy purse from his capacious pocket and held it out to her. "Here. The Countess of Morehampton's footman brought this not an hour before you arrived."

Isobel slowly extended her hand. Papa would die of mortification if he were to witness his carefully brought-up daughter acting as eager to be paid as any fishwife. Resolutely she pushed such a notion from her mind. He would just have to adjust to the idea of her earning money, for eventually people were going to be paying a great deal of money for the privilege of hearing her sing. She grasped the purse. "Thank you."

"As you can see, there is more than enough to cover several lessons," Signor Bartoli remarked. His tone was deliberately casual, but his sharp black eyes regarded her with lively curiosity.

Isobel glanced up at him and smiled shyly. Apparently he understood more about her than just her music. "That is reassuring to know. Thank you. I shall not disappoint you."

The music master smiled in return. "No, I do not think that you will. Now, off with you for I am due at Covent Garden to listen to a rehearsal. However, I want you to be thinking of other songs you would like to perform for the countess's guests besides the latest offerings from Mr. Parke and Signor Mazzinghi. Those will appeal, of course, because of the novelty, but we must have something else, should any true connoisseurs be among the audience."

Isobel nodded. "I shall think about it." She slid the purse into her reticule and allowed him to help her into her pelisse. "Thank you again."

"Think nothing of it. I would not be where I am today if I could not advance the careers of my students."

The door had barely closed behind her and she had taken only a few steps along Saint Martin's Street when isobel paused, struck by a sudden thought. Now that she had the wherewithal to pay for her first lessons and since it now seemed possible that she might earn more this way in the future, did it not make sense to go and repay her benefactor immediately so she would not remain any more indebted to him than she already was? Besides, she should at least let Lord Christian know that she had been accepted as Signor Bartoli's pupil.

Isobel refused to admit how attractive the entire proposition was, but she kept telling herself that this particular moment was as good as any to repay her debt. Since she was keeping her lessons a secret from Marthe, she could not very well send the servant to Lord Christian's lodgings with the payment, nor did she like to entrust anyone else with a sum of money. Therefore, it fell on her to accomplish the task, and what better time to do it than now when Lord Christian was likely to be out. And since it had always been her intention to repay him somehow, she had already discovered his address in Mount Street.

Filled with a sense of purpose, Isobel strode along in unlady-like haste, but the closer she came to Mount Street, the more slowly she walked, overwhelmed by an odd fluttery sensation in the pit of her stomach and a strange weakness in the knees that were as unwelcome as they were unusual. At last she found herself in front of the handsome oak door to Lord Christian's lodgings and for a moment the fluttery sensation threatened to overcome her—it must have resulted from the breathing lessons earlier that morning—but resolutely she seized the knocker and let it fall with a thump.

The door was opened by a wiry little man whose bright blue eyes were made to seem all the brighter by a skin so tan that it resembled old leather. If he was surprised to discover a young lady on his master's doorstep, he certainly gave no indication of it, but opened the door with a gracious, "Good day, miss."

Isobel cleared her throat, which was surprisingly tight, and thrust her hand into her reticule. She pulled out the purseful of coins as well as a pencil and a piece of paper and scribbled a note of thanks. Wrapping the note around the purse, she handed it back to the man. "Would you be so good as to see that your master receives this?" Then, wishing the avoid further scrutiny by eyes that were amazingly acute, she turned hastily away and began to descend the steps. It had seemed such a good idea at the time, but now, faced with Lord Christian's manservant, she felt all the awkwardness of the situation.

"But I am certain that his lordship would prefer to receive this from you himself. I shall just inform him that he has a visitor, Miss . . ."

Isobel's foot had already reached the bottom step when the servant spoke. She turned around reluctantly. "Miss Isobel de Montargis."

"Mademoiselle Isobel!" To the considerable surprise of both Isobel and the servant, Lord Christian materialized in the hall behind him. "You were quite right, Digby, in thinking that I should wish to speak to her." Christian did not elaborate on the unusual perspicacity of the batman, who was far more accustomed to informing importunate women that his master was not at home than he was to encouraging them to speak to Lord Christian.

Apparently Digby had deduced, and quite correctly too, that this was no ordinary young woman. Usually, Digby, who was paid exceedingly well to protect his master's privacy, dispensed with any unusual visitors swiftly and easily, so the fact that there had been some discussion with this one had roused the curiosity of Lord Christian, who had been well within earshot and able to recognize the visitor's voice.

"Do let us go into the library, mademoiselle." Christian gestured to the doorway just visible straight ahead at the top of the staircase. Not knowing what else to do, Isobel followed his direction and proceeded ahead of him up the stairs. Behind her, Christian paused just long enough to glance over his shoulder and nod approvingly at the batman.

Satisfied that he had correctly interpreted his master's wishes, Digby returned to his task of decanting the port that had been interrupted by the appearance of this surprising young lady. Though he always strove to maintain the wooden expression appropriate to his calling, the batman did allow himself to indulge in the tiniest of grins. Meanwhile, Digby's mind was alive with speculation. To be sure, the female sex, both proper and improper, were always running after his lordship, but the improper ones usually demanded an audience, and the proper ones rarely showed their faces, preferring to send footmen or pages with discreet missives. Nor could he ever recall that any one of them, proper or improper, had ever wished to *give* his master anything. It was quite the opposite—so much so that in his mind at least, Digby had begun to equate the word *female* with the word *demanding*.

But this female had been powerfully intent on giving something to his lordship and equally intent on leaving it without his lordship's knowledge. It was all very strange and very intriguing.

Chapter 15

In the library, Isobel was giving Lord Christian something else beside money—a piece of her mind. "It is most improper, most unacceptable of you, my lord, to attempt to pay for my lessons and I will not have it." Having refused the chair he offered her, Isobel stood in front of the fire clutching her reticule. "If I had known you were planning such a thing I should never have agreed to see Signor Bartoli."

"And what did he think of you? I'll wager he was most surprised and pleased to discover that I knew what I was about when I arranged for your introduction to him. Did you enjoy yourself?"

"Oh yes." She sighed. "It was extraordinary how in such a very short time he was able to help me attain a good deal more control and much greater force in my singing. He is very clever, is he not?" Delighted by the opportunity to share her exciting experience, she allowed herself to be diverted momentarily from her tirade. "Nevertheless"—she grasped the reticule more firmly—"I cannot allow myself to be indebted to you, so I have come to return to you the cost of my lessons."

"My dear young lady, there is absolutely no need for that. Believe me, it is a mere trifle, and I cannot think of any way I would rather spend it. Your enthusiasm is more than ample repayment for the little I have done." He saw that she was not in the least convinced. "Very well, then, think of it as my contribution to the musical public at large by furthering the refinement of an exquisite artist. No, no." He closed her fingers around the proffered purse. "I could lose as much, nay, I *have* lost as much in one evening at the card table. It is absurd for you to feel you must pay me back."

"But I *must!*" The words burst from her. "Even as it is, I can never begin to thank you for introducing me to Signor Bartoli."

Looking down into those blue eyes, dark with the intensity of her feelings, Christian was not a little touched by her desperate wish to be independent, to be beholden to no one for anything. What a singular person she was. He was not at all sure that his spur-of-the-moment gesture was worthy of such a response, and he could not help feeling a little ashamed in the face of such gratitude; after all, he had done it almost as much for himself, and to spite his brother, as he had done it for her.

Christian was silent for a moment as he tried to find the words to convince Isobel that by letting him help her she would be the one granting him a favor, giving him the chance to participate once again in something worthwhile, something valuable, something beyond the fashionable routine of the *ton*. "Of course you must pay me back."

The thick, dark lashes fluttered in surprise. She had not expected him to give in so easily. "But it will not be with money, I will take more than money." A teasing note crept into his voice as he paused to gauge her reaction. A slight blush tinged her cheeks, but she continued to return his gaze steadily, if uneasily.

"You must tell me what I may do." She spoke calmly enough, but he could tell from the rapid pulse at the base of her throat that she was afraid to hear what he would demand in payment.

"It is not entirely fair because it will take more effort on your part to repay the lessons than it took on my part to pay for them, but the only thing I shall ask in return is to see a admiring audience at your feet. It does not have to be at Covent Garden, or even at the King's Theatre or Drury Lane, but I want to be there when the rest of the world derives as much pleasure from your singing as I have. But please"—he gestured again toward the seat by the fire—"now that you are here, tell me how you found Signor Bartoli. Is he truly the ogre he appears to be?"

At last Isobel took the proffered chair, her brow wrinkled in thought. "No, I do not think so, at least he was very kind to me. In the beginning I found him rather alarming, but once the lesson began he was everything that was helpful and encouraging."

"Ah, but that is because you are a gifted musician and, therefore, worth his while; to me he was an ogre the entire time. Like you, he considers me a useless fribble at best, at the worst, an uncultivated barbarian."

"What? I have never said such a thing."

"No, for you are too well mannered, but you certainly thought it."

"Why I never . . ." Isobel paused self-consciously, remembering their first encounter in the music room at Warminster House and how annoyed she had been.

Christian grinned. "Precisely. And Signor Bartoli has exactly the same opinion. But now that I have demonstrated my taste by sending such a treasure his way, he will think better of me next time."

"I am not a treasure." Isobel felt her cheeks grow warm again. Would she never stop allowing the man to disconcert her? It was most unnerving. She was never ruffled in such a way by the Comte de Pontarlier or the Chevalier d'Entremont, people whose opinion of her did not matter in the slightest. But with this man to whom it was imperative that she demonstrate her independence and cool self-reliance, she was forever being caught off guard. He seemed to have an uncanny ability to get beneath the serene facade she worked so carefully to maintain.

"You and I both know that that is not true or Signor Bartoli would not have wasted an instant of his precious time on you."

The tense lines of Isobel's face softened and she smiled as she remembered the music teacher's words. "He *did* say that I made Mozart fresh and new for him again," she acknowledged softly.

"Ah." Christian was unprepared for the odd sense of pride that washed over him. He almost felt like a damned father watching his son take his first fence. He had not realized until this moment how very anxious he had been over the entire thing, how he had been longing to find out what had happened during Isobel's lesson with the crusty music master. It had been a long time, a very long time, since he had experienced such a sense of gratification as he was experiencing now. And it had been even longer ago that he had shared something with somebody in this special way—not since Mark. Not since Mark had he allowed himself to be so closely involved in someone else's life, in someone else's hopes and dreams. Not since Mark had he truly had hopes and dreams of his own. Now he did. He wanted to see Mademoiselle Isobel take her rightful place among the Catalanis, the Grassinis, the Mrs. Billingtons of the world. "Then you have done well indeed, for from what I saw of the man, I would say that he is not one to lavish praise or interest unless it is well deserved. And is he worthy of his reputation? How did you find his teaching?"

"Oh, he is very good, more quick, I think, than Monsieur Verbier, who was a wonderful musician, but not as good a teacher. He could tell me what I was doing wrong, but not how to correct it. Signor Bartoli sees my weaknesses in an instant and tells me how to work on them. It is truly remarkable. You have no notion how exciting it is."

"You are satisfied, then? He was not too critical?" There was no need to ask, the glow in her eyes was proof enough of her pleasure and her enthusiasm. Odd how simple it had been to make her so happy.

"Oh yes, I am. If he were not critical, then I should not trust him to help me improve."

How different she was from other women, who demanded that he make their lives easier and more luxurious. She scorned the luxuries yet welcomed the opportunity he had given her that actually gave her more work, even while it expanded her chances for achieving her goal.

Occupied by these thoughts, Christian was silent for a moment, his gaze fixed upon her in such a way that Isobel wondered at it, and pulling on her gloves rather self-consciously, she rose. "I have kept you far too long. Indeed, I only meant to leave the payment of my debt with your servant, but . . ." Her voice trailed off.

Christian rose as well, though reluctantly. He was strangely loath to let her leave. He had missed seeing her at Warminster House, though he had not known how much until this moment. He wanted to beg her to stay awhile longer or, at the very least, to ask her when he would see her again, but he knew she would take instant exception to it. He followed her to the door. "I do hope you continue to enjoy your lessons. You must let me know if there is anything more I can do."

"You have done more than enough already. But I do wish you would let me . . ."

Christian took one gloved hand and raised it gently to his lips. "Believe me, your happiness is all the payment I ask."

Isobel paused, transfixed by the look in his eyes. His voice was low and soft as a caress and she could feel the warmth of his lips on her hand through her gloves. A lump rose in her throat and the fluttery feeling invaded her stomach again. They were so close she could feel his breath on her cheek and it felt as though he were kissing her lips rather than her hand. Almost unconsciously she swayed closer to him, trying to read the expression in the gray-green eyes fixed so intently on her. She had the oddest urge to pull off her glove and trace the hard, square line of his jaw to feel the strength of him.

Isobel gulped. What was she doing? She had come to repay her debt to this man, to rid herself of all obligation to him so that she would never have to see him again, and now she was practically falling into his arms. She drew a long, shaky breath, retrieved her hand, and smoothed her gloves. "Thank you," she whispered. She turned and almost ran out the door and down the steps, not even stopping to catch her breath when she gained the street. It was not until she reached Berkeley Square that Isobel slowed her rapid pace.

She must have been mad to call on him, and even more mad to allow him to invite her in. Isobel turned into Bond Street and slowed to a properly sedate pace. She should abide by Lord Christian's wish and forget about trying to repay him since her one attempt to do so had caused her to lose all sense of propriety. She would forget about repaying him, in fact, she would forget about Lord Christian altogether, in spite of the gnawing sense of emptiness she felt at such a prospect.

Isobel drew a deep breath. It was time to concentrate on her singing, forget about everything else. Her music had always sustained her in the past. It would sustain her now. But oddly enough, she did not feel as comforted by that thought as she always had in the past.

Chapter 16

While Isobel was striving to put all thought of Lord Christian Hatherleigh from her mind, he was striving mightily to recall every tiny detail of their encounter as he stretched his long legs in front of the fireplace. What was it about her that affected him so strongly? She was beautiful, but all the women he had ever enjoyed had been beautiful. She was passionate, but most of the women he had known had been passionate. She was intelligent, and a few, very few, women with whom he had been intimate were intelligent. It was more than any one of these, and it was more than the combination of all of them, but something more rare, that drew him to her.

He smiled as he gazed into the embers, remembering the light in her eyes and the glow of her skin as she insisted on handing him the money to pay for her lessons. There was a special intensity about Isobel that set her apart from everyone else. She believed in things. She wanted to accomplish things in her life, and Christian wanted fervently to help her do so. But it was the very spirit he admired in her that kept her from allowing him to help, and it was this very spirit that would make her succeed with, or without, his help.

That was it; he admired her in the truest sense of the word, admired her in a way that he had not admired anyone since his boyhood when he had followed Potts the coachman around constantly, or certainly not since Wellington, who had been simply Wellesley at the time, had repulsed Victor's army at Talavera, and won the esteem of Christian and every other soldier.

There was a fire in Isobel de Montargis that warmed his soul, a fire he had once had, but seemed to have lost in the long period of suffering and brutality of war. He ached to pull her into his arms, to hold her slender body close to him, to caress the smooth oval of her face and touch the softness of her cheeks, to . . . What did he want? These were dangerous grounds, and at the moment, Christian was not entirely sure he wanted to explore them.

He grabbed the decanter of brandy from the table beside him and splashed it into the glass sitting on the silver tray next to it. Tossing it off quickly, he concentrated on the trickle of warmth down his throat. He set down the empty glass and rose, grabbed a sheet of paper from his desk drawer, scrawled a few lines asking Blanche to join him for supper or, at the very least, to allow him to call on her. Sealing it, he rang for Digby.

"My lord?" The batman appeared almost before Christian had removed his hand from the bellpull.

"Please see that this gets to Mademoiselle Desmoulins."

"Very good, my lord." Digby took the note, hurrying out of the room with a haste that had more to do with his efforts to conceal any possible reactions that he might betray than with an eagerness to do his master's bidding. If Lord Christian were to see his face, Digby knew that he would read the disappointment in it, for the note to Mademoiselle Desmoulins seemed to negate any interest in the intriguing young lady who had just called on Lord Christian. The batman found it odd how quickly the note to the actress followed the departure of the unexpected visitor, which suggested that in some way there was a connection between the two things, but what was the connection?

Even if he had been willing to explain it, Lord Christian could not have told his servant what had prompted him to write the note to Blanche. It was not until many hours later, as he emerged from her discreetly elegant house in Marylebone that he knew himself what had driven him to seek her out. But now, as her door closed behind him, he was well aware that what he had hoped would happen had not. Even as he drew in the first refreshing breath of the cool night air, he wondered whether Isobel had confided in anyone else about her lesson. Yes, he admitted to himself, he had thrown himself into Blanche's seductive white arms to wipe all thoughts of Isobel from his mind.

As he had slowly planted kisses down Blanche's smooth, creamy neck and inhaled her musky scent, as his hands had traced the luscious curves of her considerably well-endowed body, he had not thought at all about Isobel. And as Blanche had moaned in pleasure and he had surrendered himself up to sensual delights, he had even forgotten Isobel entirely, until he had awakened several hours later feeling pleasantly tired, but strangely empty in a way he had never before experienced. And in spite of his resolution to push aside all serious reflections, he wondered if this odd sense of hollowness had anything to do with Isobel's visit to him.

As he had pulled on his shirt he decided that possibly it had, and shrugging into his coat, he admitted to himself that he had sought out Blanche to assuage the ache left by Isobel's departure.

Why was this happening to him now? He had always been able to keep the women in his life separate. Early on, he had discovered that life was far less confusing, and certainly far more peaceful if he enjoyed one woman's favors at a time, but he had never become so attached to any woman that when the time had come to leave her he had suffered any pangs of regret. Nor had his mind ever strayed back to any one of these women after the affair was over. And he had certainly never thought of one woman when he was in the arms of another.

Christian strolled slowly home, grateful for the bracing air, and the darkness. How could a person with whom he had spent so little time affect him as strongly as Mademoiselle de Montargis affected him? And, furthermore, what was he going to do about it now that he would be seeing less of her. Since the moment she had left his brother's house, Christian had looked forward to being able to tell her about the appointment he had arranged with Signore Bartoli. After that, he had hoped that she might somehow let him know how the lessons were progressing. She had done that, but in a way that made it clear she was entirely capable of managing both her lessons and her life without any assistance from him. Now he was not even sure how she would treat him should he happen to appear at the de Montargises' modest lodgings in Manchester Street. Certainly her father would not welcome him, for he had already made it abundantly clear that only his exquisite breeding had allowed Christian into his drawing room in the first place. If the duc had known the true extent of the Englishman's interest in his daughter, he would have been outraged.

Christian smiled grimly in the darkness. He would just have to rely on his wits to discover an opportunity to see the lovely Frenchwoman again. After all, he had lived by his wits in the Peninsula, and fairly successfully too—the fact that he had survived it was ample proof of that.

Upon reaching Mount Street he hesitated, unsure of whether or not he wanted to turn in. Perhaps he had been mistaken in seeking the intimacy of another woman's boudoir. Perhaps, instead, he should have sought distraction at the gaming table, or oblivion in several bottles of port. Undoubtedly there would still be a few choice spirits left seated around the gaming tables at Brooks's. He turned, walked a few steps in the direction of Saint James's, and paused. At the beginning of the evening he had been avoiding reflection, but now, having sought out the seductive Blanche and discovered that even her considerable charms had only forestalled reflection, he realized that now that he was in the middle of this somber, self-examining mood, he would only be disgusted by the rowdy atmosphere of the gaming room in the early-morning hours. The solitary confines of his own library and the consumption of numerous glasses of brandy in front of his own fireplace were the best remedy for this sort of thing. He knew from experience that on the rare occasion when he could not distract himself from looking deep into his soul, the best thing was simply to sit down and drink brandy until the urge had passed.

Returning to his own doorstep, Christian sent the sleepy Digby to bed, poked the embers in the fireplace into a comforting glow, and tossed off two glasses of brandy in quick succession, trying all the while to blot out of his mind the picture of Isobel as she had stood proudly in front of him, thrusting the bag of coins at him, or poised on the edge of the chair across from him, leaning forward eagerly, her lovely face alight with excitement as she spoke of her lesson with Signor Bartoli. It took a good many more glasses of brandy before he felt a soothing lethargy creep over him. Christian propped his feet up on a footstool, tilted his head back, and waited for oblivion to come.

How many times had he done this in an effort to erase the horrific images of battle from his mind? And when had they become horrific? When had the excitement of the charge and the exhilaration of competing with a foe equally intent on winning given way to the corroding sense of sadness and loss. To be sure, he had mourned lives lost after every battle, but had always consoled himself with the knowledge that his fellow soldiers went, as he himself would have gone, proud to serve in a noble cause.

But over the years the excitement of the battle had dwindled into nothing and the sadness had increased until he had begun to mourn the losses of friend and foe alike. He had seen the weariness in everyone's eyes and then, as he had told Isobel, he had begun to fight, not so much to drive the French out of Spain and Portugal as to end the war entirely. Now that the fighting was over, enough so that he and parts of his regiment had been sent home, far away from the carnage and the desolation that had begun to haunt him, now he felt useless and bored. In the Peninsula fear and death, illness and hunger, had been constant companions, but at least he had known he was alive. Here in London, everyone seemed merely to be acting in some great and meaningless charade. He had almost been ready to beg Wellington to take him back as a member of his staff, a messenger, anything so long as he was doing something more than wasting time, but then he had met Isobel and things had changed. She was alive and he had begun to regain his interest in life, to feel some of his own vitality returning. Through her he had regained a sense of purpose by becoming her champion. But now that she had Signor Bartoli, a far more useful advocate for her in the musical world, his own part was over.

Christian should have been elated that his plan had worked so well and that she was now well on her way to attaining her dreams. Instead, he felt more alone than ever, knowing that she would achieve what she longed for and, achieving that, would have no need for him at all. What was he to do now?

Christian willed himself to empty his mind, to concentrate on the flickering flames in front of him, and to inhale the heady fumes of the brandy as he sipped it, slowly now. He breathed deliberately, rhythmically, forcing himself to relax as he had done the nights before battles. Finally his eyelids grew heavy and his head sank further back into the chair. The empty brandy glass slipped from his fingers and he slept.

Chapter 17

While Christian might have been seeking to obliterate disturbing thoughts of Isobel by distracting himself with Blanche and dulling his senses with brandy, Isobel was determined to throw herself into her music with so much energy that she would have no time to think of anyone or anything else. She worked tirelessly in her lessons and at home, striving over and over again to make each note perfect, to catch the precise mood and phrasing for every piece of music until even her teacher remonstrated with her. "Signorina, to become an *artista* one has to work, yes, but you are exhausting yourself. You are pale, you become thin. It is not good."

"But, monsieur, I feel I have made so much progress that I do not want to slow down. I want to do justice to all that you have taught me."

"*Certo.* And that is most admirable, but not to the point of exhaustion. When you do that, then the music becomes only work, no joy, and your singing loses its power to move. *Finito! Capisci?*" He peered at her anxiously, his dark eyes sympathetic under the bushy gray brows.

"*Oui, monsieur*, I understand, but time is so precious."

"*But?* But nothing. You must not be impatient. Great singers grow. They are not made, they grow, but their growth is like that of a tree, slow and steady, not like that of a flower. They do not grow in one season alone. But they do not die in a season either. Besides"—he smiled appealingly and a crafty gleam twinkled in his eye—"you must be not only in your best voice, but also in your best looks for the Countess of Morehampton's musicale. Go out, get some fresh air, get some color in your cheeks. These *Inglesi* they are mad for the fresh air, but sometimes it is not a bad idea, no?"

"Yes, monsieur." Isobel knew that her teacher was right. Everything he said made perfect sense, but she needed to throw herself

into her music right now. She needed to forget that with every encouraging piece of news from the Continent concerning Bonaparte's decline in fortunes, her father spoke more firmly about
returning to France. She needed to forget how frugally they were
forced to live without her regular income from the Duke of
Warminster, and she needed to forget how Lord Christian . . . No!
She would not even think along those lines. Isobel drew a deep
breath. "I shall try to do as you say. And I have been driving in
the park."

Signor Bartoli nodded encouragingly. "*Eccellente.* You have
practiced enough this week. Now you must take the air, get some
rest. Give yourself time for what you have learned to become a
part of you. You will be surprised how much you have absorbed
without realizing it. Ah, your face betrays you. It tells me, *I will
listen to this man about music, but about me, what can he know?* I
know this, signorina, you are a worker. That is good. Too many
people with musical skill think they can become artists without
working, but in you, work is too much. It can kill your music. You
need to enjoy life more. You are *seria, troppo seria, no?*" He
cocked his head in such a comical way that Isobel could not help
laughing. "*Vabbene,* I have made you smile. And, I will tell you
another thing. I will also make you a teacher again. I know that
you are no longer with this Lord Warminster, but there are many
other rich lords who need teachers for their little darlings. They
come to me all the time and I have to say no. Now I will suggest
you. Then maybe you will not worry so much."

Isobel felt warm tears prickle her eyelids. How had he been
able, in so little time, to understand so much about her? "Thank
you, monsieur. Yes, that would help, though I cannot think why
you would help."

"Signorina, you are modest. You work hard, who would not
wish to help you? There are so many in the world who have more
and deserve less than you, so many who are so much less gifted
and demand so much more in the way of praise and renown." The
music master could see she was perilously close to tears and his
heart was touched. "Yes, I will recommend you to Lord Gravetye
for his daughter this very day. Mind you, I cannot insure that he
will not have a brother also who will come to browbeat me to
make you famous." Signor Bartoli watched with interest as his
pupil's pale cheeks flushed a delicate rose. It was just as he had
suspected, Lord Christian Hatherleigh might have recommended
Mademoiselle Isobel to him because she had a beautiful voice,

but there was more to it than a connoisseur's appreciation, and Mademoiselle Isobel seemed to be well aware of it. Who could tell, perhaps she returned his lordship's interest? The music master chuckled softly. "I shall tease you no further. Go, get some rest, some fresh air. We shall have one more lesson and then the musicale. But, remember, for most of these barbarians, your looks will be more important than your voice, so you must look your best."

"Oui, monsieur." Isobel tied the ribbons of her bonnet thoughtfully. What he said made a great deal of sense. Fortunately, Jane and Emily had arranged to take her driving in the park later in the afternoon so she would be able to follow this well-meant advice. The two ladies could be counted on for distraction, for if they were not describing the latest antics of their children, then they were recounting gossip about the members of the *ton*.

"It is so delightful to you have along with us on our drive," Jane remarked later that day as the barouche rolled along Duke Street toward the park. "For we can talk about how clever our children are without fear of competition. If we are alone together, we wind up pulling caps over who is the better at sums, my Edward or Emily's Charles, or which child is more difficult at age four, a girl like my Maria, or a boy like her George."

Emily broke in laughing. "You have no idea how teasing an active four year old can be, Isobel." Her voice drifted off as she caught sight of the duchess of Warminster's carriage turning the corner into the park. "That reminds me. I hear that Warminster's brother is back from the Peninsula. I know that during my first season he was all the rage, but the matchmaking mamas soon realized that no one, not even a diamond of the first water was going to catch him in the parson's mousetrap. Of course, that did not stop several of them from flirting scandalously with him. He was so devilishly handsome and so determinedly elusive that he drove everyone quite mad with frustration. Why Eliza St. John nearly ruined herself trying to fix his attention. Have you met him yet?"

Isobel admitted that she had, in what she hoped was a manner disinterested enough to end the conversation, but Emily, who saw herself as one of the *ton's* dashing young matrons, was not about to be put off so easily. "Is he as handsome as ever?"

"I never consider these things. Perhaps he is handsome, but I really can not say."

"Oh, Isobel, you are too provoking! Did you not even notice what a fine figure of a man he makes? So tall and distinctive with that auburn hair and that damn-your-eyes air." Emily sighed dramatically. "No, Isobel, I will not let you off without a better answer than that."

"Governesses do not spend a great deal of time with the family, you know, Emily," she equivocated. Isobel could see, however, that she was not going to be allowed to evade the issue, and the sooner she responded satisfactorily to Emily's question, the sooner she would be allowed to drop the subject and move on to less dangerous topics of conversation. "He was well-enough-looking, I suppose."

"Well-enough-looking, indeed. Isobel, you are impossible. Do you pay attention to nothing besides your music?"

"Very little. It is my livelihood, you know."

Emily was instantly contrite and reached over to pat her friend's lilac-gloved hand. "Of course, and it is bad of me to tease you, but I do wish you would find some gallant who would make you forget your music just once."

"But I love my music."

Emily's brow wrinkled, making her ordinarily sunny features almost comical in her distress. "I know you do, dear, but you know what I mean. It is not natural to be so serious. I wish you would just enjoy yourself once in a while."

"We shall just have to take matters into our own hands, sister." Jane, more perceptive than her sibling, and of a more serious nature herself, could see that the entire conversation was causing distress to their friend. "Why do you not join us tomorrow evening at the opera? We shall send the carriage around for you. It is a new opera by Dibdin they are offering, *The Farmer's Wife*, with Miss Stephens performing. It may be too frivolous for your liking, but it will at least provide diversion and an opportunity for you to feel superior." She flashed a sympathetic smile at Isobel. "Do say you will join us."

"Yes, do come," her sister joined in. "You can tell us everything that is wrong with the performance so that we may act very bored and knowledgeable when our opinion is asked."

"Very well, but if I criticize it and the rest of the world is entirely swept away by it, you may find that your plan has the opposite effect and you are regarded as excessively odd."

Emily laughed. "Then it is fortunate we are not trying to take the *ton* by storm and it will be years before Maria has her come-out so the world will have forgotten any faux pas her mother or her aunt might have made. Besides, no one really goes to the opera to listen to the music. They go to see who else is there, what everyone else is wearing, and who is sitting in what box with whom. Your presence in our box alone will cause a stir because no one will know who you are and you are so lovely."

"But the world will wonder at your being seen with someone as *démodé* as I, for you see." Isobel looked down at her lavender sarcenet pelisse. "I do not frequent the best shops in Bond Street. I do not even own a proper carriage dress, much less . . ."

"Pooh!" Emily interrupted her. "You are French and the French ladies always have more style no matter what they wear. You always have had style and your face and your figure are so elegant that no one will notice what you are wearing."

"Emily is right," Jane chimed in, "You carry yourself with such an air that it does not signify in the least what you have on."

However, it did matter to Isobel, and not wishing to repay her friends' kindness by presenting a dowdy appearance, she enlisted the aid of Marthe's clever fingers the moment she returned home. Fortunately her father was dining with the Comte d'Artois that evening so she and Marthe were able to have the simplest of meals before beginning their task.

In the feeble light of a single guttering candle Isobel removed a length of blond lace from an old evening gown of her mother's and Marthe trimmed her dress of pink satin with that and a double row of white satin rouleaux which had been carefully saved from another of the duchesse's gowns.

"Eh bien, with the lace around the neck you be as *à la mode* as the *élégantes* I see in Bond Street." Marthe put a final stitch in the trim. "And no one that I have seen has the figure you do to carry it off."

"Marthe, you are far too partial."

"Non, mademoiselle. You know I pay attention to these things and I would never let you leave the house if I were not certain you would appear as well dressed as they. Perhaps you are not so richly dressed, but you have true style. The de Montargis women have always been known for their exquisite taste and they will continue to do so as long as I have a breath to draw."

Isobel smiled fondly at the old servant. "I know, Marthe, I know. I shall try to live up to your standards, but I fear I can never be as lovely as Mama."

"Not so beautiful, perhaps, but you have more spirit. And that *espièglerie* will turn more heads than her beauty. She was like a delicate flower, too delicate for this abominable climate." Marthe sighed gustily, and pausing with her needle in midair, blinked rapidly before continuing. "But you, *ma petite*, you have that certain something that makes everyone take notice of you. Rest assured, even among all those English ladies at the opera, you will be the one the gentlemen pay attention to."

"But I have no interest in gentlemen noticing me."

"Bah. Every woman cares, and so should you. Perhaps that handsome English milord . . ."

"I told you, I have no interest in any gentlemen," Isobel responded firmly, but even in the dim light, Marthe could see the faint blush that rose to her mistress's cheeks and she knew, with the intuition of an old family retainer, that that precise thought had already crossed her mistress's mind.

Chapter 18

Entering the Barford's box at the opera the next evening, Isobel was grateful that Marthe's sharp eyes were not there to observe her scanning the other boxes. She told herself that she was looking to see if the Duke and Duchess of Warminster were there or if Lord Christian Hatherleigh was as much a connoisseur of the musical world as he claimed to be, but deep in her heart she knew that she just wanted to see him again. Catching a glint of candlelight on rich auburn hair, she hastily pulled into the sheltering darkness of the Barfords' box before he could look in her direction.

Although she hated herself for caring at all, Isobel was pleased to see that Lord Christian was quite alone. Then he truly did come to the opera for the music. He had not been deceiving her with false claims. It was not until the wave of relief washed over her at this discovery that Isobel realized how important it was to her to have him be honest with her about such a thing.

However, even as she was observing Lord Christian, a rather military-looking gentleman with a woman on each arm entered the box and claimed his attention.

"There, see, I told you that all the women were mad for Lord Christian Hatherleigh," Emily hissed at her elbow. "Look at them, both of them flirting with him outrageously. Why the gentleman escorting them might just as well not exist for all the attention they are paying him."

Christian, however, was more delighted to see the gentleman than the ladies. "Solly, you old dog, when did you get back in town? And how is old Douro now that Boney's beaten?" He greeted one of Wellington's former aides-de-camp enthusiastically.

"Now, now," the pert little brunette on Major Lord Solverton's right arm wagged a coquettish finger at Christian. "The war is over, there is to be none of that talk. It is time you military gentlemen began to pay attention to the ladies again."

"Yes," her companion, a statuesque blonde agreed in a throaty voice. "But after making war against men you may need a great deal of practice learning how to make love to women." She eyed him hungrily as she licked her full lower lip. "Do let us sit down, Solly. The opera will be so much more interesting from here." She smiled suggestively at Christian as she sank down on the chair next to him and leaned toward him in such a way as to reveal her *décolletage* to its fullest extent. "Solverton tells me that all he did during the war was run errands for the generals. What did you do? I am sure it was much more interesting."

"Though he was better known for his reckless courage and fine horsemanship than for his mental abilities, Lord Solverton was clever enough to perceive that Christian's eyes kept straying to the stage and the orchestra that was tuning up in the pit. He winked conspiratorially at his friend as he held out his arms to lead his two companions out of the box. "Come along, girls, Christian likes to keep his music and his women separate. Perhaps we can convince him to join us for a snug little supper later."

Christian grinned. "Perhaps." But once the performance began, he forgot entirely about Lord Solverton and his companions. As he listened intently to the performers he kept picturing Isobel on the stage in front of him. Surely her voice was truer and sweeter than that of Miss Stephens. Or was he being too partial? He wondered how his protégée was progressing in her lessons with Signor Bartoli. It had been difficult to think up excuses to appear along Saint Martin's Street, but he had come up with enough to pass by the music master's door once or twice in the past few days, but to no avail. Signor Bartoli's most recently acquired pupil was not to be seen entering or exiting, nor anywhere in between Saint Martin's Street and Manchester Square. The more he failed to encounter Mademoiselle Isobel, the more obsessed Christian became with seeing her, so much so that he began to imagine he saw her in every tall, slim woman he saw in Bond Street or strolling in Hyde Park. He even began to think that it was she in the box opposite his, leaning forward intently to listen to the music while her companions whispered to one another in the background.

Christian edged forward to get a closer look, but the woman, apparently sensing his interest in her, drew back hastily into the shadows. He must have been mistaken, for surely Mademoiselle de Montargis would have acknowledged him in some way. Or would she?

Isobel could have kicked herself for becoming so interested in the music that she forgot everything and leaned forward, her elbows propped on the edge of the box, and gave herself up to the pleasures of the music. It was not until a sudden movement in the box across from her distracted her attention from the stage that she realized the occupant was studying her closely. With a stifled gasp she pulled back. The less she saw of Lord Christian Hatherleigh, the better. The mere sight of him set her heart pounding uncomfortably as she recalled the warmth of his lips on her gloved hand and the look in his eyes the last time she had seen him.

Those eyes had seemed to warm as he had looked at her, sending a secret message meant just for her. Undoubtedly she had been mistaken, undoubtedly he adopted that same intimate air with every woman, and therein lay the devastating attraction for which, according to Jane and Emily, he was famous. Certainly it had seemed to captivate the two women who had just visited him in his box. Isobel had not been close enough to read anyone's expression, but from the way the blonde had practically thrown herself at him, Isobel could well imagine the approval in his eyes. She grew uncomfortably warm herself recalling the way he had looked her up and down that first day in the Duke of Warminster's music room. It had made her breathless and given her the oddest sensation as though she were standing before him dressed in nothing but her chemise, or, perhaps, not even that.

"Why, Isobel"—Emily leaned over to whisper conspiratorially, "I do believe Lord Christian has recognized you. He appears to be looking in this direction. If you but nod to him, perhaps he will call on us after this act."

"I most certainly shall not do anything so vulgar or so forward. I told you, I have barely met the man." In her annoyance, Isobel forget to lower her voice.

Jane turned around in some surprise. It was very unlike their usually self-possessed friend to be so vehement. Meeting her sister's mischievous glance, she frowned and shook her head ever so slightly. If Isobel de Montargis wished to have nothing to do with Lord Christian Hatherleigh, then it was up to them to respect her wishes.

Emily sighed and leaned back in her chair. Jane could be such a spoilsport sometimes. It was as plain as pikestaff that Isobel was more aware of the Duke of Warminster's brother than she let on, for more than once her eyes had strayed toward his Warminsters'

box and she had appeared uncharacteristically agitated since
Emily had called attention to Lord Christian and his visitors.

A sly little smile crept across her face as Emily glanced again
at their guest. Jane might have interfered for the moment now, but
she, Emily, was not going to give up this intriguing line of inves-
tigation. She would just have to proceed more carefully. If Isobel
was not going to acknowledge Lord Christian when it was obvious that she was interested in him, why Emily was going to have
to make sure that they came across him some other way. Yes,
Emily's smile broadened, she was just going to have to take Isobel about with her more—to Bond Street, to the park, all the
places where encounters with members of the *ton*, such as Lord
Christian, were unavoidable.

However, it was not Emily, but the Countess of Morehampton
who was responsible for the next meeting between Isobel and
Lord Christian. Knowing, from his attendance at the vocal concerts at the Hanover Square Rooms that Lord Christian was a
dévoté of fine music, the countess made sure to include him in the
invitations to her musicale, for which Signor Bartoli had
promised to provide a new performer who could be counted upon
to impress her audience.

Greeting Isobel and her teacher before the guests began arriving, the countess had been somewhat surprised by the young
lady's proud bearing and her air of quiet elegance. In fact, she
confided to Signor Bartoli as Isobel went off to a corner of the
room to review her music, she looked more like a guest than a
performer.

"Do not be deceived by Mademoiselle Isobel," the music master reassured his patroness, "she may look to be a gently born
young lady, for she is, after all, the Duc de Montargis's daughter,
but she is first and foremost a musician and an artist of great
power and agility as you will see."

"If *you* say that about her," the countess wheezed, her ample
bosom heaving under the confines of her tight, green satin corsage, "then she must be outstanding indeed, for your taste is the
most exacting. But now I must leave you, for it is time to meet
my guests." She opened her fan and waved it vigorously in front
of her flushed face for several minutes, then snapped it shut,
pushed one damp curl into place under her imposing turban, and
proceeded majestically across the room, looking like nothing so
much as a battleship under full sail.

Signor Bartoli returned to his pupil, who was reading her music and humming beneath her breath. "Come, let us get into the anteroom and procure a glass of lemonade that the countess has so kindly set out for us. Besides, it would not do for you to be seen by the guests as you are to be the chief attraction and a surprise."

"But, signor, how can I possibly be an attraction with Signor Tramezzani and Madame Bertinotti on the program. With the two of them preceding me, I wonder that I dare open my mouth."

"Do not worry. Bertinotti and Tramezzani do well because they are together, but you have power and range that neither one of them can hope to equal. Trust me, my child, we have chosen music that will provide a contrast to what the other musicians have to offer. Compared to you they will appear stale, and this audience is always in search of something new."

Indeed, when the Countess of Morehampton, hastily wiping a perspiring brow, stood before her guests after the two singers had finished, an expectant buzz of conversation flowed around the room. The countess clapped her hands for silence and the buzz died to a hush of anticipation." I have confided to many of you that I am introducing someone entirely new to our musical scene." The countess paused for effect, relishing every minute of suspense. For someone who had no looks, no grace, and not a great deal of conversation, she relied on her musical taste and the fortune that allowed her to produce such evenings as her only claims to the attention of the fashionable word and she exploited them to the fullest. "She is new not only to this musical scene, but to any musical scene, as she has just been discovered by that well-known cognoscente of musical talent, Signor Bartoli."

Not the cognoscente, Signor Bartoli, but the connoisseur, Lord Christian Hatherleigh was Christian's first thought as Isobel, regal and poised in her exquisitely simple gown of pink satin, gracefully acknowledged the welcoming applause. But all thought was quickly banished from his mind as he waited tensely to judge the crowd's reaction.

There was the usual continued whispering as Signor Bartoli played the opening bars of "The Soldier Tir'd" which ceased almost entirely as the first liquid notes spilled forth from Isobel's throat. The countess's audience, though genuinely interested in music, were first and foremost members of the *ton*, and it would take a great deal of talent to stop the delicious exchange of scandalous *on-dits*, even during a performance.

Isobel finished the song to enthusiastic applause, which, blue eyes sparkling, she accepted charmingly. As she launched into "I Know That My Redeemer Liveth," the whispering stopped completely, and by the time she began the first notes of "Der Hölle Rache kocht in meinem Herzen" the silence was so profound that the measured breathing of the dowager seated next to Christian sounded almost deafening.

As her voice soared brilliantly to the highest notes, Christian was transported to the music room at Warminster House and the afternoons he had sat gazing into the garden, the pale winter sun gleaming on the parquet floor, and he was struck by a pang of nostalgia which he could not explain until after the concert when the well-wishers and admirers made an impenetrable throng around Isobel and he caught the words "brilliant, exquisite, incomparable," all the words he had used to describe her to Signor Bartoli. And now she was no longer his private secret. She belonged to everyone and anyone who could appreciate music, and even those who could not. It was sharing her with the rest of the world that was responsible for the odd sense of loss he was now suffering. He longed to throttle the young buck at his elbow who remarked to a friend. "What a voice! And with a face and figure like that, she will make Catalani look to her laurels. The elegance of her shoulders and arms alone are enough to make a man lose his senses."

With a barely concealed snort of disgust, Christian turned away and headed toward the supper room. The less he heard of this fawning cant, the better. What he needed most was a bracing glass of something—several bracing glasses, to be exact.

The supper room was deserted except for the footmen, who were delighted to provide his lordship with the countess's excellent Madeira. Christian tossed off one glass and then slowly sipped the next, savoring its fumes while trying to decide on his next step. Should he return and join the crowd of well-wishers or should he simply leave?

Instinct, tested by years of fashionable gatherings, told him to leave, that he would find no satisfaction now that the music was over, but something else held him there. It seemed so long since he had last seen Isobel, in spite of his best efforts to cross her path. He wanted to know how she felt about this evening's success, what she was planning to do next, how he could help her take the next step toward her goal.

"My lord, I had no notion that something as tame as a musicale could interest a hero of the Peninsula," a silvery voice interrupted his thoughts. Christian turned to see Lady Selina Atwood tripping eagerly toward him. He groaned inwardly. She must have set her sights on him during the concert and worked out her strategy accordingly because no one else seemed to be in any hurry to enter the supper room.

"Mama is a dear friend of the Countess of Morehampton so our attendance was unavoidable, though I was dying to attend Lady Southbridge's rout instead. But now I am delighted that we came." The young lady bit her lower lip and fixed him with a provocative look from under pale eyelashes.

Christian struggled to hide his dismay. Surely society had not changed so much since he had been away that it was proper for young misses to stalk single gentlemen in the supper room? Apparently not, for before he could reply to Lady Selina, another voice boomed from the doorway, "Well, it is Lord Christian, is it not?" and Lady Selina's mother, resplendent in a diamond parure that overshadowed her dress of outmoded design, sailed into the room in pursuit of her daughter. "It is so gratifying to see that modern youth still has an appreciation of fine music. So many young men are quite worthless these days and do nothing but closet themselves with their tailors or waste their time and their fortunes at the gaming tables. But you, young man"—she delivered an approving buffet to Christian's shoulder that nearly caused him to lose his footing—"appear to be different."

"So it would seem," Christian responded meekly. "But I have not had the opportunity to congratulate the countess on the success of her evening. It would be most remiss of me not to. Please excuse me." And feeling like the veriest of cowards, Christian escaped back to the ballroom, where the crowd around Isobel appeared to be dwindling.

Glancing up at this particular moment, Isobel felt her stomach lurch as she caught sight of a broad-shouldered figure in the doorway. So he *had* been here after all. At first she had been concentrating so hard on the music that she had no thought for the audience, but as the silence descended and she knew that she had captured everyone's attention, she had surveyed the room in front of her. She told herself that she was just getting a feel for those listening to her, but in her heart of hearts, she knew that she was really looking for one listener in particular, one auburn head that would tower above the rest, but she had not seen it. He must have been over to one side or too far back for her to make out.

Now he was here, approaching her purposefully, a conspiratorial smile on his face that somehow made it feel as though he and she were the only two occupants of the entire room. Isobel smiled and nodded mechanically to the hatchet-faced lady speaking to her. She could barely make out the woman's words over the pounding of her heart. Her palms felt sweaty. What on earth was wrong with her? She had never suffered this nervous reaction before and she had sung many times for audiences at the gatherings at Madame de Sallanches's, even for the illustrious crowd at Monsieur's formal dinners held on New Year's Day, His Name Day, and the feast of Saint Louis. Why was she feeling agitated now?

"Mademoiselle Isobel." Warm with approval, Lord Christian's voice was like a caress. Isobel's knees threatened to buckle under her. She drew a long, steadying breath and lifted her chin. Agitated she might be, but she was certainly not going to let on that she felt anything, but coolly self-possessed.

"Your performance was exquisite. The delivery was . . ." Christian paused and cleared his throat. Even to his own ears his voice sounded unnaturally high, his praise as fulsome as that of any of her other admirers who sought to win the approval of the woman destined to be the *ton's* newest sensation. "Er, your performance is precisely what I would have expected."

"My lord!" The slender, wasp-waisted macaroni at his side protested in horror. "How can you say such a thing? Why, Mademoiselle was superb! She was a veritable siren, a . . ."

"Exactly." Christian cut him short as he winked at Isobel. "But one expects nothing less from Mademoiselle Isobel."

"Thank you, my lord." His bluntness had had a most steadying effect on her. It reminded her that they were friends, that she could trust his opinion, no matter how badly it was stated.

The dandy shot Christian a venomous look and turned away as Christian edged closer.

"Are you pleased? You certainly caused quite a stir."

"I think so, but then I am new to the audience, and anything new is bound to attract a certain amount of attention."

"So young and yet so cynical," he teased.

"You forget, my lord, that I have spent a great deal of time among the members of the French court. Exiled they might be, but they are courtiers nevertheless, and in that milieu, novelty, flattery, and reputation, are the driving forces. One can fall in favor as quickly as one can rise. I have seen it happen time and again."

"Too true. But though it is fashionable to be seen at the Countess of Morehampton's, one is not invited unless one has a good understanding of music, so, to a certain extent, praise expressed here is more valid than praise expressed elsewhere."

"Which is precisely what I have been telling her," Emily chimed in. She and her sister had been invited at Isobel's request and had been trying to make it to her side since the moment she had made her last bow. They now appeared to flank her like two guard dogs, ready to spring to her defense should anyone fail to give Isobel her due.

"She will soon be all the rage and our drives in the park will become nothing more than a chance for her to acknowledge her admiring public." Emily fixed Christian with a meaningful stare. She had observed the look in Christian's eyes and the conscious expression on Isobel's face that her friend tried unsuccessfully to hide, and Emily had barely been able to refrain from hugging herself in delight. So he *was* interested in Isobel. She had thought he might be, and she was now going to do her utmost to see to it that the two of them were thrown together as often as she could manage it.

Isobel jumped at the sound of Emily's voice. She had been so mesmerized by the look in Lord Christian's eyes and her own happiness at seeing him again that she had entirely forgotten her two companions. "I beg your pardons. Jane, Emily, may I present Lord Christian Hatherleigh. Lady Mordiford and Lady Verwood are old family friends. It was their mother who offered us shelter when we first came from France and who introduced me to the Duchess of Warminster."

Christian's eyes twinkled as he caught sight of the speculative expression on Emily's face. There was no doubt in his mind that she had already linked him with her friend and, oddly enough, this incipient matchmaking pleased rather than annoyed him.

Chapter 19

It was in the interests of carrying out this scheme of throwing Lord Christian and Isobel together that Emily insisted that Isobel accompany her to Bond Street for a shopping expedition the next day, followed by a lengthy drive in the park, and Isobel, though she could think of many more useful things to do with her time than saunter along the fashionable thoroughfare, was grateful for Emily's genuine interest in seeing that her friend enjoyed fresh air and lively conversation.

"Now tell me," Emily began in her usual direct fashion as the door of a shockingly expensive millinery establishment closed behind them. "What do you hear from Auguste these days? I always thought he was so dashing and so gallant. He was the hero of all my girlish fantasies, and I am sure I cried my eyes out when he left for France. Has your papa forgiven him for throwing his fortunes in with the Corsican monster?"

"No." Isobel sighed. "And I dare not mention his name to Papa because it upsets him so. The doctor says we should keep Papa as calm as possible because his heart is weak. Auguste has been able to get word to me from time to time, but I worry, now that the Allies have nearly arrived in Paris. I have no idea what has happened to him. I do not know if he is in Paris now with Marmont or if he is with Bonaparte himself, for Bonaparte has fled the city and will continue to fight, but who can be sure."

Indeed, no one was sure of anything these days, and the little community of émigrés that formed the de Montargis's circle of acquaintances was in a fever of anticipation.

"Who knows," the Comte de Pontarlier had crowed gaily to Isobel as they sat together at another one of the Comtesse de Sallanches's eternal salons, "in six months' time I may at last be able to consult a French tailor."

"A great relief to you, I am sure." Impervious to the acid note in Isobel's voice, the comte had nodded happily. Isobel could not work herself up to the same level of excitement and it pained her to see her friends, their faces worn by years of suffering and worry, acting as though a return to their beloved France would eradicate the years of their exile and restore them to their original selves. There was no one to whom she could turn, no one in whom she could confide these misgivings, for Jane and Emily, though sympathetic listeners, were so preoccupied with their families and the Season that it was difficult for them to project themselves into the larger events taking place in the world and Marthe, loyal servant that she was, would not listen to a word of doubt or uncertainty that might reflect on the royalist cause. When Isobel had even ventured to hint that they might be returning to something rather different from their previous glory, the old woman had snorted in indignation. "*Non*, mademoiselle, Monsieur and the king will see to it that everything is *comme il faut* when we return. You will see."

In fact, there was only one person Isobel knew to whom she felt she could speak with the expectation of receiving a rational response and that was Lord Christian. He had seen enough of the world to be able to understand her concerns.

Fortunately for Isobel, he had taken Emily's obvious hint and was now to be seen riding in the park at the fashionable hour along with the rest of the *ton*. For several days he and Ajax had endured the crush with no success, but patience was rewarded and the minute Emily's barouche entered the park, Christian, recognizing its occupants, maneuvered his way to them with such skill that Isobel could not help remarking on it.

Christian smiled and patted his mount's neck. "As an old cavalry horse, Ajax is accustomed to coping with indescribable crowds and confusion. To him, this is all very tame and I am afraid that he blames me for having made his life so dull."

"Rather he should blame the Duke of Wellington and the Allies. But you, my lord, must be glad that the conflict you fought to end is nearly over. Or do you think Bonaparte will be able to rally?" Isobel's anxious expression bespoke someone who had more than casual interest in international affairs.

"I think that brilliant though Napoleon may be, his generals are tired of war, as is France."

"But is France tired of him? Is it tired enough of war that it will welcome back the old régime?" There was no mistaking the anxiety in Isobel's voice or the tension in the hands that gripped the side of the carriage.

A chill washed over Christian as he realized the full implications of her question. "I can not say, but I do know human nature well enough to know that when the future looks uncertain, the past always seems more wonderful than it actually was, so perhaps the French, after years of revolution and war will look upon the old days more favorably now than they did before. Are you looking forward to returning to your homeland?" Christian told himself that it was none of his concern, but he still could not help himself from asking, nor could he keep the concern out of his voice.

He had not realized until he envisioned London without her how important a role Mademoiselle Isobel de Montargis was beginning to play in his life. True, he did not spend much time with her, but their few conversations had been so deep, they had discussed so many important things, shared their sentiments on topics of such a personal nature, that he felt closer to her than he did to many people he had known all his life. He did not want her to leave. He wanted her to stay and pursue the career that had begun so auspiciously at the Countess of Morehampton's musicale, and he wanted to be right there beside her, encouraging her and sharing in her success.

"I suppose I am," Isobel replied slowly, breaking into his train of thought. "But I do not know what to expect. I was so young when we left France that England feels more like home to me than France does. But Papa and all his friends are, and that makes me very happy." She did not sound entirely convinced of this, however.

"For you, I suppose it will be as foreign as England was for your parents and you will miss such warm friends as Lady Verwood here." Christian flashed Emily a smile that left her quite breathless. La, the man was attractive. If she were not so determined for him to fall in love with Isobel, she might have enjoyed setting up a mild flirtation with him herself, but there were other fish in the sea and she had quite decided that he was the one who was going to awaken her serious friend to all the delightful possibilities that existed between a handsome man and a lovely woman. In fact, she had even decided that he was going to rescue Isobel from that stiff rump of a father of hers and the drudgery of being a governess, or, to be more exact, the Countess of Verwood had decided that she was going to do her utmost to see to it that Lord Christian Hatherleigh did.

Isobel remained thoughtful, savoring the warm feelings she got from knowing that she was understood, that there was someone who would not dismiss her misgivings about the return to France as either absurd or traitorous.

"If you return to France, will you continue with your music, mademoiselle?"

How easily he identified another of her worries about the possible return to France. "Naturally I shall. Just because I am in another country does not mean I shall change my interests." Isobel wondered if she sounded as falsely optimistic to him as she did to herself. If the truth were to be known, she was dreading the possible restoration of the *ancien régime* more for this reason than for any other. The prospective loneliness of a strange land did not bother her as much as the thought that if she were restored to her position as the daughter of a wealthy and powerful member of Louis XVIII's court, she could have no reason to become an opera singer, no need for the money or the acclaim it would bring, and, therefore, nothing that would counter her father's and their friends' certain disapproval of such a course of action. She had seen enough of Louis XVIII's household at Hartwell to gain a sense of the stifling and rigid etiquette that prevailed in the king's entourage. If it were dull and regimented in England, where poverty, at least, kept the ceremonial atmosphere from being too excessive, how much worse it would be once he had returned to Versailles or to the Tuileries.

"Ah"—Christian spoke softly enough so that only Isobel could hear—"but there you will be invited to sing like some clever child performing. Everyone will applaud because of who you are and what your family represents rather than because of your accomplishments command attention. Surely that is not for you, not after your triumph the other evening."

"But that too was before friends, and though they were friends of the countess, they honored her by honoring me."

"That is not quite the same thing, for the only connection you have with the Countess of Morehampton is that you are a performer recommended to her by Signor Bartoli. To the audience, Mademoiselle Isobel de Montargis was nothing, except that you were French, and therefore not one of them. It would be the greatest of pities should you be forced to leave now. Perhaps I should speak with Signor Bartoli, and between the two of us, we could make sure that you were on the next program to be held at the Hanover Square Rooms."

"Oh," she breathed, entranced by the very possibility and touched by his confidence in her, "but I am not nearly good enough. Why, Madame Catalani and the Knyvetts were there not long ago. I do not think that after . . ."

"And so was Mrs. Vaughan and Miss Travis, who cannot compare with you. No, we must plan something to follow your introduction at the Countess of Morehampton's, both to satisfy the interest and curiosity raised by your appearance there, and to keep you from fretting over what will happen in France."

The anxiety in the dark blue eyes looking up into his faded somewhat, but Christian could see that she was still uneasy. "I am sure that, while things will not be the same for your family and friends as they were a quarter of a century ago, much of the bitterness will have been forgotten. I have spoken with enough French prisoners to know that. Those who were most violently against the *ancien régime* fell victims to the revolution themselves long ago."

"But I am not sure that I wish for it to be the same. Of course for Madame de Sallanches and Madame de Saint Veran, I wish an end to their sadness and their suffering, but to return to a world where birth, and only birth determines one's lot in life is not . . . not . . . to my liking," she finished lamely. And beyond all that she had spoken of lay a fear that Isobel could not even acknowledge to herself—what would happen to Auguste should the king be restored? Would everything think, as her father did, that he was a traitor?

"It would seem that you have become infected by our own more free and easy ways." Christian's tone was teasing, but inwardly he was delighted at her lack of enthusiasm for returning to France. Perhaps it meant she would miss him just the tiniest bit.

No sooner had the thought entered his mind than he squelched it ruthlessly. He was a soldier, albeit one who was home for the moment, and a wanderer. Part of the reason he had become a soldier was that he had chafed under the expectations of society in general and the expectations of women in particular, and he had sought to avoid these by being constantly on the move, from camp to camp in pursuit of the enemy. Yet here he was, talking about the prospect of someone else being on the move and he was longing to make her stay. He was hoping to meet her in the park tomorrow, and every day thereafter, as he had today. It was hopes like that, on the part of others, hopes that he had spent so much of his life trying to discourage, that had made him known as an incorrigible bachelor, and, therefore, much to his great satisfaction, had eventually caused the matchmaking mamas of the *ton* to give up on him.

"Perhaps I have," Isobel agreed. "Though, in truth, I often feel more English than French, having spent my childhood at Barford Court with Emily and her sister." She smiled fondly at her companion. "But I should never admit such a thing in front of Papa, who left Paris twenty years ago expecting to return in a few weeks when tempers had cooled, and so, he has lived his life accordingly, ready to return at a moment's notice as though it were but a brief, unpleasant intermission. Mama, on the other hand, knew that things were changed forever, and she was very grateful to Lady Barford for giving her a home. I believe that she actually preferred the simple, less rigid existence here to the excessive ceremony of court life in France. And as for me, Jane and Emily were the sisters I had always longed to have. Even now, I am excessively grateful to them for drives in the park and evenings at the opera."

"Then it was you I saw at the opera the other night. Perhaps you are attending again this evening?" Though he tried his best to sound as offhand and as bored as any self-respecting man-about-town, Christian was not able to disguise the eager note in his voice or mask the interest in his voice. Nor could he ignore the faintest twinge of jealousy as she spoke of her gratitude toward her childhood friends who, as far as he could tell, had not recognized her true ambitions, nor had they done anything to promote her very obvious talent.

"I, ah . . ."

"Of course she will be," Emily replied with a sly smile that forestalled any response from her friend.

Chapter 20

Though Isobel had protested to her friends during the ride home from the park that there was absolutely no need for her to attend the opera that evening with them, even to her own ears, her protests sounded halfhearted. That evening as she allowed Marthe to fuss over the fall of lace around the bodice of her simple white satin evening dress made up some years ago from one of the few court dresses the Duchess de Montargis had brought with her from France, she admitted to herself that it was not the opportunity to evaluate the ability of Madame Grassini, or to learn what she could from the singer that was making her look forward to the evening so much as it was the possibility of seeing Lord Christian.

Noticing the sparkle in her mistress's eyes and the flush of excitement in her cheeks, Marthe too could have told her that music had very little to do with her mood of eager anticipation. Certainly Isobel had not been in such a flutter of expectation on her previous visit to the opera. A knock at the door and the appearance of a young lad bearing a roll of music tied in white ribbon early that afternoon had aroused the servant's suspicious and, watching a secret smile light up Isobel's face as she had untied the ribbon and read the bold handwriting on the note inside, Marthe had no doubt that the handsome English milord who had once called on the duc was planning to be present at the opera that evening.

Isobel had sat for some time gazing at the music and the note that read, "Would that it were you instead of Madame Grassini, but perhaps now that you have the music, you will be performing it next Season. Hatherleigh." Even if she had not seen the bold "Hatherleigh" scrawled at the bottom, Isobel felt she would have recognized the identity of the sender, for the script was as impetuous and dashing as the man. The Comte de Pontarlier had once sent her some snowdrops on her birthday and one of the young courtiers who made up the Duc de Berri's retinue had had the audacity to address some flowery verses to her charming complexion, but these gestures had both been more calculated to call attention to the giver than the receiver. Isobel could not think when anyone had given her a present more truly suited to her tastes, more indicative of an understanding of who she was than this. Indeed, it was not until Marthe's sharp "Mademoiselle!" had called Isobel's attention to the proximity of her foot to the kitchen fire where she was waiting for water to boil in order to steam some crumpled ribbons that she awoke from her reveries to realize just how much her thoughts were being taken up with Lord Christian Hatherleigh—entirely too much.

Having recalled her mistress to reality, Martha went back to chopping carrots, a secretive smile lighting up her dour face. So the *Petite* was going to be seeing the English milord at the opera after all. *Bon*. It was about time she became interested in a gentleman though what would come of all this when they went back to France, the old servant would not hazard a guess, for surely Monsieur le Duc would not want anyone for his daughter, but a Frenchman of the highest nobility. Marthe had seen enough of the world and the devastating changes that could occur overnight that she asked for nothing more than someone who could make her mistress happy. Certainly, the package that had just been delivered had done precisely that.

Isobel was so touched by the gift of the music that she was barely able to express her thanks that evening when Lord Christian, resplendent in an exquisitely cut coat and intricately tied cravat appeared in the Barfords' box. "It was extremely kind of you to think of me, though there was not the least need for it," she stammered, frustrated by her inability to find just the right words to convey how much his gesture had meant to her.

The glow in her eyes was all the thanks Christian had been hoping for though it rather pleased him that her cool self-possession seemed to have deserted her for once. It had come as a rather unwelcome shock to him to discover how upsetting the idea of her return to France was to him, but even more upsetting was the distinct possibility that she might not be as affected by this prospect and the thought of never seeing him as he was. He had sent her the music in the hope that he might learn from her reaction something about how she felt about him. Judging from her halting speech and heightened color as she thanked him, Christian could see that she was not accustomed to receiving presents from gentlemen. Good. "I am delighted that it pleased you. I wish I were able to do more to help you toward your heart's desire, for though I enjoy being able to speak with you here, I should be a great deal happier to see you down there." He nodded in the direction of the brilliantly lit stage.

"Why thank you, my lord, but you have already done so much toward that end. Signor Bartoli has helped me to improve a great deal and it now truly seems like a possibility instead of a dream." Isobel glanced anxiously at Jane and Emily, but neither one appeared to have overheard. They had applauded her appearance at the Countess of Morehampton's, but Isobel was not at all certain they would have felt the same way about seeing their friend on stage at the opera.

"If you do not return to France."

"If I do not return to France," she echoed somberly. Isobel was silent for a moment, but she soon recovered to inquire in a brighter tone, "But you, my lord, what will you do now that Bonaparte is very nearly beaten once and for all? You once told me that you fought to end the war, and therefore, you must feel some reward in seeing this accomplished, but now what will you do? I can not picture you becoming a Bond Street beau or rusticating at a country estate." A provocative dimple hovered at the corner of her mouth.

"Ah." It was Christian's turn for serious reflection. What would he do? He had joined up in order to avoid the very pursuits she now mentioned.

"There is always India, I suppose." She paused to consider the idea. "Affairs always seem to be in an uncertain-enough state there to need experienced leaders and it would offer you opportunity for adventure."

"Yes, there is India." How well she understood him. Most women, most people, in fact, assumed that the life of a fashionably bored man-about-town was the pinnacle of perfection, the life everyone was striving to achieve. The very idea of it was one that had always filled him with horror. However, haring off to India, or some other far-flung colony did not hold the appeal for him that it once would have. Conversations like this one had made him see how pleasant it was to share things with a congenial companion. How very enjoyable life might be if it were shared with someone sympathetic and understanding, someone like Isobel.

Christian shook his head slowly. He must be going soft in his old age to be entertaining thoughts such as these. Lord, he was sounding practically domesticated, and it was all the fault of Old Duoro. If Wellington had not stopped beating the French on a regular basis, he might still be out there leading cavalry charges and bivouacking in one inhospitable place after another. True, he had lost his taste for the glory of it all, but it was the only life he knew. He glanced up to find Isobel looking at him curiously, her head tilted to one side, her eyes questioning, but at the same time sympathetic. Christian smiled ruefully. "That is the damnable thing, I do not know what I shall do now. What does one do when one stops being a . . . er, *barbarian,* as you put it."

"I never called you a barbarian."

"No?" He chuckled. "Well, not precisely, perhaps, but you certainly thought that when I happened in on your practice session at Warminster House."

"Intruded, more like." A flush stole over Isobel's cheeks as she recalled the lazy amusement in his eyes as they had traveled the length of her body.

"I did not intrude, I observed. And I was most appreciative." Christian grinned at the memory. "I still am. You have grown even more lovely since I have come to know you."

"I . . ." Isobel did not know what to say. He was sitting at least a foot from her, but she felt as though she were in his arms. His eyes were warm with admiration, and something else she could not quite identify, something else that made her feel *quite* breathless as his eyes searched her face. They lingered on her lips in such a way as to make it seem as though he were kissing her, caressing her. Isobel had never known that a single glance could be so intimate, so . . . unsettling. Her heart thudded against her ribs as the breath was squeezed out of her lungs. She felt quite dizzy. What on earth had come over her?

A slow smile stole over Christian's face as he watched her lips part. So she felt it too. It was all he could do not to crush her to him, to cover her lips with his, to plant kisses down the smooth white column of her throat. Lord, he wanted her in a way that he could not remember ever having wanted a woman before. She stirred his soul, she touched his heart and mind in a way no woman had ever managed to do and now he was lost.

He had known he was lost the moment he had heard her singing, had seen her at the pianoforte pouring all her energy and passion into the song that rose from her lips. He had known it then, but had not admitted it to himself until now.

Isobel remained transfixed by the look in his eyes, unable to move or to think about anything except the way the light from the stage accentuated the lean, strong lines of his face and the broad outline of his shoulders. She had never really noticed a man in quite that way before, had always concentrated so much on what was being said that the physical appearance had never made any impression on her. Now it seemed she could think of nothing else. How broad and strong his chest looked under the closely fitted coat. The firm lips and piercing gray-green eyes only added to the powerful physical impression he made, and one knew instantly that Lord Christian Hatherleigh was a man to be reckoned with. Despite her own considerable height and proud carriage, Isobel felt small and weak in comparison to this man and she suddenly had the maddest urge to cast herself against his chest and feel the strength of his arms around her.

The crash of cymbals and the blare of a trumpet brought her rudely to her senses and, hot with embarrassment at the direction her thoughts had been taking, Isobel glanced hurriedly around, but neither Emily nor Jane had seemed to notice a thing, being too involved in their discussion of Lady Silverton's outrageous *décol-letage* and the audacity of Lord Wilford, who seemed to have brought his mistress with him to the family box, for surely that overdressed person next to him was no one he knew socially.

Isobel heaved a sigh of relief and turned her attention back to the stage before her. Try though she would, however, she could not lose herself in the music as she ordinarily did. No matter how much she studied the style and range of each singer, no matter how hard she concentrated on visualizing herself in their roles, she was aware of nothing else but the man beside her and of the fact that his eyes never left her face during the entire perform-ance.

Christian remained seated next to Isobel throughout the rest of the opera, and if the other occupants of the box noticed this un-usual circumstance, they never let on by so much as a glance that they were conscious of his interest in their guest. In fact, he did not leave the ladies until he had handed them all into Lady Ver-wood's carriage.

Isobel was the last to climb in and he held her hand just a frac-tion of a second longer than was necessary, looking deep into her eyes. "Thank you. I hope to see you in the park soon."

"I hope . . . that is, I do not know," she responded, incapable of retrieving her hand from that warm and reassuring clasp. Once again, his eyes were fixed so intently on her that she felt as though he were kissing her. She wished he were kissing her. Again, a hot wave of self-consciousness enveloped her. Where were these thoughts coming from? She had never entertained such thoughts about a man in her life.

But as the carriage rolled away, Emily offered her own explanation for Isobel's erratic behavior. "La"—she fanned herself as she lay back against the squabs of the carriage—"I vow that man is handsome enough to make even the coldest of hearts beat faster. Those eyes, they look right through one. And the smile is enough to melt one's very bones. Small wonder the matchmaking mamas do not want him anywhere near their impressionable daughters. But you, my dear"—she directed a sly smile at Isobel—"seem to have made quite an impression on Lord Christian Hatherleigh for a change."

"I? Oh no. It is merely that he knows that I can carry on an intelligent conversation about music and the opera."

"If you ask me"—Emily turned to her sister for confirmation—"he did not hear a note, for his eyes were fastened upon you the entire time. Were they not, Jane?"

"I did not notice, for my eyes were directed toward the stage," Jane responded firmly. Then, seeing that their guest truly was being made uncomfortable by the entire conversation, she changed the subject slightly. "But tell me, what did you think of the performance, Isobel?"

Flashing a grateful smile at her, Isobel was opening her mouth to respond when the hideous realization came over her that indeed, she had not heard very much of the opera at all after Lord Christian had come to sit beside her. Gathering her wits about her, she was able to make enough credible observations to deter any further discussion of Lord Christian Hatherleigh until they reached Manchester Square.

Once inside her own bedchamber, however, she was unable to put aside the memories of the evening and the strange, breathless feeling that had come over her every time he had looked at her. She did not know whether she hoped to see him in the park the next day or not. On the one hand, the restless, excited feeling was quite delicious. On the other, it was rather unnerving, for she found herself wanting more and more of it. At first, a sympathetic glance had been enough to gratify it, then a touch of the hand.

Now, she was wondering what it would feel like to be held against the powerful chest and encircled by those strong arms. Where were such ideas coming from?

Resolutely, Isobel thrust these upsetting thoughts aside, and as she climbed into bed, tried instead to recall the music rather than the man sitting next to her, but she was not at all successful, for as she fell asleep, she could hear a deep voice murmuring, *You have grown even more lovely since I have come to know you.*

Chapter 21

Even if Isobel, beset as she had been by confusing emotions as Lord Christian had helped her into the carriage, had not paid attention to his remark about seeing her in the park, Emily had, and she made certain to send a footman around to Manchester Square the very next morning to inform Isobel that she would be calling to take her for a drive in the park the following day, and every day after that while the weather was good.

The weather was exceedingly fine the next afternoon as Isobel climbed into the Marchioness of Verwood's barouche so that Isobel, while admiring her friend's fashionable Circassian turban of crimson velvet, was glad for the shade afforded by the brim of her straw-colored satin bonnet. Isobel was too preoccupied with her own thoughts on her lessons with Signor Bartoli that morning to notice the secret smile that would keep breaking out on her friend's face despite Emily's best efforts to look unconcerned.

But as they rolled down Oxford Street toward the Stanhope Gate, Isobel's mind turned gradually from reviewing the difficult piece of music she had struggled over that morning to Emily's chatter about the previous evening. This brought with it thoughts of Lord Christian, and almost unconsciously she scanned the crowds in the park for a tall figure on a powerful horse, while half paying attention to what Emily was saying.

The Marchioness of Verwood noted this fit of abstraction with a great deal of satisfaction and correctly attributed its cause to the gentleman who had spent time in their box the previous evening, but her attention was truly fixed on quite another gentleman, tall, slender, elegant, but with a military bearing, who was steadily making his way toward them on foot, his eyes casting about over the crowd as though looking for someone in particular. Emily's smile deepened as the gentleman recognized them, raised his curly beaver, and hastened to join them.

"Isobel, my dear"—Emily laid a hand on the sleeve of her friend's green sarcenet pelisse—"here is a gentleman come to see you, I believe."

Isobel looked around. "Auguste! Oh, oh, stop the carriage," she begged as the coachman, already alerted by his mistress, pulled the team to a halt. Heedless of the throng of carriages and horses, Isobel jumped down and threw her arms around the gentleman's neck, laughing and crying at the same time. "Oh, Auguste, it is you. You are safe."

"*Mais bien sur, ma petite*. Of course I am safe. We de Montargis are men of great ingenuity and fortitude."

"But how, when, what are you doing here?" She grabbed his arm, pulling him toward the barouche. "Emily, look, it is Auguste, is that not a miracle?"

"Of course it is Auguste. He came to see me this morning after having journeyed down to Barford Court and back. Papa and Mama gave him my direction and he came straight to visit me to see if we could arrange a meeting with you. And here he is."

"I am sorry to surprise you this way, *Petite*." Auguste took her hand under his arm and led her a little way from the carriage. "But I did not know that things would happen so quickly. I was with Marmont in Paris when he surrendered and I could see, in spite of Bonaparte's desire to continue fighting, that the rest of the marshals, even Ney, were unwilling to march from Fontainbleau to save Paris and continue the struggle with the Prussians and the Russians. I knew the end was near so I asked Marmont for permission to come see you, and Papa, if he will let me. It remains to be seen whether the Allies will ask Louis to be King of France in the emperor's place. I had hoped on my visit here to speak to those courtiers surrounding Louis to beg him to be moderate in his policies. I believe that France is ready to welcome him back if he is not harsh. However, if he acts as Monsieur does, it will not go well, for people say of the Bourbons that they have *learned nothing and forgotten nothing*. I was hoping to speak to Papa and convince him to make Louis understand this."

Isobel shook her head slowly. "Papa will not understand. He is not so blind as the others perhaps, nor was he so blind as they were in the first place—as a soldier, even a soldier of the *ancien régime* he was more realistic than the courtiers, I think. But the only France that he will acknowledge as France is the France of his forefathers with Louis as King Louis XVIII of France and Navarre. I know this, for he and his friends have talked on nothing else since the Prussians and the Russians began advancing on Paris. He and the others are old, Auguste, they have been through a great deal, and they do not know how to change, even if they wanted to."

"Am I still a traitor in Papa's eyes, then?" Auguste's tone was clipped and his eyes hard and bright. "Even though many of us who went back fought honorably for the glory of France, the country of our ancestors, even though we swore the oath of fidelity to the emperor so we could win back the lands that had been in our families since the time of the Crusades?"

Isobel smiled sadly and shook her head again. "I know, Auguste, you have never been a traitor to our country or to our family, but Papa . . ." She glanced at the budding trees in the distance, trying to collect her thoughts, to make her brother see it from their father's point of view. She had long since given up trying to make her father see Auguste's side, but Auguste was young, he had lived through times of great change and had learned to be more accepting of those who held different opinions, who had different pasts from his. If she could get him to see it all through Papa's eyes, perhaps he could ask for forgiveness, perhaps they could be a family once more. "Papa has nothing left but his pride. It is this, and his sense of honor, that have sustained him all these years when he lost everything else. If he were to say that you are not a traitor, it would be the same thing as acknowledging Bonaparte as the rightful ruler of France. To do that would be to fly in the face of his very existence. For if Bonaparte is ruler of France and not Louis, then who is the Duc de Montargis? Do you understand, *mon frère?*" She fixed him with a pleading glance.

"I do." He patted her hand. "But he must understand that what I did, I also did out of a sense of pride and honor—pride and honor that I learned at his knee, I might add. And if he does not accept that, then who am I? Certainly not his son."

Auguste's pleasant, open countenance hardened with a resolve as obstinate as his father's. Indeed, Isobel thought that in that moment he looked remarkably like the duc. She sighed. "I shall try. At any rate, I am glad to see you."

He smiled down at her. "And I you, *petite soeur.* Now, tell me, how goes the singing?"

"Ah, it goes." The dark blue eyes lit up with joy and a secret smile played on her lips. "Actually it goes very well. I have a new teacher, a Signor Bartoli, who is well thought of in musical circles and . . . he likes my singing," she finished with quiet pride.

"Of course he does. You sing like a nightingale, *Petite*. But what of your pupils, the daughters of the so-important Duke of Warminster?"

"Shh." She held a finger to her lips. "No one knows, not even Marthe, that I am no longer there. She thinks I am at the Duke of Warminster's when I am actually at Signor Bartoli's. You know, she is almost as bad as Papa is about my singing anywhere except for our friends. But, Auguste, Signor Bartoli has arranged for me to sing at several select musicales and he thinks I can be another Catalani. That is what I wish to be more than anything. I do not wish to be married to the Chevalier d'Entremont or the Comte de Pontarlier or Madame de Colignac's foolish son and just become Madame la Comtesse or Madame la Duchesse, even if we go back to France and everything returns to the way it was. I do not want that, Auguste, you must see that, you must help me keep that from happening." In her anxiety, Isobel gripped his sleeve with surprising strength.

He smiled fondly at her. "Ah, Isobel, always passionate whether you are five and telling Papa you *will* ride a horse instead of a pony or twenty-five and telling me you intend to be an opera singer. I will do what I can, but if Papa will not talk to me because I am a traitor, then he is hardly likely to listen to me when I tell him he should allow my little sister to become an *actrice d'opéra*. But come, I see Emily beckoning to us. If we do not return to the carriage, I fear she will die from curiosity. She never could abide being left out of anything."

"And she has not changed in the slightest. She knows every *on-dit* there is to know," Isobel responded, grateful that her brother had been too distracted to ask the reason for her departure from the Duke of Warminster's household or how she had happened to engage the illustrious Signor Bartoli to give her singing lessons. Her face flushed as she thought of the answer to both of those questions and, in spite of herself, she scanned the throng of horses and riders again looking for a tall figure on horseback.

Chapter 22

Meanwhile, the rider that she vainly sought sat in the shadows of a grove of trees, struggling valiantly to overcome the thoroughly unpleasant sensation that resembled being kicked in the midriff by a cavalry charger. In all actuality, nothing had happened. Christian had entered the park from Park Lane, hoping to catch sight of Lady Verwood's elegant barouche. Though the previous evening Isobel had blushed and dissembled at his mention of a possible encounter in the park, Lady Verwood had directed a knowing look at him and had nodded ever so slightly.

He knew he had an ally in the Marchioness of Verwood and that she could be counted upon to do her best to promote an interesting situation between her friend and one of the *ton's* most notorious bachelors. Personally, Christian did not understand the attraction of a man who preferred to run his own life rather than put it entirely in the hands of some female, but his sister-in-law had assured him time and again that such was the case. "Believe me, Christian," she had confided to him before Lady Boroughbridge's rout, and several times thereafter, "the fact that you never stand up with the same woman twice and that your name has never been linked to anyone's only makes it all that much more of a challenge. The matchmaking mamas will avoid you like the plague, but their daughters will flock around you like sparrows around bread crumbs in an effort to attract your interest. Any young woman who manages to attach to you, even for more than one dance, will have put a considerable feather in her cap and will be hailed immediately as an incomparable. No young lady worth anything would pass up the opportunity to win such renown for herself, so you may expect to be the center of much attention wherever you go."

Lavinia had been all too accurate in her predictions and he had been dimly aware of languishing looks cast in his direction whenever he made an appearance in the ballrooms or the drawing rooms of the fashionable world. Though the Duchess of Warminster was highly gratified by her brother-in-law's status as a much sought-after bachelor, Christian himself remained unmoved by this dubious distinction. However, he knew that the Marchioness of Verwood would see things the same way Lavinia did and would extend every effort to throw her friend together as much as possible with such a notable catch as Lord Christian Hatherleigh.

Christian had not been in the park long when he spied the deep maroon panels of the Verwood barouche and though he was too far away to make out the coat of arms on the side, the occupants resembled Emily and Isobel. He urged Ajax in their direction, but he had not gone more than a few paces when the carriage stopped and the two ladies leaned over to greet a gentleman of military bearing and superior height. As he observed them, the lady, whom he had now positively identified as Isobel, descended and, with all appearances of delight, threw her arms around the neck of the military-looking gentleman.

Christian gasped as if the wind had been knocked out of him and a cold wave of some unidentifiable emotion swept over him. So, the Marchioness of Verwood *had* been promoting an assignation between Isobel and a gentleman, but he himself was not the gentleman in question. Unable to drag his eyes away, Christian watched as Isobel took the gentleman's arm and, clinging tightly to it, her head nearly resting on the gentleman's shoulder, she walked slowly along with him, deeply absorbed in conversation. From time to time, she would seem to break off and glance eagerly at her companion as if to feast her eyes upon him.

When he was at last able to breathe again, Christian gathered the reins tightly in his hands as if to urge Ajax forward, but he could not move. He could not make himself do anything except remain frozen in the saddle watching the couple, all his muscles tensed in concentration. Who was the man? Was he some lover from the past?

You fool, he berated himself silently, *why would she have mentioned a lover to you? Why would she mention a lover to someone who was a mere acquaintance, the brother of an employer who had insulted her to the point that she left his employ.* Christian's intellect told him that it was ridiculous to think that a woman he had met only a score of times, if that, would confide something so intimate to him. However, his heart told him something quite different. His heart told him that every time he had looked into Isobel's eyes, he had felt as though he were looking deep into her soul. That was what had drawn him to her, what made her so different from other women. And having looked into those eyes, so innocent, so free of coyness or guile, he could have sworn that no lover existed, there was not even the thought that a lover could exist. Had he been so wrong, then? Had Lord Christian Hatherleigh, lover of scores of women on the Continent and in England been duped? Had he lost his touch entirely?

It was not until the couple had climbed into the carriage and it had rolled off to join the impressive procession of fashionable equipages circling the park that he was able to overcome his terrible inertia and ride slowly back toward his lodgings in Mount Street, too stunned to contemplate doing anything except sit in front of his fire and try to sort out what had happened to him, because something had definitely happened. He had never felt this unnerved in his entire life, not even facing his first cavalry charge at Talavera. What had come over him?

Even Digby, opening the door for his master at a most unusual time in the afternoon, knew immediately that something was wrong. He had not seen Lord Christian looking that way since they had lost Major Lord Calvert at Vitoria. Then, and only then had he seen his master's face looking so white and set, his mouth grim, the graygreen eyes so dark they looked like slate. Without a word, he took his master's coat and went to rekindle the fire in the library, where Christian was already tossing off a glass of brandy.

Slowly warmed by the brandy and the fire, Christian began to examine what had happened to him and to ask himself why he felt so betrayed by it, so oddly bereft at the thought of Isobel with a lover. For him, she had come to represent a purity, a spirituality that he had not known in any other woman. Perhaps it was her dedication to her music, perhaps it was her independence, perhaps it was the ideals she had expressed when discussing the insular, tradition-bound lives of the émigrés among whom she lived, he could not say for certain, but something about her set her apart from the rest of her sex.

At the Countess of Morehampton's musicale, clad in her plain, but elegant dress of pink satin, her hair simply done, her only ornament the pearls around her neck, Isobel had seemed as beautiful and remote as an angel among the chattering, overdressed throng of fashionable women. And that was how he thought of her—as something better, finer than the rest of the females of the *ton*, someone who had thought about life, someone who had set goals for herself beyond marriage and children, someone who was striving for perfection rather than a wealthy husband. And now, in the space of an instant, she had lost that special unattainable quality that had set her apart. She had become attainable, and she had become attainable to someone else other than himself.

That is the damnable part of the matter, you fool, he muttered savagely under his breath. *You want her to remain aloof and apart from the rest of the world except from you. And now what are you going to do about it?* He had to see her. That much he knew. He could not let her disappear from his life without knowing why. Did she have that special sympathy and understanding that had touched him so deeply for everyone? Surely she did not. Surely the interest and concern he had seen in her eyes whenever they talked about his life had been for him alone.

All of the many women Christian had known had been adept at making the man they were with at the moment feel important. Some of them had even been skilled enough to make several men feel that way at the same time, but no one had touched his soul in the way that this woman had. He had to know if it was real, or if it too was an act, albeit a very clever act.

He had to see her. Once he had settled that in his mind, the next thing would be to take action. Never one to brood over anything, Christian resolved to deal with the problem immediately. Setting down the empty brandy glass, he strode over to his desk and riffled through the unopened stack of invitations that had arrived that day. Ordinarily he would have tossed them all into the fire the moment they arrived, but since he had met Isobel he had gotten into the habit of saving them, sorting through them, and selecting ones where she might possibly be appearing.

At last he found one card for a ball at Carlton House given in honor of the émigrés. With the Allies now in Paris, suddenly all the world was remembering those who had fled France more than a decade ago, and the Regent was not to be outdone in recognizing Louis XVIII now that Csar Alexander was finally referring to him as the King of France. Surely the de Montargis would not miss such an important event as a ball at Carlton House?

Having decided upon a plan of action, Christian was left with nothing to do but wait with as much patience as he could muster. As he did in times of stress, he sought relief in physical activity, which he found boxing at Gentleman Jackson's.

Chapter 23

They had dropped Auguste off at the Stanhope Gate and proceeded toward Manchester Square. All the way home from the park, while Emily chattered on about who had been seen with whom, and whose carriage dress was done in last year's style, Isobel had sat clasping and unclasping her hands in her lap in a state of silent agitation. She had not realized quite how much she had missed Auguste until she had seen him standing there, his dark curls ruffled by the breeze and his brown eyes warm with affections for his *petite soeur*. She had not realized until that moment just how much she missed being part of a family or how lonely she had been after he had left and her mother had died.

Now, having discovered this, she was not about to let it slip away again. But what was she to do to recapture it? Her father was a man of principle and honor above all else; he would never go back on his sworn word that he would not allow a traitor to the king to enter the de Montargis household. How was she ever going to make him change his mind? Isobel was not even sure whether or not he secretly missed the son who had been the pride of her father's life until he joined Napoleon's army. Once Auguste had agreed to fight for *le Monstre*, he had simply ceased to exist for the Duc de Montargis.

The Verwood carriage halted in front of the house in Manchester Square. "Thank you, Emily," Isobel murmured distractedly as she allowed the footman to help her down. She remained standing on the pavement, collecting her thoughts for some moments as the carriage rolled away. Then taking a deep breath, she opened the door and slowly climbed the stairs to the drawing room.

The duc was seated at his desk, gazing out of the window. "Papa?" Isobel hesitated, trying desperately to choose the words that would make him see that it was time to welcome Auguste back into the family. The duc remained immobile, staring out the window. "Papa?" she began again.

Her father turned around. His face, usually so grave was taut with some emotion she could not read, his pale blue eyes strangely alight with excitement. *"Le Monstre* is beaten at last! He is gone. France will live again," he exulted. He rose, his lean cheeks flushed as though he had a high fever, and waving one hand over his head as though brandishing a sword, he exclaimed, "They will see, La France never gives up. We shall return to the land of our fathers. We shall triumph after all. The years in exile have only made us stronger."

"Papa, *calmes-toi.*" Isobel hurried across the room to force him gently back into his chair. The duc had not shown such energy and animation since the evening before he had left with the Comte d'Artois to lead the royalist uprising in the Vendée. She had been barely six at the time, but she still remembered how handsome he had looked in his uniform, how proud and straight he had held himself as, drawing his sword, he had declared to his wife and children, "I shall not return until we avenge the death of our king and queen."

But he had returned, a gray, defeated man, and a shadow of his former self, his health badly weakened. He had continued to rally around the Comte d'Artois and to work for the royalist cause, writing his memoirs and making regular contributions to the *Courrier de Londres* or by translating into French for the *Courrier d'Angleterre* the acts of the British government published in the *London Gazette*; however, he seemed to have lost his fervor in the aftermath of the Vendée, until this moment.

Isobel was alarmed by his flushed face and rapid breathing. Her father was an old man now with failing health, and any excitement, good or bad, presented a threat to a heart weakened by the trials and tribulations of the Revolution. She seated herself on the low stool at his feet. "Now, Papa, tell me what has occurred."

"Monsieur sent a boy with a message to say that the Corsican is beaten. He abdicated and the Senate had declared in favor of the king. Louis will be returning to France as soon as he can ready his household. We must prepare ourselves as well. How glad I am that I had not yet contracted a marriage for you. Now you can be married from the Hôtel de Montargis with a respectable dowry and all the proper arrangements instead of some poor sort of affair in the chapel at the Spanish embassy here in Manchester Square."

Isobel's heart sank as she felt the stifling walls of the *ancien régime* conventions closing in on her. How was she going to resist them if she could no longer use their extenuating circumstances and the precariousness of their finances for excuses to do the thing she loved the most—singing. Surely none of the rigidly formal young men her father had considered a worthy match for the daughter of the house of de Montargis would ever let their wives indulge in music except in the most frivolous and decorative fashion. Isobel racked her brains for some excuse to delay the inevitable. "Perhaps, Papa, but we do not even know if it is possible to return to Paris and the Faubourg Saint-Germain, or if any of the estates are still in our possession. Your health is not strong so we must wait until the weather is good and everything is in readiness for our return. We must write to Auguste to see what he has been able to accomplish."

"Auguste! I have told you, you are never to mention that traitor's name in this household." The duc's high color deepened with rage until his complexion looked truly alarming.

Isobel grabbed the decanter of water on his desk, poured it into a glass, and held it to his lips. "Here, Papa, drink this. You must not agitate yourself so." She had been afraid it would be like this. The guiding principle in the Duc de Montargis's life, the one thing that he had never lost, the one thing that could not be wrenched away from him by the Revolution was his honor. And to him, being honorable was, purely and simply, being loyal to the king. It was unthinkable to him that a son of his could have been anything but ready to die, as he was himself, for Louis XVIII. The country that Auguste had been fighting for was not France because, to the duc, France was not France until the king had been restored to the throne.

The duc's angry flush faded and his rapid breathing slowed as he drank the water his daughter had given him. Observing these encouraging signs, Isobel tried another line of reasoning. "I shall speak to Madame de Colignac to see when she is planning to return, for surely she will leave as soon as possible. I shall ask her to assess the state of affairs and to write to us. Perhaps she could even take Marthe with her to ready things for us." The vexed topic of Auguste would just have to wait until they had made the long journey to France and she was reassured that her father had recovered from the journey. It might be best to arrange for her father and her brother to encounter one another unexpectedly, for surely when confronted by the son he had not seen in over a decade, the Duc de Montargis would not be so proud as to reject him out of hand. And if the sons of other émigrés who had joined Auguste in Napoleon's army were seen welcomed back into their families, perhaps her father could be prevailed upon to do the same.

"If Marthe goes, that leaves no one to see to our establishment here."

"I can do it, Papa. I have been helping Marthe for years."

The duc snorted. "It is not fitting for a de Montargis to concern herself with such lowly details. What would people think of such a thing?"

"They will think nothing of it; many émigrés have no one to serve them and have been attending themselves to such mundane matters for years."

"*Non! Absolument.* I will not have my daughter working like a common servant. Marthe will stay with us."

"Very well, Papa." Isobel sighed. "I will ask Madame de Colignac to look into things for us in Paris." With a resigned shrug of her shoulders she turned and was heading for the door when Marthe came up the stairs, puffing mightily, a heavy cream-colored note in her hand. "Monsieur le duc, mademoiselle, a messenger, all in livery of the most magnificent brought this." She placed it reverently in the duc's outstretched hand.

A smile of grim satisfaction settled on the duc's face as he read the gilt-edged missive. "At last they deign to recognize us. The Prince Regent has invited us to a ball at Carlton House, *ma fille.*" He reached in his pocket and pulled out a small packet of faded silk. "You must use this to see that we are suitably attired for such an occasion."

Isobel gasped as she unwrapped the package. "But it is Maman's diamond necklace! It is worth far more than a court dress. I shall . . ."

"I wish you to spend it all. We shall not disgrace ourselves on the first occasion in so many years to show the world who we are."

"But, Papa, with the money from that we could have . . ."

"I will have no argument, Isobel. It is essential that you make your first appearance at the English court *en grand tenue.* When we return to France, a diamond necklace will again be the merest trifle to the de Montargis."

Biting her lips to keep back any further retort, Isobel wrapped up the necklace and fled from the room, too angry to remain another minute. All those years he had been hoarding thousands of pounds worth of diamonds and for what? So she could look her best at one miserable ball! Even for the Duc de Montargis, this seemed excessive. All those years when they could have paid for medicines and doctors to help her mother, to keep them warm in winter instead of shivering under layers of coarse chemises and petticoats. It was beyond belief! Not for the first time, she wondered if her father were a little mad, but if he were, it was a collective madness, a ruinous pride that she had seen exhibited by their friends many times before. There was the duchesse who had invited friends to dinner and spent all her money on flowers, leaving nothing to pay for the food, the chevalier who had been court-martialed by his peers because he had been forced to become a servant in order to survive, the countesse who had sold all the jewels she escaped with so she could have Rose Bertin, the Queen's dressmaker, make her dresses and then had no money for food or lodging. All of them seemed to possess a pride so strong that it precluded all else. Isobel had nothing against pride if it were justly earned, but this, this was pride stemming from a whim of fate. To have pride in one's own accomplishments was one thing, to have it over a mere accident of birth was quite another, and she found it nearly impossible to have patience with such foolishness.

Too furious to think, she paced her narrow room in a vain attempt to exorcise some of her frustration. There was no one in whom she could confide her anger. Marthe, whose family had served the de Montargis for generations, would see nothing wrong in this misplaced sense of honor. A genius of practicality herself, Marthe never expected to see such a trait in her master. In fact, she would occasionally take issue with Isobel's insistence on descending into a realm that most of her peers scorned to visit. "But Mademoiselle should not be troubling herself with such things. Mademoiselle is a great lady," she would occasionally protest. It was only by pointing out that even the greatest of ladies had to eat that Isobel could silence her. To Marthe, allowing one's family to suffer the strictest of economies unnecessarily so one's daughter could appear *en grand tenue* for one court ball would not seem at all unreasonable.

The only person Isobel could call to mind who would share her righteous fury would be Lord Christian Hatherleigh. He too had lived a life where food, shelter, and survival, rather than fashion and image were the issues controlling his life. He would understand her resentment of her father's absurdities; in fact, he would be the only person of her acquaintance who would see them as absurdities.

You must calm down. You must calm down, she repeated to herself as she turned corner after corner in her tiny bedchamber. No
one would understand her anger; they would only regard it as
being excessively ill-bred. The only thing to do was to swallow
her annoyance, obey her father's wishes, have a suitable dress
made up, and bide her time. But for what? Isobel sank down on
the narrow bed and clasped her head in her hands. What was there
to look forward to but becoming the wife of some equally rigid
husband who would expect her to live the same narrow, formal
existence that her father did, demanding that she appear out-
wardly elegant and charming, but inwardly empty and docile with
nothing more to enliven her days than idle chatter and the occasional interaction with servants who would cater to her every
whim? She could hardly bear to contemplate it. If only she were a
man, she would run away and join the army, become a diplomat
to foreign lands, anything to escape the stifling routine she saw
stretching endlessly before her.

I won't! She lifted her head and straightened her shoulders defiantly. *I won't give up and I won't give in*, she vowed as she rose
and made her way downstairs to help Marthe in the kitchen.

Chapter 24

In the end Christian found no relief at Jackson's. Even sparring with the champion himself, though it tired him out, had not calmed the welter of emotions raging inside him, and he returned home as upset as he had been when he left. After rereading the Prince Regent's invitation, he decided that he must see Isobel before the ball, for it had become quite clear that he was not going to be able to wait until then to discover the identity of the mysterious lover. He would find some way to encounter her and demand an explanation. With a muttered oath, Christian crumpled the invitation and tossed it into the fire. He had no right to demand anything of her, much less an explanation of her conduct.

How could he have felt so close to her if she were in love with someone else? How could the last look that had passed between them at the opera have felt so much like a kiss if there were someone else with whom she shared real kisses? And why was he torturing himself thinking about such things?

It would pass. She was just another woman among many. It would pass. It always had before. But—he leaned against the mantel, staring fixedly into the flames—he had never cared so much until now. He had never cared if a woman he had flirted with kissed anyone else or not. Frequently he had simply assumed that they had other lovers and it had not bothered him in the least. Perhaps that was because he had only shared their bodies with other lovers. With this woman, for some inexplicable reason, and for the first time in his life, he had shared his soul.

Furiously he rang the bell for Digby, who materialized so quickly as to make Christian suspect that, well aware of his master's uncertain frame of mind, and knowing Christian to be a man of action, the batman had hovered near the library door in anticipation of orders that were sure to come.

"Sir?" Digby's features were more wooden than usual as a result of his intense struggle to hide any indication that he recognized the urgency of his master's summons.

"Digby, I wish you to go to a Signor Bartoli's establishment in Saint Martin's Street, and I wish for you to discover, without anyone's realizing that they have divulged it to you, precisely what time Mademoiselle Isobel de Montargis is expected at her next lesson, and how long these lessons usually last. Do you think you can do that?"

"Of course I can, sir. Believe me, no one will even realize they have had a jaw with me." He gave his master a broad wink. "Just like old times, won't it be, sir?"

Christian smiled faintly. "Yes, just like old times." But it was not. He had never known a time when he had been so confused, so torn up inside over the actions of another person, especially a woman.

Closing the door gently behind him, Digby was coming to much the same conclusion. "He's in a bad way, he is," he muttered to himself as he finished brushing off his master's many-caped driving coat, hung it up, and put on his own coat before heading off to Saint Martin's Street. "Never seen him upset over a woman since I've known him." Digby stepped out into Curzon Street, pulling his coat close against the sharp breeze that had sprung up. "If I had to say it, I would say the master is in a fair way to being in love, though he's in too much of a pucker right now to realize it." A sly smile stole over the batman's wind-reddened features. "Aye, that's it," he addressed the pigeon that fluttered down to grab a crumb in front of him, "top-over-tail he is, and with no more an idea of it than you, Mr. Pigeon, have of wishing me a *good day*."

Later that evening, the batman was able to report that Mademoiselle de Montargis was expected at ten o'clock the very next morning and that her lessons lasted an hour. "And the little maid whose parcel I carried had no more idea that I was asking about the particular young lady in question than the man in the moon. 'Course now I know all about every blessed person that calls on the signor, but she is none the wiser," he reported with barely concealed pride.

"Thank you, Digby. You always were a first-rate man for intelligence."

Now there was nothing to do but wait until morning. A long evening of gambling at Brook's was in store for him. Ordinarily,

Lord Christian did not go in for deep play, considering it a waste
of time when one's mind could be put to so much better use, but
in this case, distraction of the highest order was called for and the
only way he could put off thinking about tomorrow was to risk
enough money tonight to capture his full attention.

At last, as the sky was showing the faintest signs of light in the
east, he felt exhausted enough to stagger home for a few hours of
sleep before confronting Mademoiselle de Montargis.

Promptly at eleven, freshly shaved and looking as elegant as
though he has spent several hours dressing in a leisurely manner
after enjoying a full night's sleep, Christian sauntered down Saint
Martin's Street. Anyone passing by would have put him down as
a nonpareil, a Corinthian who had not a care in the world beyond
the set of his exquisitely tied cravat, until they looked in his eyes
and then they would have seen the haunted look that revealed the
unrest in his soul.

At last the door of Signor Bartoli's house swung open and a
slender figure in a lavender sarcenet pelisse and a straw-colored
bonnet trimmed with lavender ribbons emerged.

"Mademoiselle Isobel," he called hoarsely.

She turned in some surprise and alarm. Could it be that she was
discovered, that somehow her father knew she was no longer giving lessons at the Duke of Warminster's? Her expression softened
into a shy smile when she recognized Lord Christian. "Good day,
my lord. This is certainly a surprise."

"I had to see you." Driven by forces stronger than he, Christian
plunged in without preamble.

The delicate brows rose in surprise. The blue eyes were wary
now as Isobel surveyed him uneasily. The taut set of his shoulders, the dark expression in his eyes, and the urgency in his voice
were foreign to the self-assured Lord Christian Hatherleigh. She
searched his face for some clue to all this, but could find none. "Is
something amiss?"

"Yes, er, I mean no, I mean, I do not know. It is just that I was
concerned for you." He struggled for the right words, but none
would come. "Who was that with you," he burst out at last.

"With me?" Her blank expression should have reassured him.
If she had a lover, she would have known instantly to whom he
referred, but he was too far gone to notice.

"Yes, in the park. Who was he?"

"In the park? Oh, that was . . ." Dawning comprehension gave
way to another sort of revelation. "How dare you! What is it to

you who my associates are? I am not your sister. I am not your niece. I am not even a distant cousin, and even if I were, I should most certainly take exception to your questioning my conduct, especially when it was perfectly unexceptionable, in a public place, and in the company of one of my oldest friends, the exceedingly respectable Marchioness of Verwood." Isobel paused to draw an angry breath. "How *dare* you, sir!" She reiterated it fiercely and then, without another glance, she turned on her heel and strode off furiously in the other direction. Angry tears stung her eyes, making it nearly impossible to see, but she kept on, determined to get away from him, to put as much distance between her and Lord Christian Hatherleigh as possible before she was tempted to turn around and . . . and . . . Isobel would have given anything in the world at that moment to be able to draw a sword and challenge him to a duel. Of all the . . . how she longed to be a man, someone who could settle affairs of honor with the clean slice of a blade, or at least someone who could work out some of his righteous anger by doing battle. But no, she was constrained to an ignominious exit, stalking off with only the disdainful set of her head and her proud carriage to register her indignation at such an outrageous affront to her character.

"Isobel, wait. I wish to ex . . ." Christian began. But what was it he wished to explain? How could he possible explain this totally irrational, totally unwarranted intrusion into the affairs of a young woman with whom he was only casually acquainted? No, that was not true. It was not a casual acquaintance. The first instant he had looked into her eyes, he had felt as though he had known her all his life, that he could tell her anything and everything about himself, and that she would understand, would accept it all. No, it was no casual acquaintance—quite the contrary, it was the most intense acquaintance he had ever had—but it still did not give him the right to demand an accounting of her actions as though she were some servant in his employ. What had he been thinking?

Experienced as he was in the ways of the world in general, and women in particular, he should have known that no one, particularly a proud, independent woman of ancient lineage, one accustomed to supporting herself and her family, accustomed to enduring hardship and deprivation for loyalty to what many believed to be a lost cause, would take kindly to being questioned about her conduct. After all, how would he have reacted to such an impudent and ill-judged questioning of his affairs?

Christian cursed himself bitterly as he turned to retrace his steps. Isobel's reaction had been mild in comparison to what his would have been. Why, any gentlemen who had had the audacity to question his conduct might have lived to see the dawn of another day, but not the one after that. The only question would have been whether he would have chosen swords or pistols to defend himself for daring to offer such an incalculable insult.

He had been a clumsy, overbearing fool, ruled by passion instead of intellect. Even a schoolboy would have known that such an approach would not only infuriate Mademoiselle Isobel, but it would also fail to elicit the information he was seeking. In fact, he was worse off than he had been before. Why had he done it? He knew better than to act that way. For years he had maintained a cool superiority in the most trying situations by suppressing his emotions and relying on his intellect, but today he had bungled it like any hotheaded young subaltern facing his first test of fire.

Lord Christian turned into Piccadilly, barely missing a costermonger pushing a barrow of fruit. Why had he done it? What had prompted him to act like such a benighted fool? It was not until he reached Bond Street that he admitted to himself that it had been jealousy pure and simple. And it was a jealousy so strong and so irrational that he knew it did not spring from disappointment in Isobel's character alone. He was not marching along in a blinding fury simply because she had not told him that she had a lover. It was because he was in love with her himself.

Lord Christian stopped dead on the pavement. He was in love? How the lads in his regiment, and quite a few ladies of a certain racy reputation, would have hooted at the thought that the man who was more often than not doing his level best to avoid jealous women or their jealous husbands, was suffering from that same ridiculous ailment himself. He had never, even in his wildest dreams, though he would fall in love, but on the rare occasion when he had entertained such an absurd notion, he had never imagined it would be like this. He had envisioned, rather, something quite pleasant and seductive, not the infuriating, confusing, and thoroughly upsetting range of emotions that he was experiencing now.

"My Lord, how delightful," a silvery voice intruded on these unsettling thoughts.

He looked up to recognize the smiling features of Lady Emily, Marchioness of Verwood.

"Lady Emily."

La, what was wrong with the man, Emily wondered. He was scowling like a veritable thundercloud. She devoutly wished that nothing serious was amiss, for she had had such high hopes for him and Isobel. There had seemed to be some sort of understanding between them when he had joined them in their box at the opera. There had been the special language of shared interests, the intimate glances that suggested previous conversations and a relationship more special and deeper than mere acquaintance. She had congratulated herself for having contributed to the development of that relationship by providing opportunities for them to meet. Now, however, he wore the look of a man disappointed in love, for Emily could think of no other passion strong enough to disconcert as experienced a lover and as hardened a soldier as Lord Christian.

She refused to be daunted in her campaign. Gathering her courage, she declared, brightly, if irrelevantly, "Is it not famous that Isobel has been invited to perform in the New Rooms in Hanover Square next month? It is truly such an honor and, though I have the utmost regard for her talent, I do believe it is owing in some degree to Signor Bartoli's connections. Isobel says he is very influential in the musical world. It is such a pity that her brother can not hear her, but I gather it is imperative that he return to France within the sennight."

"Her brother? So that was the gentleman . . . ah, well, never mind. Yes, that is an honor for her."

Emily directed a shrewd glance at Christian under her lashes. The man looked as dazed as though he had been struck by a bolt of lightning. There was more to this than met the eye. She was dying to discover more, but she could see she would get no further in this particular conversation. "I beg your pardon, but I agreed to meet my sister at Madame Celeste's to look at a particular bonnet that has caught her fancy."

"Oh . . . er, yes, good day." Christian remained standing stock-still as the Marchioness of Verwood tilted her parasol to hide a sly smile and sailed up Bond Street.

Her brother! Good God, what had he done!

Chapter 25

But in spite of the enormity of his mistake, Christian felt almost lighthearted as he headed off to Tattersall's to see the crop of hunters that were being shown there by a well-known Irish stable. Her brother! Then Mademoiselle did not have a lover! She had not been playing him false. He had not been entirely wide of the mark in hoping she was as drawn to him as he was to her. Or at least, she had been. Had his boorish behavior—for there was no wrapping it up in clean linen—ruined his chances completely? There was only one way to find out and that was to put it to the touch. He would just have to wait with as much patience as he could muster until the ball at Carlton House.

Christian dressed with more than usual care the evening of the ball. His cravat, so skillfully tied, was blinding in its whiteness, setting off the deep tan of his skin and the rich auburn highlights of his hair. The black coat molded to his broad shoulders and trim waist made the cravat appear even more dazzling. He wore no jewelry except for a heavy gold signet ring on the little finger of his finely shaped right hand.

More than one female drew her breath and eyed him hungrily as he stood somewhat apart from the rest of the elegant crowd that was making its way to the octagon at the foot of the graceful double staircase and upstairs to the state apartments.

He ignored all of them as he scanned the throng for one slender, elegant young woman with rich brown hair and deep blue eyes. Though his height allowed him to survey the richly dressed multitude without obstruction, he was unable to locate Mademoiselle Isobel and was forced to proceed slowly along with everyone else up the staircase, mustering his patience as best he could. Everywhere blue silk hangings embroidered with gold fleur-de-lis proclaimed the Prince Regent's intent to honor the restored monarch and his loyal followers, but Christian had eyes for only one of those followers.

At last, as he shouldered his way into the Great Crimson Room, he saw a small crowd gathered around a large, portly gentleman whose blue uniform was bestrewn with military orders. He was smiling graciously and chatting affably with all those who approached him. A little behind this gentleman, and off to one side, he recognized from engravings he had seen, Monsieur, talking with an older gentleman resplendent in a green uniform reversed with scarlet and laced with silver and gold. But his eye was caught by the woman standing at this gentleman's elbow. She was standing next to the little group, yet somehow she appeared aloof and remote from it all. The feathers that waved gently in her hair as she turned her head to gaze coolly out over the assemblage added to her height and were held in place by a pearl bandeau that circled her head like a crown. Indeed, of all the royal party assembled around Louis XVIII, she appeared more royal in her bearing than the rest of the party put together. Her dress of white satin trimmed in gold tissue that matched the gold fluer-de-lis embroidered on the white satin train, was cut so as to show off her elegant figure. The Elizabethan ruff standing up around the back of her neck called attention to the long, white column of her throat encircled by a magnificent double strand of pearls. There were more pearls trimming the corsage cut low across her bosom.

She stood so still, proudly erect and distant, that she could have been a marble statue except for the touch of color on her cheeks. Then she languidly turned her head to observe the crowd pouring into the room, eager to congratulate the king. Christian's breath caught in his throat. It was Isobel. There was no mistaking the brilliant blue eyes surrounded by a heavy fringe of dark lashes or the delicately arched brows raised in faint hauteur at the *ton's* sudden enthusiasm for a man they had, to all intents and purposes, ignored for the past twenty-five years.

It was Isobel and yet it was not. She seemed to have donned an air of regal aloofness with her finery. She had always carried herself proudly, but there had been an alertness about her, an understanding in her eyes that had made her seem approachable. Now she seemed as remote and unreachable as a goddess.

Christian swallowed hard. He had always known that she came from an ancient, respected family, but until this moment she had been for him, Mademoiselle Isobel, instructress and dedicated musician. Now it was very clear that she was Mademoiselle de Montargis, daughter of the Duc de Montargis and a member of Louis XVIII's court. It should not have mattered, but it did, and that, coupled with the memory of the last time he had spoken with her was a little unnerving.

He grimaced at his own misgivings. Since when had rank and privilege ever meant anything to him? Since when had he ever been unsure of making a woman do exactly as he wished her to? Since when had he been nervous as a schoolboy? He knew the answer—since he had fallen in love. And now, just as he was acknowledging this upsetting truth to himself, the object of all this anguish had transformed herself into someone who was practically unrecognizable.

To be sure, the beautifully sculpted face, the exquisite complexion, the elegant figure, belonged to Isobel, but the air of a grande dame did not, and it made her seem as though it were a total stranger inhabiting her body.

Little did he know that Isobel was feeling very much that way herself. When she had surveyed her image in the looking glass during her final fitting at the modiste's, she had barely recognized the richly dressed young woman who stared back at her. And this evening, as she had glanced at her reflection in the small glass that Marthe held up, the transformation was even more complete. Her father had wished for her to appear *en grade tenue* and she had obliged. Now she was hating every minute of it, the people who pressed eagerly around the stout monarch, anxious to wish him well and to assure him they had always supported him, the members of Louis' court and her father's friends smiling in gracious condescension as though they had left Versailles only last week instead of barely escaping with their lives a quarter of a century ago and existing hand-to-mouth ever since.

Had everyone forgotten everything? Had no one learned anything? Was she the only one who knew it was all the merest charade until they returned to France, were accepted by their people, and were once again established in their *hôtels* and chateaux, if their *hôtels* and chateaux still existed. Glancing around at the Comtesse de Sallanches, dazzling in a gown of silver tissue embroidered in fleur-de-lis, or at the Comte de Pontarlier sporting the uniform of the Comte d'Artois *guet des gardes* as though he had the slightest idea of what to do in a situation that demanded something more courageous than choosing a new tailor, Isobel felt utterly and completely alone. Was she the only one among them who was not looking forward to the return to a life of empty formality, meaningless rituals, and exaggerated civilities?

And to make matters worse, she had been betrayed by one of the few people who seemed to understand her, someone she had come to regard as one of her closest friends. No, she resolutely pushed aside the image of gray-green eyes boring into her as Lord Christian had demanded the identity of her companion in the park. No, she would not remember the anger and the hurt she had suffered at his intrusion into her private affairs, his assumption that she had behaved with anything but the utmost propriety. No, she would not think of him again.

But even as she vowed this, she turned slightly and her eyes fell on a tall broad-shouldered figure making his way through the crowd toward her.

Isobel clutched the edges of her train with her gloved hands as she struggled for control. Her heart was thudding in her chest, her breath was coming in ragged gasps, and her cheeks felt as hot as though she had just run a race. She was furious at the gentleman, but she was even more furious at herself for reacting to his presence, furious at the uncontrollable burst of happiness that washed over her the moment she caught sight of him.

"Mademoiselle." Christian's voice caught in his throat as he fought to gain control over his own breathing, which had become extremely erratic. Now that he was here, next to her, she did not seem so unreal, but that made it worse. Now he could see the pulse throbbing in her throat and smell the faint scent of rose water that clung to her skin.

"Yes?" Isobel was pleased with herself for sounding so normal when so many emotions were warring within her. She wished to remain cool and detached, to remind him that she still resented the liberty he had taken in questioning her actions. At the same time, she had to fight to keep from smiling a welcome to him, to keep from laughing with him at the absurdity of the role she was being forced to play, a great lady wearing a fortune of jewels and the dressmaker's art, when she did not have the wherewithal to pay more than two months' rent at the most, and very little extra for food and the other necessities of life. Who would understand better than Lord Christian how frustrated she was? Who could know better than a soldier what it was like to maintain a position when there was no guarantee of supplies? He had been in the field long enough to appreciate the difference between appearance and reality.

"May I have this dance?"

"What?"

"We *are* at a ball, you know. I was wondering if you would care to join me in the waltz?"

"Papa?" She looked around to see her father totally absorbed in acknowledging the greetings of the *ton*. In this, his hour of triumph, his daughter, the daughter whose music and French lessons had made it possible for them to rent a house near the Comte d'Artois, the daughter who had looked after him while he wrote his memoirs, was nothing more than an ornament in the kings' retinue. Once he had assured himself that her costume would not disgrace him, he had forgotten her existence entirely in the festivities being held to honor his king.

Lord Christian glanced at the Duc de Montargis, whose attention was entirely taken up at the moment by Lady Crewe, and held out his arm.

As if in a dream, Isobel laid one gloved hand on his arm and he led her to to the floor. Even with the prescribed distance between them she felt as though her body were molded against his. She tried to avoid his gaze, to glance over his shoulder at the bejeweled throng, but despite her best efforts, she could not look away, could not take free her gaze from his and the questioning look in his eyes.

Skillfully he guided her to the stairs and down them toward a doorway opening into the garden.

"My lord, I thought you wished to dance."

"Shhh." He pulled her into the shadows. "I did, but I wish even more to apologize to you for my incredible effrontery in asking you the identity of your companion. It was none of my affair and I am fully sensible of the offense I gave you, first, in assuming that it was my concern and second, in assuming that your companion was one with whom you . . . er . . . enjoyed a certain degree of intimacy.

Isobel did not know whether she felt gratified or infuriated. "You are correct. It was none of your affair. And yes, you are also correct in assuming that there is a degree . . . in short, it was my brother, Auguste, who had his own reasons for walking with me in the park."

"I know that now, and that . . ."

"You *know*? *That* is why you are apologizing. It is not that you came to the conclusion that you could trust me to behave honorably and respectably, it is that now you know the identity of my companion you feel ashamed enough to apologize for your ill-bred behavior. But if you had not discovered that singular fact what then, my lord?"

"Isobel, please try to understand."

"I am trying, my lord. And what I understand is that you do not trust me to behave honorably, that . . ."

He held up a hand. "No, Isobel, you do not understand. I barely understand it myself. But what I know now, and it is not to my credit, is that I was jealous. Purely and simply put, I saw you laughing and talking with a man as though he belonged together with you and I realized that for some time I have been thinking that we, you and I, belong together."

"You presume a great deal, my lord." But Isobel's protest lacked conviction and she could not move or break her eyes away from his steady gaze, though she knew she should have.

"Yes, I did, but I do not think that I was mistaken, was I, Isobel?" His long fingers tilted up her chin and he pulled her close to him.

"You . . . you, had no right."

"I know I had no right except that I have shared more of myself with you than I have with any other human being, and I think—I hope—you feel the same way."

"I . . ."

"Do not deny it, please do not." His lips came down on hers and he felt the warm response in her lips as they parted underneath his. She yielded for just a moment and then he felt her struggle to pull away.

"I . . . you . . . you have no right to . . ." She wrenched herself from his arms and he barely caught the look of desperation in her eyes as she whirled away and fled back toward the brilliantly lighted staircase, leaving him with the taste of her on his mouth.

"No, I have no right, only the hope that you will understand someday that we belong together. But how is that to happen?" He addressed her retreating form. Then, with a sigh of despair he made his way to the door and, welcoming the blast of cool evening air on his face, he began to walk home.

What was he to do? It would take a long time to explain it all, to prove to her that he was right. Did he have that time? Political events were crowding one upon another—Napoleon'a defeat, the Congress of Vienna—they were all against him. At any moment Louis and his court, the de Montargis included, could be returning to France, and he needed time. Would he get it?

Chapter 26

Isobel was shaking as she reached the stairway. She grabbed the railing and, gasping for breath, slowly mounted the staircase, trying desperately to look normal, as though she had been forced to retire from the ballroom for nothing more serious than the adjustment of her coiffure or the repair of a torn flounce, instead of the way she felt, which was that her entire world had suddenly turned upside down. For the first time in her life, she truly did not know what to think or how to feel. For every other upsetting situation in which she had found herself she had always possessed a clear picture of what she should do. Her idea of what this was might not be something that other people considered proper or fashionable, but she always had known what felt right for the sort of person she was. Now she did not have the faintest idea of what to do. She felt as lost as a sailboat that she had once seen on a seaside visit with Jane and Emily. It had come loose from its mooring and bobbed away from the shore, driven by the wind and the tide. She was much the same as the sailboat, caught off guard by the tumultuous forces of emotion that she had not even known existed.

She had never experienced such hurt and fury as she had suffered when Lord Christian, a person who had in so short a time seemed to understand her better than anyone she had ever known, not only appeared to think so ill of her that he assumed she had a clandestine lover, but then had had the impudence to think he had the right to question her about her conduct. Isobel had told herself again and again that she did not care about the opinion of a man who misread her so and she had spent several sleepless nights trying to adopt her own coolly rational advice without much success.

Just when she thought she was able to put him out of her mind, he appeared and she found herself reacting to him so strongly that she knew she had been deluding herself completely. To make matters worse, he had not only proven to her that she was not immune to his charm, but that she was far more drawn to him than she had even realized. The touch of his hand on her waist as he had led her out onto the dance floor had made her knees weak, and when he had pulled her away from the crowd toward the garden she had found herself longing for him to hold her closer. At last, in the shadow of the doorway he had held her close and she could feel his heart beating against her breasts, and revel in the strength in the arms that drew her closer to him. Still she had wanted more. And when he had turned her face up to his and kissed her slowly, languourously, she had barely been able to breathe with the longing that washed over her. So overwhelmed was she by all these sensations that she had hardly heard his words *I had been thinking that we, you and I, belonged together.*

For her entire life Isobel had been desperate to belong to something. She had longed, as only an exile could long, for a home, a country, a sense of place. Until that moment, however, only her music had given that to her, and even her music had not exerted the powerful urge that this man did over her. But she was afraid. To give her life to her music was one thing; to give it to a man was another, especially a man who, according to Emily, made a practice of loving women.

Music enlarged her soul; this man might diminish it; he might take it away altogether. How much she had already been hurt by his mistrust of her. Her pride had been insulted, and pride was what gave her much of her strength. It was not a pride in external things—birth fortune—like the pride for which she condemned her father and his friends, but a pride in herself, her independence, her ability to work hard, to learn, to sing, to make a reputation for herself. In her anger over the misunderstanding with Lord Christian she had very nearly forgotten all this. She could not risk forgetting that again. Unconsciously Isobel knew that this justifiable pride was something that drew him to her and that if she allowed it to vanish she would not only lose herself, but him in the process.

All these thoughts jostled together in her head as, gripping the railing for support, she finished climbing the stairs and made her way back into the ballroom to her father's side. More than anything she wanted to escape somewhere where she could sort these things out in peace and quiet. The last place she wished to be was in a throng of brilliantly dressed people intent on seeing one another and being seen by the Prince Regent and his illustrious guests.

Fortunately, Isobel's father, intent on acknowledging the well-wishes of the *ton*, had not noticed his daughter's absence, but as she returned to his side he turned to her. "The king has asked us to accompany him to the reception being given to him by the citizens of London at Grillon's Hotel and then, at last, we shall return to France. He has also made arrangements for us to join his party traveling to Paris. But now, my dear, you must dance. The Chevalier d'Entremont and the Comte de Pontarlier are most anxious to show these barbarians how a true courtier dances, and you are the perfect partner for this. Go, show *les Anglais* how gracefully it can be done, how it *should* be done.

Sighing inwardly, Isobel allowed the Comte de Pontarlier to lead her onto the floor. Personally she thought he moved with far less grace than Lord Christian, who possessed the assurance and coordination of a natural athlete as well as a sensitivity toward his partner that was totally lacking in the comte, who insisted on escorting her around the floor with needlessly showy flourishes. Isobel did her best to look interested and attentive to her partner's incessant flow of conversation, but in truth, she did not hear a word as they whirled around the floor. All she could think of was her previous partner and the unsettling revelations that had followed her last waltz.

In fact, she barely heard any of the conversations directed at her for the rest of the evening, so absorbed was she in the tumult of emotions awakened in her by Lord Christian. Hating herself for doing it, yet longing to know what had happened to him after her precipitate departure, she surveyed the crowd from time to time, but no tall, broad-shouldered gentleman stood out. She was forced to conclude that, having come to the ball to see her, he had left after their dance. Even though she told herself that his presence was of no interest to her, she could not help but be gratified by this.

"La, Isobel, you look like a queen of France yourself," a gay voice at her elbow broke into her thoughts. "I have been trying to reach you this age, but there is such a crush of people around His Majesty that it is nearly impossible." Emily was still gasping from the effort of working her way through the crowd of people surrounding the French court. "You look as fine as fivepence. I vow, Hatherleigh must have been completely undone. Yes, you sly girl, I saw you dancing with him. He could not take his eyes off you the entire time. He was like a cat looking at a cream pot. He must have filled your ears with more than one pretty compliment. It is said, you know, that he has a silver tongue, and that is a goodly part of his charm, for no woman can resist being told she is beautiful. At the very least, he must have told you that you look like a goddess."

"Er, no."

"No! He danced the waltz with you and did not say that you outshine every woman in the room, which is perfectly true."

"Ah, no."

"My dear, the man must be blind!" Emily paused and directed a searching look at the blush rising to her friend's cheeks. "Either that or he must be so in love that he dispensed completely with pretty phrases." The blush deepened. "So that is it. Very well, I shan't tease you, but you do look remarkably elegant. I vow that every man in the room has his eyes on you. Even Verwood, who has gone off to find the card room, said that you looked *devilish fine* and for him, that is high praise indeed. Did you see the absurd turban Lady Ashworth is wearing? She looks like a perfect quiz. And why she would choose that dreadful color of green for a gown, why she looks positively hag-ridden."

As Emily preceded to discuss one costume after another, Isobel nodded absently, not hearing a word she said. He had not said she was beautiful. In fact, he had never attempted to offer her Spanish coin. Did that mean he did not find her attractive, or did it mean he considered her above such things? Perhaps he had meant what he said after all, that they belonged together. Perhaps there was something special in their friendship, something that meant she was not just another one of his flirts. The rush of happiness that accompanied this thought was ruthlessly quelled. What did she care? She was not about to fall in love with someone who had behaved as high-handedly with her as Lord Christian had. She was a de Montargis, after all, and much as it infuriated her to hear her father say it year after year, even when the de Montargiess had nothing else, at least they had their pride.

Isobel glanced over at her father as he exchanged words with the king in between receiving congratulations and good wishes for the future. There was color in his face, energy in his movements, and a liveliness about him that she could only dimly remember from her childhood. Even if she were feeling overwhelmed and lost, she could take comfort from the fact that he at least was happy, and that he would be able to live out the rest of his old age in his own land among his own countrymen.

She could concentrate on that and put all her energies into their return to France. That would leave time only for her music and little else. Certainly it would leave no time for reflection about a certain tall gentleman with strong arms, a broad chest, and compelling gray-green eyes.

Chapter 27

True to her resolve, Isobel approached her father the next day to inquire about plans for the impending move.

"The king and the court are leaving in a fortnight. After the reception at Grillon's, there is to be another dress party given in our honor by the Prince Regent and the day after that, or perhaps the next, we shall proceed to Dover and then to France."

"But, Papa, I am not sure that everything will be in readiness by then. Madame de Colignac is not leaving for a sennight and even if she were to arrive in Paris several weeks before we did I am not confident that she or her servants would be able to insure that the Hôtel de Montargis is available for us to live in."

The duc waved a dismissive hand. "That is no matter. The king assures me that we are to have apartments at the Tuileries for as long as we desire and that even now they are being readied for our arrival.

Isobel's heart sank. They were to leave so soon, when there were still so many things she wished to do. There were lessons with Signor Bartoli which she was loath to give up and there was a coveted appearance at the New Rooms in Hanover Square. She had been unable to believe her ears when her teacher had announced that he had secured her a place on the program for a concert being held the last week in April. At last she truly seemed to be on the road to her dream. How could she leave now? She knew what her father's answer would be even before she posed the question, but an opportunity to appear in the Hanover Square rooms was too important to let slip from her grasp. Drawing a deep, steadying breath and clasping her hands tightly in her lap, she took the risk. "Papa?"

"Yes?" The duc gazed curiously at her. It was unlike his independent and decisive daughter to sound so tentative.

"Papa, I have been asked to sing in the New Rooms in Hanover Square the last week of April. May we not postpone our departure until after that?"

The duc's aristocratic nose quivered as he snorted in disgust. "A daughter of the de Montargis singing like a common *actrice d'opéra? Non, et non, et non!*"

"But, Papa, all the best people can be seen there, even the Prince Regent himself. And Madame Catalani is giving concerts there. It is a great honor to be asked. You were not displeased that I sang at the Countess of Morehampton's musicale."

"That was different, a private affair held at the *hôtel* of one of the *ton's* well-known hostesses. But a public concert? For money? It is beneath you. No de Montargis would dream of such a thing."

"Very well, Papa." Isobel sighed and refrained from pointing out that the handsome payment given to her by the countess had, in addition to repaying Lord Christian, been responsible for more fires in more fireplaces at the house in Manchester Street and more meat for the delicious pots-au-feu with which Marthe had managed to whet his appetite. Tears stung her eyes as she left to consult with Marthe about the packing. It was difficult to admit, even to herself, how bitter her disappointment was, and she had no one in whom to confide. Marthe, though proud of her mistress's accomplishments, was inclined to agree with her master. "To be sure, it is an honor to be asked to sing at the New Rooms, mademoiselle, but Mademoiselle is a great lady once again. It would never do to compromise her reputation in such a way," she had responded when Isobel had first shared her dilemma with her.

"Mademoiselle is no grander a lady now than she was a few weeks ago and she will not be a grand lady in the future if there is nothing left to be a lady of," Isobel replied with a good deal of asperity. Did no one see the irony and uncertainty of their future besides herself?

And Emily and Jane, though they were not so vehement as the duc, could not sympathize with her very strongly either. "What is one concert, compared with being in Paris?" Emily wondered out loud as they had discussed it at the ball.

Jane, more perceptive than her sister, saw the distress in her friend's eyes. "Do not worry, Isobel. They say that Napoleon has restored the capital to the way it once was. Mama's friend, Lady Edgerton, went to Paris after the Peace of Amiens and she reported that it was as elegant as it had ever been, if not more so. I should not fret about it. Did you not say that Auguste had reported that the Hôtel de Montargis had not been destroyed. From what I understand, he rented it to one of Napoloen's marshals?"

"Shhh." Isobel glanced nervously at her father. "He must not know this. It was the only way to save the Hôtel de Montargis and return it to its former elegance. It is all owing to Auguste's energy and perseverance that we can return to it at all, but Papa will not so much as allow the whisper of Auguste's name in his presence.

In fact, the only one who sympathized with Isobel's dismay at being deprived of the opportunity at the Hanover Square rooms was Signor Bartoli. "Ah, signorina, it is the greatest pity." He laid a comforting hand on her shoulder the next day when she finished her lesson. "But all artists have these unfortunate moments, and sometimes, in the end, it proves the better for them."

"But, monsieur"—Isobel's eyes were bright with unshed tears—"my lessons. What shall I do about my lessons? When I go to Paris I shall no longer have you to teach me or to encourage me."

"That is true, signorina, and it is not only you who will be sorry for this." The old man smiled fondly at her. He would miss her, her passion, her dedication, her willingness to learn, and her humility. In the music teacher's vast experience he had discovered that God had created few creatures as rare as Isobel de Montargis and he, Giulio Bartoli, had been fortunate enough to meet her. Most young ladies would have been overjoyed to be returning to a life of elegance and ease in France, but he knew Isobel well enough that he did not insult her by congratulating her on her change in fortune.

Signor Bartoli sat down at the pianoforte, fingering the keys idly while he racked his brains for some way to help his student. "Ah, I have it." He strode over to his marquetry desk, pulled out pen, ink, and paper and scribbled furiously. "When you arrive in Paris, you must seek out Signor Gasparo Spontini. I knew him many years ago in Napoli, but he is now in Paris. If I do not miss my guess, he will be delighted to meet you, not only because you are a singer of the highest caliber, but because he has been director of the Italian Opera in Paris under Bonaparte, and I am sure he wishes to remain there. To have a pupil who is also a member of the court would be a situation of the most helpful to him."

"Oh, thank you, signor." In an uncharacteristic display of enthusiasm, Isobel flung her arms around her teacher's neck. "You do not know how worried I was."

"There, there, signorina." He patted her awkwardly on the shoulder. "It is but a temporary reverse. I have the utmost confidence that you will achieve your dream in time."

"Thank you, monsieur." Isobel took the slip of paper and put it in her reticule. "You have given me some hope, something to look forward to, and now I am equal to the task of preparing for our departure."

Despite these bold words, Isobel found the task somewhat daunting. While there were very few things that they wished to take with them—her father's desk, her mother's triptych, the watercolors the duchess had painted while at Barford Court—there was still a great deal to accomplish, and Isobel found herself running hither and thither on last-minute errands. Occupied with these, she was not at home any of the times that Christian attempted to call on her in Manchester Street.

Reporting to her mistress these unsuccessful efforts, Marthe could not help wondering at the strange agitation these messages induced in Mademoiselle. To be sure, it was most distressing to miss the opportunity to speak to such a handsome and distinguished gentleman, but Isobel's agitation went beyond that. Marthe did not understand. A lady could, without being thought forward, give some indication as to when she might be found at home, but Mademoiselle did none of this. On the contrary, she seemed to wish to put all thought of the gentleman's visits out of her mind, even going to the length of snapping, "It is of no importance" at Marthe when the servant had ventured to speculate when he might return.

Isobel participated halfheartedly in the events leading up to their departure. She refused to join the crowds in Piccadilly that watched the procession, led by the Eleventh Dragoons and ending with the Prince Regent's carriage, that swept out toward the Paddington turnpike to the village of Strathmore, halting at the Abercorn Arms, where they met King Louis. She was waiting at Grillon's Hotel with the rest of the French court, but while the others were watching from the windows as the Prince Regent's carriage, drawn by eight cream-colored horses, drew up in front, she remained aloof. And once the king had arrived and began to receive the well-wishers crowding around him, she glided unobtrusively to a place by the windows so as not to be seen as part of the court and the celebrations for which she could muster no enthusiasm.

Exhausted by her preparations, Isobel went through the Prince Regent's dress party the following day in a fog, barely even noticing the moment when Louis was invested with the Order of the Garter.

It was almost with relief that, two days after this ceremony, she lay back against the squabs of the post chaise hired to take them to Dover. They spent the night at the Red Lion and joined the king and his entourage boarding the English frigate that was to take them to Calais. Worn out with the emotions of the last few days, saying good-bye to Emily and Jane and their parents, who had journeyed to London to offer their best wishes and their farewells to Isobel and her father, visiting all the places which had been her home for the past years, and parting from Signor Bartoli, Isobel sought solace in the solitude of the open deck, as she leaned on the rail watching England and the white cliffs receding behind them. Long after the shoreline had disappeared from sight, she remained there feeling the salt spray on her face and listening to the lonely cry of the seagulls.

Isobel did not begrudge the other émigrés their rising excitement and happy anticipation as the shores of France came into view, but she could not share it with them. Nor could she share their joy at stepping ashore onto French soil to the sound of French voices and French church bells. As the others fell to their knees to kiss the ground beneath them, Isobel thought she had never felt so alone in her entire life.

The trip to Paris passed as if in a dream. They stopped at Compiègne, where Louis received Czar Alexander and various deputations from the government. Isobel allowed Marthe to dress her for the reception held in honor of the czar, the man who had been so instrumental in Louis' restoration, but she exhibited no more interest in it all than if they had been back in Manchester Street and Marthe had been handing her her pelisse. At the reception she made her curtsies to foreign dignitaries mechanically, responding automatically to the often repeated phrases of congratulation.

When at last they arrived in Paris, Isobel was able to overcome her lassitude enough to see them installed in temporary quarters in the Tuileries, but even the pianoforte so thoughtfully procured by Madame de Colignac failed to rouse much enthusiasm in her. This was how her parents must have felt upon arriving in England so many years ago, lost and aimless, but infinitely poorer.

I must pull myself out of this lethargy, Isobel told herself again and again. *I must find something to interest me. After all, when he was in exile, even Papa was able to inspire himself with the hope of a return to France.*

Slowly, as the days passed, she recovered from the physical exhaustion of the move and the days of celebration, and as her fatigue wore off, some of her natural energy returned. Bit by bit she began to return to her music, reveling in the luxury of having a pianoforte at her disposal and available for practice any time she might wish it. Gradually she began to feel more like herself again, enough so that at last she felt prepared enough to send a footman with a note to Signor Spontini. After years of having only Marthe or the occasional stable boy to run messages, she was finding it difficult to adjust to the army of servants available to her at the Tuileries.

Isobel soon discovered that living at the palace meant that one was constantly immersed in a hive of activity, of comings and goings, intrigues and cabals, and discussions among the many courtiers jockeying for position and a chance to win the king's favor.

Even her father, though he never complained of it, found the increased activity and increased society fatiguing. There was many a state dinner when he asked that his daughter might be seated next to him. He explained it to her. "I tell them that it is so I may help you to be better acquainted with court etiquette, but, *du vrai,* it is to make sure that you keep me awake. I am not so young as I was the last time I was at court."

Chapter 28

Isobel was not the only one experiencing this strange feeling of lethargy. After the ball at Carlton House, Christian had found it difficult to put his mind and his energies toward anything. The truth of the matter was that he was finding it difficult to well nigh impossible to think about anything else except Isobel. Everything else in life seemed of little consequence compared to her and her happiness.

Was it simply because she had rejected his advances that he could think of nothing but the trembling of her slender body as he had held her or the brief moment when her lips had parted beneath his so invitingly? Surely he had not become as big a coxcomb as that? Even though he could not recall it, there must have been other women who had rebuffed him and he had not become obsessed with them.

He thought about her constantly and looked for her everywhere he went, picturing her in every tall, graceful young woman he saw in Bond Street. Naturally, the first thing he had done the day after the ball was to call in Manchester Street even though he felt relatively certain that he would not be received. The duc had looked askance at him when the de Montargis were poor exiles, he would undoubtedly refuse to speak to him at all, now that the de Montargis were on the verge of returning to their former exalted status. It had been no use. Every time he had called, both Isobel and her father had been out and, judging from the regretful expression on the stolid face of the servant who answered the door, they truly had not been at home. If he had not been so distressed, Christian might have wondered at the servant's seeming change of heart as she encouraged him to try again, but he was oblivious to it.

He rode in the park regularly and though he had observed the Marchioness of Verwood's barouche taking part in the slow procession of vehicles parading through the park, he had also noticed that the only other person who accompanied the marchioness was her sister.

Throwing his pride to the winds, Christian even took to haunting Saint Martin's Street in the mornings in the hopes of catching Isobel as she went to her lessons at Signor Bartoli's, but to no avail. The horrible premonition that she was preparing to depart, or had already departed for France, took possession of him and finally, driven by desperation, he accosted Lady Verwood in the park.

Dispensing with pleasantries, he plunged right to the point. "Mademoiselle de Montargis is. . . ."

"Gone to France, my lord." Seeing the haunted look in Christian's eyes, Emily also dispensed with pleasantries and gave him her answer as briefly and quickly as possible. "She and her father left with the rest of the court." Emily watched as the grim expression on his face became even more bleak and she could have hugged herself with delight. So he *did* care after all. And, if she did not miss her mark, her friend Isobel's distress at leaving had almost as much to do with leaving Lord Christian Hatherleigh as it had to do with parting from her singing teacher. Emily smiled sympathetically at the unhappy man in front of her. "However, I shall be delighted to furnish you with Isobel's direction. I shall send my footman around with it as soon as I return home." A sly twinkle crept into her eyes as she watched a dull flush creep over his lean, tanned cheeks.

"Thank you." Without further comment, Christian left her as abruptly as he had appeared.

She had gone to Paris without a word to him. Could he have been mistaken in thinking that he meant something to her? Had he been wrong about the response he had felt in her body when he had kissed her, or the warmth in her eyes whenever she spoke to him? Surely she would not have been so angry at him for coming to the wrong conclusions about Auguste's identity if he had not meant something to her. If she did not feel anything for him, she would simply have been indifferent to his interference in her life, and she had not been indifferent when she had broken away from his embrace at Carlton House—upset, yes; furious, certainly; but indifferent, no.

Lord Christian rode slowly back to Mount Street, his mind numb. He was completely bereft of energy or interest in anything except Isobel. Never in his life had he felt himself to be at such a loss as to what to do with himself. Wordlessly he handed Ajax over to the stable boys, failing, in his abstraction to give his usual final pat to the horse. He even failed to acknowledge Digby's

"You are home early, sir" as the batman took his curly brimmed beaver and his York tan riding gloves.

He entered the library, poked halfheartedly at the glowing coals, then strode over to stare blindly out the window at the street below. When he had first returned to London, Isobel and her quest to become the next Catalani had captured his interest. He had allowed their friendship and his attempts to further her career to keep his mind from facing the inevitable question of what he was going to do with his life now that Napoleon was beaten. He had discussed this topic with Isobel, but had not really given it serious thought. For a moment, the pleasure of her company and the anticipation of seeing her, talking with her, helping her, had made him feel alive and useful.

Now she was gone and he was faced with not only the ache of losing her, but with a vast empty future. He had fought to end the war and now, at last, it had ended. Where was he to look now for purpose and meaning in his life?

The question remained with him during the ensuing weeks as he numbly followed the routine of a London gentleman—boxing at Jackson's, shooting at Manton's, and trying to distract himself with deep play at Brooks's until one afternoon at Tattersall's as he idly strolled from one stall to the next a voice boomed in his ear. "Hatherleigh. Do not tell me you are seeking a replacement for the noble Ajax?"

Christian turned around to see the handsome face of Charles Stewart smiling at him. Delighted to see a fellow cavalry officer, Christian was about to launch into reminiscences about the Peninsula when he remembered that the last time he had seen Stewart it had been in Wellinton's headquarters in Torres Vedras where the commander in chief had been giving Stewart a severe dressing-down for his letters criticizing the campaign that had been appearing in the *Morning Chronicle*. Not even Wellington's friendship with Stewart's brother, Lord Castlereagh, had saved the hapless commander from his superior's wrath. Glad to have caught himself just in time before he brought up an unfortunate memory, Christian responded, "So you still remember Ajax. I am happy to report that he is in prime twig, eating his head off, and in danger of becoming thoroughly bored with his peaceful existence. And you, what are you doing?"

"Taking the opportunity to feast my eyes on fine English cattle before I leave again for the Continent."

"The Continent? That sounds intriguing, and certainly more enlivening than London." Christian did not bother to hide his interest.

"Yes, Robert has asked me to help him in Vienna sorting out all those fellows who are wanting to divide up the spoils now that Bonaparte is safely out of the way."

"You and your brother have your work cut out for you. Dealing with all the various ministers and potentates vying for power, each one more jealous of his influence than the next, is likely to be far more dangerous than leading a cavalry charge. Still, I envy you for you, at least, will be doing something."

"These situations are always so fraught with intrigue that one is never really assured of accomplishing anything."

The conversation then drifted to the horses on view for sale, but the encounter had given Christian the idea of offering his services to Stewart and his brother. Surely they could put him to some use in Vienna and it would take his mind off other things, such as Isobel de Montargis.

The ache of her absence had not lessened over time; in fact, it had increased, and he found himself thinking of her several times a day, wondering how she was adjusting to Paris, whether she had begun to enjoy court life or if she had simply resigned herself to it, if she was continuing with her singing. He had gotten so desperate that he had even sat down to write her several times, but found himself at a loss as to what to say. He wanted to apologize for angering her, but he was always stopped by the memory of the look in her eyes as she had broken away from him that night at Carlton House. It had been a look of desperation, perhaps even of fear, and the question remained with him; was she afraid of him or of her feelings for him. He had tortured himself endlessly with this question until he could stand it no longer and decided that the only thing to do was to forget her. He had forgotten women before, he would do it again. He could not understand what had happened to him, the man who would never allow a woman to upset his equanimity. It was all this peace that was responsible for it. When he had been at war he had never had this problem. Now he had time on his hands and nothing particular to do except think.

Having decided on a course of action, and feeling that a great weight had been lifted from his chest, Christian strolled over to Brooks's to watch the dedicated gamesters trying to break the faro bank. He even played a few hands of whist before returning home to compose a letter to Stewart, asking for the opportunity to join him in Vienna.

That done, there was nothing left to do but wait for an answer and review all the information he could lay his hands on concerning the present political situation.

The more Christian read, the more intrigued he was and he came to the conclusion that the one field in which he was experienced, war, was merely the result of failed diplomacy, or diplomacy gone wrong, and that diplomacy was often a written codification of all that had been decided physically on some battlefield somewhere. During the war he had studied the strategies of Napoleon and his commanders enough to be able to predict their moves with as much accuracy as anyone else; understanding what was going on now among the Allied Powers at the Congress of Vienna was not so very different.

His patience was eventually rewarded some weeks later when he received a travel-stained letter from Charles Stewart, promising him that he would be put to use if he could make his way to Vienna.

Laying down the letter, Christian felt as though he had just swallowed a reviving tonic. For the first time in weeks, his head felt clear, his energy returned, and he looked forward once again to what the next day would bring. "Digby!" he bellowed uncharacteristically, carried away by his newfound exuberance.

"Sir?" Digby materialized immediately. He too had been intrigued by the letter from abroad and, after having delivered it, had lingered close by in the hope that he would learn something.

"Pack our bags; we are headed for the Continent."

"Paris? Very good sir." Digby permitted himself a hopeful smile.

"Paris? Why Paris? No, my man, we are headed for Vienna. The Allied Powers have left Paris; the Congress is being held in Vienna."

"Very good, sir." The hopeful note vanished from Digby's voice and demeanor, but his master was too busy rereading the letter to notice his servant's expression.

The batman closed the library door quietly behind him. Drat! He had been hoping that the letter had come from Mademoiselle Isobel and that it would signal the end of his master's moping about. Digby had heard through the same sources that had revealed information about Mademoiselle Isobel's lessons with Signor Bartoli that the Mademoiselle had returned to Paris with her father who, according to these sources, was a great favorite of the restored King of France. Digby had been sorry to learn this for, though he wished Mademoiselle Isobel all the best and though he was happy to hear that she had been returned to her rightful position, he had secretly hoped that she would find her future happiness with Lord Christian Hatherleigh instead of at the French court. But her departure did at least explain his master's curious lack of interest in anything and everything.

With the arrival of the letter, Lord Christian seemed to have reverted to his usual self. Digby was rarely, if ever, wrong about things where his master's welfare was concerned, but he was forced to admit to himself as he set about making arrangements for their departure, that perhaps he had been mistaken in thinking that the lovely, young Frenchwoman was crucial to his master's happiness, and that realization saddened him.

Chapter 29

Signor Spontini, summoned by a note from Isobel, proved to be as effusive as Signor Bartoli was reticent. He was honored to be invited to the palace to give Mademoiselle her singing lessons, delighted to make her acquaintance, enchanted by her exquisite beauty, and charmed by her voice.

At first, Isobel was inclined to dismiss him as nothing more than a sycophantic opportunist who owed his success to his way with women, for it was widely rumored that it was Josephine who had procured his directorship at the Italian opera. However, she soon discovered the real warmth under his effusiveness, for once they began to work together, this effusiveness dwindled into a more temperate, more accurate appreciation of her qualities as a musician. She began to understand that much of his gallant air was a nervous habit adopted over the years for dealing with potential patrons who had it in their power to make or break his career. Indeed, all the while that he had been showering her with compliments, she had been aware of his eyes steadily fixed on her and later she realized that he had been observing her closely, trying to form an opinion about her.

When they began to discuss music and her hopes for their lessons, he realized that she was in earnest and he grew more frank with her. "You must understand, mademoiselle, that many fine ladies are convinced that they sing very well and they expect me to agree with them. Naturally, I do not wish to offend them, but I am a musician, after all, and I can not lie about my art. It can be difficult if these ladies are related to powerful men, and, at the moment, there has been a change from one group of powerful men to another which leaves me in a most delicate situation as I owed my position to a man who has now lost his power completely. For me, music is more important than politics, but"—he shrugged eloquently—"everything is political, and a man must eat, nonetheless. I do you the honor of saying in all honesty that if you are pleased with what I teach you, it would help me greatly if you could mention that to your friends at court. However"—he smiled slyly—"if you had not included in your note the letter from Giulio Bartoli praising you as one who sang like the nightingale and possessed the soul of an *artista* I might have discovered a thousand reasons why I was too busy to take you on as a pupil. But Giulio is a hard man, and if he says you could be the next Angelica Catalani, then you could be the next Angelica Catalani. Now, mademoiselle, to work."

Working with Signor Spontini became the bright spot of Isobel's days, all of which seemed to be consumed by dressing and undressing for one elaborate court function after the next. One reception succeeded another with such dizzying speed that the days seemed to run into one another, with each one being like the last except for the change in costume. And changing costume meant that she was subjected to hours with the dressmaker choosing patterns and materials—a discomfort that she had largely avoided when she had been too poor to afford more than a few serviceable walking dresses and one dinner dress. Isobel pored over designs and trimmings until her head ached and she longed for the cool woods at Barford Court or the peaceful music room at Warminster House.

Her one other joy, besides the lessons with Signor Spontini, was her visits with Auguste. Disregarding his sister's dire predictions, Auguste, still an officer under Ney, had called at the Tuileries in hopes of reuniting with his father now that he was able to reassure the duc that the de Montargis lands in Burgundy had been restored and he had made arrangements for the tenants in the Hôtel de Montargis to leave by Assumption Day.

His father had refused to see him, informing the servant who had brought up Auguste's card that, *"There is not such person as Auguste de Montargis."*

Isobel, however, refused to join her father in his denial of her brother's existence. "You may stand by your stubborn and ill-judged pride, Papa, but I shall not, and I tell you now that I *will* see my brother. He has done nothing wrong, and whatever he did was for us. The Comte de Neuilly returned to France with Auguste and his family does not call him a traitor." Isobel spoke firmly enough, but she was trembling all over at her own temerity in standing up so boldly to her father.

The duc gripped the arms of his chair, half rising out of it in his anger. "You will do as I say, Isobel. I am your father and I am still head of this family, such as it is."

"I know, Papa, but I am old enough now to make my own decisions and I say I wish to see Auguste." Her voice quavered slightly, but her chin was held high and her shoulders thrust back. At that particular moment she looked so like her fearsome grandmother that the duc caught his breath. The girl had the proud blood of her ancestors in her veins, there was no denying that. "You dare to disobey me? No proper young woman would even think of questioning her father's wishes."

"Have care, Papa, that I do not become so distraught over your refusal to let me see my brother that I do something desperate or, worse yet, improper. I am of age, you know."

The duc knew when he was defeated. His daughter had grown too independent, too strong for him to do anything about it now. If her mother had lived, Isobel might have been influenced by her gentle, ladylike example, but he rather doubted it. Isobel had always been strong-willed. "Very well, but do not think you can coax me into seeing him, for I will not."

"Very well, Papa. Thank you, Papa." Marveling at her own audacity, Isobel hurried to her own bedchamber before her shaking knees gave out under her.

Once the Duc de Montargis had lost this battle, he never mentioned the episode again. In fact, he was rather relieved that his daughter had found someone to escort her for he was mostly preoccupied with affairs of state and quite unable to introduce her to the capital of her native land. He would have been less relieved if he had known the liberal nature of the salons to which she was introduced by her brother. Madame de Staël, Benjamin Constant and their friends were all ready to welcome Auguste's sister even if she were the daughter of the reactionary Duc de Montargis. Soon Isobel's own spirit and charm made her a general favorite in the society that had accepted her for her brother's sake.

Isobel was gratified to find these soirees much more to her liking than those held by her father's coterie. There was an energy and a purpose about all these people that was lacking among the adherents of the ancien régime. Auguste's friends talked of the future rather than the past, of ideals rather than antecedents. But despite her enjoyment of the society in which Auguste moved, despite her music lessons, and despite becoming accustomed to France, Isobel felt hollow inside. She did not want to admit it to herself, but she was forced to come to the conclusion that it was the absence of Lord Christian Hatherleigh's companionship that was at the root of this empty, restless feeling.

Every time her mind conjured up the picture of the tan face with the alert gray-green eyes, every time her pulses quickened at the sight of a tall, broad-shouldered man, she would quickly try to think of something else, anything else. These unwanted thoughts were made all the worse by her certainty that he had never suffered from such things himself. Undoubtedly he had forgotten her entirely by now and was enjoying numerous flirtations with the sophisticated flirts of Vienna. Emily had mentioned in one of her letters that he had joined Stewart and Castlereagh in the Austrian capital, where all of Europe had gone to decide the fate of the territories conquered by Napoleon. Emily wished that she could convince her husband to think of some way in which to be useful there because she was longing to visit the Continent. Her letters complained that everyone who was anyone had left London to waltz until dawn in Vienna, but Verwood could not be made to see that there was any other spot in the world as comfortable, salubrious, and well-mannered as England and therefore, he saw no earthly reason for departing for foreign parts which were all thoroughly inferior to England.

But Isobel was completely mistaken in her assumptions. While it was true that Christian was in Vienna, and he was, of necessity, a guest at all the most brilliant gatherings, he was avoiding rather than indulging in amatory adventures. This took a great deal of skill and forethought, for many of the ladies who satisfied their craving for power by flirting with the older, more important statesmen longed to indulge their physical appetites in an affair with the handsome Englishman. His total lack of interest in the many feminine charms displayed for his benefit only added to Christian's attractiveness and to the challenge of capturing his interest.

As he moved among the ministers and foreign dignitaries, Christian had no thought for the attractions of their wives, daughters, or mistresses, but concentrated entirely on the information that could be gleaned from conversations with them or those that he overheard. These he would report once a day to Stewart or Castlereagh. The rest of the time he spent poring over reports from other observers like himself or interviewing various spies that the English were paying to keep an eye on the foreigners. As an officer experienced in evaluating intelligence information offered by partisans in Spain and Portugal, Christian had, over the years, gained an innate sense for judging the credibility of both the informant and the information.

Though Lord Christian Hatherleigh could been seen dancing at balls and receptions with the most alluring of women, a truly sharp-eyed observer would have noticed that his partners were women such as Wilhemina of Sagan and the Princess Bagration, who were involved with powerful men, women from whom he could learn a great deal. For their part, the women danced with him because he appeared to be a man who was not only charmingly gallant, but bent on enjoying himself and therefore he offered a great contrast to their more important lovers, who were intent on gaining any political advantage that they could.

"I do like waltzing with you," Princess Bagration confided one evening as they whirled around the ballroom of the Hofburg, "because you know how to make a woman feel appreciated and you do not fume over Talleyrand or make sarcastic remarks about Metternich."

"Ah, Princess, that is because I came to Vienna for the beautiful women that were rumored to be found here. For me, politics is a secondary concern, if it is any concern at all." Even someone as accustomed to flattery as the princess experienced a frisson of pleasure as the gray-green eyes smiled into hers and the mobile mouth crooked into a mocking half-smile. Christian's explanation of his presence was accepted without question by these ladies, who saw him dancing with first one and then another of them. Each one assumed that he never presumed to do anything more than waltz with them because he was more seriously involved with someone else and when he disappeared after a ball, they pictured him following that someone else discreetly to her boudoir instead of returning to the headquarters of the British delegation in the Minoritzenplatz, where he related to his superiors everything of value he had learned that evening and where he helped to write the dispatches to be carried back to England by one of the king's messengers. That done, he would conclude by burning everything. It was a tedious and often monumental task, but a critical one, for he never knew when Hager's spies would find the opportunity to sift through the wastepaper. They never caught these spies, but it was well known that the Austrians were keeping an eye on all their guests.

Christian welcomed the exhaustion that washed over him after the long, intense days, for it often meant he would fall asleep in a chair or slumped over his desk to be wakened later by Digby, who would help him stumble to bed. He welcomed it because it meant he did not lie awake fighting off memories of Isobel or speculating on how she was doing. And it meant he was too tired to dream of wrapping her in his arms and covering her face with slow, gentle kisses. It was bad enough that every woman he danced with he compared to her, remembering her lithe, graceful figure moving in perfect harmony with him as they had waltzed that first and only time at Carlton House.

Yes, he was managing to fill his days and nights, to keep his mind occupied with politics and his senses alert as he parried the questions of delegates, their wives and their mistresses as he probed for even the tiniest scrap of information. But the thought of Isobel was always with him, a dull ache that would not go away, and the more he fought against it, the more he asked himself if he wanted it to go away.

At last, Christian realized that when he had offered to join the British delegation he had been hoping against hope that Isobel and her father might appear with Talleyrand and the French diplomatic representatives, but now he knew that that was a vain hope, inspired more by his own need to see her than by any realistic expectation. The Duc de Montargis was a courtier who would remain with his king in Paris. After months of missing her, Christian began to feel the distance between Vienna and Paris lessening and at last, driven by the desperation of uncertainty, he had resolved to ask Castlereagh for time off to accomplish this journey when the diplomat was recalled to London to defend his policies to Parliament. Wellington arrived to take Castlereagh's place and Christian could not bring himself to ask for leave from a man whose dedication to his troops and his country had won the war, nor could he deprive someone newly arrived in Vienna of his own experience in the seething cauldron of intrigue that was the Congress.

In the end, it was Napoleon himself who solved Christian's dilemma. In little over a month after Wellington's arrival in Vienna the duke was asking Christian to join him as an aide-de-camp when he left to take command of the British army in Belgium and to plan for the battle that was bound to occur.

Chapter 30

For Isobel too, the Corsican Monster provided a means of escape from the stifling court routine that threatened to sap all her energy.

During the first months of Louis's return to France the Duc de Montargis had spent most of his time close to his royal master, assisting him in the selection of his ministers, the granting of peerages to fill the upper and lower chambers of the Chamber of Deputies, organizing the household troops to take the place of the Mousquetaires and the Chevau-Légers that his brother had disbanded a generation ago, and assisting in the preparations for the solemn ceremony honoring the transfer of the bones of Louis XVI and Marie Antoinette from the cemetery of La Madeleine to the customary burial place of the Royal Family in Saint-Denis.

Once these tasks had been accomplished, however, the duc had turned his attention to his daughter's future. Isobel received some idea of what he was about when he began to insist on joining her as she made calls on many of their old friends who had returned to their hôtels in the Fauborg Saint-Germain and when he encouraged her to increase these calls. Isobel had begun these visits out of politeness, but once she had started with her singing lessons she had curtailed her calling drastically. Now her father began taking such a serious interest in her activities that she was not allowed to get away with this reduced schedule. Isobel also began to notice the presence of highly eligible young men of illustrious lineage who were suddenly to be found at home when the de Montargis, in a carriage lent to them by the king, pulled through the entrance portals into the courtyards of these imposing *hôtels*. Her suspicions were confirmed one afternoon as they were returning to the Tuileries along the rue de Varenne and passing in front of the high walls that surrounded the Hôtel de Montargis when the duc remarked, "It will not be long before we are home again and then we shall hold a ball to announce your engagement."

"But I am not engaged, Papa."

"You will be," her father replied serenely as if he had just told her he had decided to order new hangings for the ballroom of the Hôtel de Montargis.

"But, Papa, there is no one . . ."

"Of course there is someone. In fact, there are many someones who have approached me on the subject now that life has returned to normal. The Comte de Pontarlier has always been a member of our circle and the Chevalier d'Entremont has also expressed his admiration for you. Though the chevalier's lineage is no so pure as the comte's, he is master of several estates that seemed to have survived the depredations of the *sans culottes*. And there is the Duc de Montmorency, though I do not know so much about him or the Comte de Reverdy."

Isobel could no longer contain her exasperation. "But, Papa, I am not in love with any of them, nor am I that well acquainted with any of them."

The duc opened his eyes in astonishment. "What does love or even acquaintance have to do with alliances made among people like us? And you have known the Comte de Pontarlier and the Chevalier d'Entremont since we lived in London."

It was useless to argue and equally useless to point out that ex-changing polite pleasantries with young men who abhorred dis-cussing anything more serious than the cut of their coats or the ability to select a good tailor hardly amounted to knowing them. Now she understood the meaningful look in the Comte de Pontar-lier's eye and the slight squeeze he had given her hand the other day as he had helped her into the carriage after his aunt's salon. With a sinking feeling she realized that the moment she had been dreading had arrived. She could no longer avoid the fate of all well-bred young women of her class. Her father would choose a husband for her. The thought of relinquishing her freedom and her independence to some man was so upsetting that she decided she did not care which man it was, as they were all equally uninspir-ing.

But that evening the Comte de Blacas called on the duc and Isobel in their apartments in the Tuileries to tell them that another gentleman was about to play a far more important role in their lives than either the Comte de Pontarlier or the Chevalier d'En-tremont, for news had reached the palace that Napoleon had es-caped from Elba along with an escort of twelve hundred officers and men of the Old Guard and had landed at Golfe Juan. "I have only come to tell you this because the king wishes his most loyal subjects to be fully informed." The Comte de Blacas smiled reassuringly. "But I assure you that there is no need to be alarmed by the Corsican's mad enterprise. The king will publish a proclamation in the *Moniteur* asking all loyal subjects to lay their hands on Bonapate wherever he should happen to appear. There are sufficient troops in the south to rout the invaders and the Comte d'Artois and the Duc d'Orleans have been sent to Lyons, so you see, there is no cause for alarm.

However, Auguste, who knew when Isobel was most likely to walk with Marthe in the gardens of the palace, sought her out to voice a very different opinion. "You must convince Papa to leave at once. It is dangerous for a royalist to remain in Paris."

"But the Comte de Blacas told us not to worry that there are troops who will stop him, and . . ."

"Isobel, *attends-moi,* the troops who are being dispatched to stop Bonaparte are the same troops who helped him conquer nearly all of Europe. They are men to whom he brought a glory they had never dreamed of in their entire lives. Now tell me who do you think they will follow, the man who gave them so much of the world or an ineffectual king who can not make up his mind without consulting his ministers? I tell you, *petite soeur,* that man Bonaparte works magic, and until you see him, you can have no idea of his power. You know I am not an alarmist and I should not suggest a journey that will be exhausting for you and for an old man in frail health if I were not convinced that Napoleon will soon be in Paris. I have friends who can help me procure you a traveling carriage and horses. You *must* listen to me, and you *must* leave before anything happens. Go north, away from Napoleon and his army, to Belgium, where you can get a packet to Dover. Do not try to leave from a French port or you may be stopped."

"But, Auguste, surely you do not think that Bonaparte can take over all of France that quickly?"

"This man is a genius, Isobel. I have seen him work miracles before. You yourself have heard enough at Madame de Staël's and the salons of her friends to know that the royalists are not making themselves popular. Now, go home and prepare to pack. I will send you a reliable coachman as well as a carriage and horses."

"But, Auguste"—Isobel clutched at her brother's sleeve in an agony of indecision—"what about you? What will you do? Will you not come with us?"

"*Petite,* you know I can not do that. Papa would never allow it. And I am still a soldier, you know. I must obey orders. I do whatever Marshal Ney commands me to do. At the moment he is just returned from leave and is perhaps even now meeting with the king. Now I must go and await his instructions, but I want you to promise me you will do what I ask."

"I will."

"Good. *Bonne chance, Petite,* I shall be thinking of you." He kissed her tenderly and hurried off, leaving Isobel and Marthe to look at one another in some dismay as they contemplated the work ahead of them.

"I must convince Papa to flee, but I have not the slightest notion how I will do so. I believe that Auguste knows what he is about in wanting us to leave, but I can not breathe a word to Papa of what Auguste said, for that will make him resist the idea of departure all the more."

"*Angleterre,*" Marthe exclaimed gloomily. "These old bones can not face it again. *Les Anglais,*"—she shrugged—"I can get along with them, but their weather, it is of the worst."

England. The very word sent a tremor of excitement through Isobel that she could not attribute to the hope of seeing Jane and Emily or escaping the rigidly formal atmosphere of the Tuileries, or even the opportunity to show Signor Bartoli the results of the new breathing exercises that Signor Spontini had taught her. She tried unsuccessfully to ignore the vision of a tanned angular face and gray-green eyes looking deep into her soul and a deep voice that said, *You and I belong together.* Shaking her head to clear it of these disturbing images, she turned and began to walk briskly back toward the palace and their apartments. "Come, Marthe, we must began packing."

But Auguste was not the only one who thought that flight was the proper choice for the king and his supporters. That evening at a reception at the Tuileries, Aimée de Coigny, who once had tried to convince Talleyrand himself to support the Bourbon cause, admitted to Isobel that even the Duchess of Courland, Talleyrand's mistress, had left Paris. "She says that she wishes to visit her daughter, Dorothea de Talleyrand-Périgord, who is in Vienna with her husband and Wilhelmina, but *I know* that the real reason she has left is that she fears Napoleon will return to Paris."

There were others who spoke of leaving. By the time Isobel and Marthe had surreptitiously packed their personal belongings, word came that Marshal Ney, who had journeyed to Lons-le-

Salnier with a force of eight thousand men, had thrown in his lot
with Bonaparte. The king sent immediately for the Duc de Montargis, and the rest of his advisors. While her father was occupied
with the debate that raged over whether or not to proceed to La
Rochelle and try to raise loyal troops there, to remain and fortify
the Tuileries, or to ride out surrounded by all the nobles and
deputies to face the Corsican upstart, Isobel and Marthe finished
the remainder of the packing.

When her father at last returned, gray and exhausted, to report
that Louis and his household, along with Monsieur and the
Gardes du Corps, were to leave at midnight the next night in
twelve traveling carriages and make their way north, Isobel and
Marthe were ready. By that time, the duc was too worn down by
worry and the tense hours of discussion to do anything but eat and
fall asleep in a chair in front of the fire. The next evening he was
still too tired to question the two women as they helped him into
the traveling carriage sent by Auguste. He simply lay back against
the cushions and stared blankly ahead as they joined the solemn
procession leaving the Tuileries.

This second flight from France seemed to have robbed the Duc
de Montargis of not only his energy, but his powers of thought. As
they rolled north to Soissons, Cambrai, Valenciennes, he sat
dumbly watching the scenery pass by, his face expressionless except for the deeply etched lines of exhaustion. The de Montargis
carriage followed the royal cortège to Ghent, where Louis, unable
to face the finality of returning to England, decided to remain as a
guest of the Governor of East Flanders at his elegant Hôtel
d'Hane-Steenhuyse. The duc would have been content to remain
there with the rest of the court, but the *hôtel* was too small to ac-
commodate them all so they were forced to make do with the dubious comforts of a small inn on the Vrijdamarkt.

It was Marthe who, returning from the market where she had
made a few small purchases, suggested that they move to Brussels. "For they say that now there are as many English milords in
Brussels as there arc in London. The Duke of Wellington has arrived along with the Earl of Uxbridge and the Duke and Duchess
of Richmond and many others are arriving each day, for everyone
is expecting that a great battle will be fought here."

"The Duke of Wellington, Lord Uxbridge, so soon?" Isobel
turned pale.

Marthe, who had seen her mistress through countless troubles
and some danger could not ever remember her looking so

alarmed. Wisely she held her tongue, but it was as clear to her as the nose on her face that it was the thought of the handsome English milord, who was also a soldier, that was at the root of Mademoiselle's concern. *Bon!* At least now Mademoiselle looked alive again. For the past months, ever since they had left England, Marthe had been worried about her mistress. It was not like the independent Mademoiselle Isobel to be so languid and uninterested in her surroundings, and to Marthe it had seemed as though her mistress had been living in a dream. She had walked, talked, dressed for and attended balls and salons, but she had lost her sparkle. There was no expression in her eyes, no passion in her voice and it was as though she had retreated into some sort of place where nothing and no one seemed to touch her or even reach her. Now, in an instant, with news of the arrival of the English in Belgium, that shell had disappeared and her mistress had come back to her, worried and afraid perhaps, but at least she was alive and herself once again.

Chapter 31

After spending several nights in Ghent they set forth on the road to Brussels, arriving late one evening, too exhausted to do anything more than take the two remaining rooms at the Hôtel d'Angleterre in the rue de la Madeleine. Marthe insisted on bringing her mistress supper in her room and making her rest after the journey. "Tomorrow you will remain in the hotel, mademoiselle, while I look for some suitable lodgings for us. It may take some time for everyone says that the British are arriving in great numbers—mothers and sisters are anxious about their sons and brothers in the army, wives wish to be with their husbands before the battle that is to be fought—everyone is looking for a place to stay and not much is to be had.

"Thank you." Worn out by the trip and worry over her father's health, which seemed to be weakening, not to mention speculation as to the likelihood of Lord Christian's joining his old commander in the fight to stop Napoleon, Isobel had no strength for anything at the moment and gratefully allowed Marthe to take over.

A night's rest restored her natural energy, however, and she was able to join Marthe the next afternoon as they went to look at lodgings she had found for them in the rue du Musée. The house belonged to the widow of a banker who was only too delighted to rent it to them while she went to stay with her married daughter in Antwerp, safely away from the impending conflict. The house was small and easily managed by Marthe and the young serving girl Madame Hubert left behind, but its chief recommendation to Isobel was that there was a pianoforte in the drawing room that Madame Hubert was happy to have her play.

The duc might deplore the fact that most of the French court remained in Ghent, but his daughter reassured him that it was far safer for them in Brussels. "Papa, we are only a few streets away from the headquarters of Wellington himself; surely *they* will not fall into the hands of Bonaparte." Not the least of Brussels' attractions, at least for Isobel, was its distance from the Comte de Pontarlier and the Chevalier d'Evremont.

Not long after their arrival, Isobel discovered another advantage to staying in Brussels when, walking in the park with Marthe, she heard the sound of a familiar voice hailing her. "Isobel, is that you? My dear, how delightful that you are here and not in Ghent, for surely it is far more amusing to be here. Why there are so many people come over from England that a walk in the rue Royale is like a promenade on the Steyne in Brighton. I do believe that the only one who is not here is Prinny."

"Emily! Whatever are you doing in Brussels?"

"Is it not delightful? I could not convince Verwood to go to Vienna which is quite a good thing as it turns out, what with that shocking Corsican loose again, but Verwood's youngest brother, Reginald, insisted on buying a commission in the Guards and, as he is so young, Verwood's mother begged us to come look after him, so we are here. And everyone who is anyone is here as well. We are going to the Wallingfords' tonight, where we are sure to see Wellington himself. You must come with us. I am sure that Lady Wallingford would be thrilled to have you sing for her guests."

Isobel demurred, but Emily was so insistent that at last she promised to consider it. When later that afternoon she received a note from Lady Wallingford herself, she was left with no excuse not to accept. Her father, however, could not be persuaded. The trip and the threat of another exile had exhausted him to such a degree that he was content to sit in the drawing room and work on his memoirs. "If we were in Ghent, I should be a great deal easier about your going out, for there you would be among friends," was his only comment.

"I *am* among friends, Papa. I have known Emily as long as I have known the Comtesse de Sallanches, and longer than I have known Monsieur, for I did not meet him or the Duc de Berri until we moved to London. And it is far safer here for the Duke of Wellington and the entire army is here, while in Ghent we have only a few officers from the *Maison Militaire* to protect us."

The duc did not deign to reply and his daughter was forced to content herself with her own belief that she had done the right thing in coming to Brussels and to comfort herself with the thought that at the Wallingfords' she would have the opportunity to sing. She spent a good deal of the afternoon at the pianoforte, lost in her music as she prepared for her performance, delighting in a reason for throwing herself into her music.

The Wallingfords' drawing room was a crush of people abuzz with gossip and speculation as to Napoleon's movements. Though in many ways it resembled gatherings of the *ton* that Isobel had occasionally attended in London, the presence of so many scarlet coats and a certain intensity in the conversations revealed that at the back of everyone's mind lay the very real possibility that at any moment, half the men in the room could be called into battle.

Without even being aware of what she was doing, Isobel found herself examining the men in uniform, almost afraid to recognize one soldier in particular, yet certain that he was not likely to miss what was sure to be the final struggle with Bonaparte.

Just as she was being led to the pianoforte by her hostess, Isobel became aware of a heightened excitement in the crowd and a commotion in the doorway. "It is the duke," Emily whispered. Glancing in that direction, Isobel could just make out the tall figure surrounded by admirers. However, it was another equally tall figure just behind the duke's shoulder that caught her attention. Almost before she recognized Lord Christian she gasped as her knees weakened and a warm flush spread over her face. He was here! She had known it, and now she admitted to herself, she had longed for it.

In a daze she sat down at the pianoforte while her hostess called her guests' attention to the performer. In a daze she allowed her fingers to move over the keyboard of their own accord until the power of the music took her over and she was able to lose herself in the song.

At the far end of the room, Christian was answering an anxious dowager who was expressing her concern over the army's state of preparedness. "I assure you, madam, the duke is doing . . ." He broke off as the first liquid notes of Isobel's song soared over the crowd, which had fallen into a hush the moment she had begun to sing. She *was* here after all. His heart pounded so heavily that he was sure Lady Cholmondely could hear it, or even see it beating under the gold facings of his uniform. "Ah, er, excuse me. There is something I must attend to." And without further ado, he turned and made his way toward the pianoforte, leaving the astonished woman staring after him.

From that moment on, the crowd in the room disappeared entirely for Christian. All he could see was Isobel seated at the pianoforte casting the spell of her music over her audience. He moved toward her, drawn inexorably by the spell of her music and the longing he had endured for so many months.

The final round of applause awoke Isobel to her surroundings. She rose and acknowledged her audience, looking desperately around for some means of escape. Her emotions were in too much turmoil for her to be able to face anyone with any degree of equanimity. She must get away, at least for a moment, to gather what shreds of composure she had left. At last she spied a window, its draperies billowing gently in the night air, and, nodding mechanically, she excused herself from her enthusiastic admirers, "I must get some fresh air." She made her way to the window with the desperation of a rabbit seeking its burrow. At last she felt the cool breeze on her face and, gliding behind the velvet draperies, let it fall to block the glitter and the noise of the ballroom behind her.

She stood motionless, gulping in the night air for a few minutes only before she felt the draperies billow behind her. "Mademoiselle Isobel." A deep voice spoke softly, almost in her ear. She fought the urge to turn around, though she could feel the warmth from his body. As she brought her hands forward to clasp them tightly in front of her, she felt the scratchy wool of his uniform rub against her elbow. She closed her eyes, willing him to go away, but it was no use.

"Mademoiselle, I came . . . I am here . . . to apologize."

Still she did not look at him until a warm hand, gentle, but firm reached around to grasp her chin and turned her to face him. At last she was forced to look into his eyes. Her heart turned over at the haunted look in them, at the dark hollows underneath them, at the lines of fatigue running from his nose to his mouth, barely visible in the diffuse light from the ballroom. She longed to reach up and smooth those lines away, to tell him that she had been thinking of him constantly since she had left London, but she could not. She was still angry at the presumptions he had made about her brother and his interference in her life, and she was afraid that if she gave in to her feelings he would only become a greater part of her life than he was at the moment and she could not afford that. She had to think of herself and her father.

Isobel drew a deep breath, and clenching her hands at her sides, she spoke at last, "Your apology is accepted."

She bowed her head gracefully and slipped away before Christian could stop her, but not before he had caught a glimpse of tears welling up in the dark blue eyes and clinging to the long lashes. There was nothing for him to do but let her go. He sighed and let the drapery fall behind him as he too returned to the ballroom. He did not remain there long, however, but made his way unobtrusively to the door, down the stairs, and out into the street.

The neighboring houses were dark, the hardworking Bruxellois having gone to bed at a respectable hour, but English officers were hurrying here and there; carriages carrying people from one distinguished gathering to another rattled over the cobblestones.

Christian strolled slowly down the rue du Musée into the Place Royale, and then into the park, where at last he paused, drew a deep breath, and, hands clasped behind his back, began to pace along the carefully laid-out walks.

The moment he had caught sight of Isobel, he knew with a clarity he had not thought possible, that he was in love with her. It all seemed so simple now and so obvious that he was astounded he had not realized it before. But how was he to convince her of it, and, even more difficult, how was he to make her love him in return? He smiled mockingly in the darkness. Making women fall in love with him had never been a problem in the past; it had always been quite the opposite as he had tried to extricate himself gracefully from relationships where the expectation had all been on the woman's side.

Still, he had hope. The pulse at the base of Isobel's throat would not have been so noticeable, her breathing so rapid, nor her hands so nervously clenched at her sides if he did not affect her in some way. Of course, he acknowledged miserably to himself, those signs could have been just as indicative of anger as of attraction. However, if she had been angry, would there have been tears in her eyes as she left him? He traced and retraced the patterns of the walks in the park, trying to decided if it was anger or attraction, the stress of seeing someone again who had annoyed her, or her distress at not knowing how to deal with her feelings for him that was responsible for her agitation.

So many times in the past her words had echoed his own thoughts. Was it not possible that she too was feeling the way he was, overwhelmed at the sight of someone whose absence had left a hole in his soul, a dull gnawing loneliness ever since they had parted? He had to know. He had to find out.

Resolved on following her until he could make her talk to him, Christian stopped his pacing and headed back to his quarters in the house nearby Wellington's headquarters in the rue Montagne du Parc to try to sleep. He, along with the rest of Wellington's staff, had been burning the candle at both ends, rising early to read reports of troop movements, to review troop strengths, and to struggle over planning a variety of alternative actions depending on where Napoleon chose to cross into Belgium. At the same time, they all knew that their commander was counting on them to maintain the atmosphere of normalcy and avoid panic among the hordes of British visitors by appearing unconcernedly at one ball after another, as though they had nothing more serious on their minds than the next waltz.

Christian and all the rest of the officers had done their best, but the strain and the mounting tension as reports of attacks on Prussian outposts near the Sambre River were closely followed by confirmations from well-paid peasants that Napoleon had indeed massed troops along the Sambre and the Meuse was beginning to show. They all looked forward to action of any sort to relieve the agony of waiting and watching.

Chapter 32

Isobel was silent as the Verwoods' carriage clattered home; even Emily's enthusiastic praise for her performance failed to rouse her. "You were magnificent, my dear." Emily patted her gloved hand reassuringly. "And Lady Conyngham asked me, as a particular friend, if I would beg you to sing at her party on Wednesday. Will you not enjoy that? Isobel, Isobel, what on earth is ailing you? It was a veritable triumph this evening.

Isobel massaged her aching forehead. "It is just that the crowd, the heat, has given me a headache. I . . . I shall be better in the morning." She fell silent for some time, but feeling her friend's eyes on her full of concern, and not a little curiosity, she continued, "It is the worry, as well, over what will happen—Papa, what if we have to flee again, so many things. But never mind, we are all faced with that worry. Yes, tell Lady Conyngham I shall be happy to sing at her party."

"My dear, of course you worry, and I am a brute not to see that," her friend hastened to reassure her. "But thank you, I shall convey your message to Lady Conyngham."

Isobel had reason to bless both Lady Wallingford and Lady Conyngham more than Emily could know, for their invitations forced her to think of something other than Lord Christian. Whenever the vision of his haunted face appeared before her, she would struggle to replace it with a mental image of the music she planned to perform. And whenever the sound of his voice, deep and caring, intruded into her thoughts, making her shiver with an odd kind of longing and sadness, she would force it out by mentally rehearsing arias or scales, anything to fight the overwhelming urge she had to seek him out, to throw herself into his arms and tell him how empty her life had been without him.

Lady Wallingford had also eased her mind another way, for the morning after Isobel's performance, a footman had appeared bearing a gracious note of thanks and a small leather bag of gold sovereigns which he had handed to the Belgian serving girl. The Duc de Montargis did not see the bag, which Isobel hastily thrust into her pocket, but he did question his daughter about the note. "It is merely Lady Wallingford thanking me for singing at her ball."

"Bah." The duc snorted. "My daughter acting like a common *actrice d'opéra*. I will not have it."

Isobel rose, her eyes dangerously bright. "And would you have me insult our protectors by refusing the kind invitations of these English who have given us a home for all these years and are now waiting to spill their blood to protect us once again while our leaders hide themselves at Ghent?" She drew a long, shaking breath and her voice quavered dangerously close to breaking as she continued, "You speak of pride and breeding, Papa. Well, I have the de Montargis pride as well, and it will not let me repay their kindness with ingratitude. I am far too proud to act the boor and refuse the invitations of my friends' acquaintances because of some misguided vision of what is due to a name that is no more illustrious than theirs. I *will* sing for these ladies who ask me to do what I can to calm and reassure everyone during these difficult days."

Her voice steadied and then rang out proudly as her father gazed at her in silent amazement. However he might disagree with her, he was forced to admit that she was magnificent, and as she swept from the room, he acknowledged to himself that she had the air of a true de Montargis.

Isobel's performance at Lady Conyngham's was greeted with even more enthusiasm than it had been at Lady Wallingford's. "I have never heard "Porgi amor qualche ristoro" sung half as well by anyone," the man introduced to her by her hostess as Mr. Creevey, congratulated her. "You sing like an angel," a turbaned dowager declared, wiping her eyes. And more than one person compared her favorably to Catalani or Mrs. Billington.

But pleased as she was by these compliments, Isobel found that all her attention was focused on one tall scarlet-coated figure that hovered outside the circle of well-wishers. What was she to say to him? How could she avoid speaking to him with so many eyes upon her?

At last Christian reached her side. "Mademoiselle, they are beginning the waltz in the next room. It would be the greatest honor if you would grant me this dance."

With Emily standing at her elbow smiling slyly, there was nothing to do but accept with as much good grace as possible and allow him to lead her into the next room, where the musicians were playing one waltz after another.

"Mademoiselle Isobel," Christian began as he maneuvered them over to a less crowded corner of the room. "I can not live with a mere apology. It was presumptuous of me to intrude into your affairs as I did, but believe me, I have chastised myself for my behavior a great many times over since that day. Please, can you not put it behind you and let us continue with the friendship I thought we shared."

"But of course, my lord. I have already told you that I accept your apologies."

Even to Isobel's ears, her reply sounded utterly false. She felt Christian's right hand increase its pressure and tighten its grip on her waist through the thin silk of her ball gown, while his left held hers more tightly.

"No, Isobel, I will not be fobbed off in that manner. How can you insult our previous acquaintance by dismissing it so lightly? I missed you desperately." He stopped by one of the open windows and looked down at her searchingly, daring her to evade the issue with politely facile replies.

Again, tears welled up in her eyes as she looked up at him. "And I you, my Lord."

The whispered reply was so low that he felt it rather than heard it. He whirled her into an alcove and held her close for a moment. "By God I have been lonely without you to talk to, to consult about so many things, and to hear how you would answer."

He released his hold on her as another couple glided close to them. "Tell me, do you ever walk in the park, oh, about ten in the morning? It is not yet the fashionable hour and one can enjoy the grass, the trees, the flowers, and the birds in peace, and one can even forget that we are about to go to war."

"And will it come soon?"

"Very soon."

"Ah." She signed sadly. "Yes, I do walk in the park."

"Good."

They finished the dance in silence and he restored her to Emily, who smiled archly at both of them. Then, not wishing to be forced to pay any attention to anyone else or think about anyone else, Christian left the room and went back to headquarters to pore over maps, read the latest reports, and think about the upcoming meeting in the park.

It was gray and cloudy and threatening to rain the next morning and the headquarters on the rue Montagne du Parc was a scene of frenzied activity, for information had just arrived that General de Bourmont, wearing a royalist cockade on his hat, had ridden over from French lines and revealed to a Prussian officer that the French had crossed the Sambre and were planning to attack Charleroi that afternoon, but Christian would let nothing keep him from slipping out just before ten and, hoping against hope that Isobel would be there, hurrying over to the park.

He had no difficulty picking out her graceful figure accompanied by the short square one of Marthe. Marthe had seen the expectant look in Isobel's eyes as she pulled on her straw-colored satin bonnet and green sarcenet pelisse, and she knew immediately that something beyond ordinary importance was involved. Loath though she was to intrude upon her mistress, she also knew her duty, and grabbing up her own bonnet and joined Isobel. "Mademoiselle, you must let me accompany you. This is not London and there are soldiers about. I shall not intrude, but I must accompany you."

"Very well." The significance of Marthe's tone was not lost on Isobel, who not for the first time, realized that there was very little about her that the old servant missed.

When they reached the park, Marthe looked around and, just as she expected, she caught sight of a tall, scarlet-coated figure hurrying toward them. Offering her thanks to *le Bon Dieu* who had seen to it that her *Petite* and the handsome English milord were once again brought together, she fell a good distance behind Isobel as Christian joined them.

"Mademoiselle." He smiled down at Isobel in a way that turned her bones to water. The gaunt lines of his face seemed to have softened and the gray-green eyes lost some of their sadness as he gazed down at her.

"Are they . . . is there any news?"

He nodded grimly. "Yes, they have crossed the Sambre. We are bound to meet them soon."

"Oh." There was a sharp intake of breath and she grew pale. "Do you know if . . . I mean, is Marshal Ney crossing the Sambre as well?"

"I believe so." Christian was puzzled.

"It is Auguste. I know that he is with the enemy, but I . . ." Isobel's voice caught in her throat.

"Auguste? Oh your brother. He is with Ney?"

She nodded. "Yes, he fought with him in the Peninsula, and he was with him in Paris before Ney joined Bonaparte. Papa thinks Auguste is a traitor, but I do not."

The words tumbled out so defiantly that Christian smiled. She looked so fierce, ready to do battle with him should he dare to think anything dishonorable of her brother. "Mademoiselle, if he is fighting with the one they call *le brave des braves*, then I am quite sure that your brother is no traitor. And if he has fought under Ney in the Peninsula, then he is as experienced and battle-hardened as a man can be. In a test such as the one we are about to face, a respected leader, plenty of experience, and a good horse, are the best protection a man can have."

She smiled gratefully at him. "Thank you. Auguste went back to France thirteen years ago, after the peace was signed, to see if he could reclaim some of our property. He did, but before he could do more, he was made to join the army. What could he do but submit? At least by choosing the cavalry he was able to ride. But as he fought beside these men, he came to like them for their dedication to their country and to their work, and he began to admire all that Napoleon had done for France, a man who was not born to the position of emperor, but who had worked to earn it. Auguste and Papa had never agreed about the absolute rights of the king and now Auguste, after having lived through the horrors of the Revolution, which was the fault of a king who had inherited the throne and governed poorly, was seeing how powerful and strong France had become in just a few years under the rule of a man who taught himself to lead and to govern. If he could have, Papa would have disowned Auguste. As it was, he would no longer allow his name to be mentioned in our house, but I would not forget the big brother who helped me to climb trees and taught me how to ride. So I wrote to him year after year. And, I had not seen him in over ten years, until I saw him that day in the park." She flushed self-consciously at the uncomfortable memories associated with that meeting.

"Mademoiselle Isobel, if I could have cut my tongue out before I had said . . ."

"It is no matter. I just wish you to know how much Auguste means to me. He is the only one of all the émigrés in our community who agreed with me that much of their pride was based on nothing but worn-out titles, and petty rules of precedence in a court that no longer had a country to rule. And he is now to fight a battle, and who knows . . ."

"Hush." Christian took her hand in a strong, reassuring clasp. "Your brother is doing as I am, he is taking a risk to do something he believes in. Not many of us is given that opportunity. If he does not survive, you will know that he died doing something he wanted to do, not something that he was forced into by an accident of birth. That is the most that any of us can hope for. Surely you, as you follow your own dreams, can understand that. Now"—he tilted her head to look at him—"I must go, but I want you to smile at me before I do."

Isobel summoned up a wavering smile.

"Good girl. Do you attend the Duchess of Richmond's ball tonight? I do not imagine that the Marchioness of Verwood would miss it for the world."

Isobel nodded.

"Good, then I shall see you there." He lifted her gloved hand, kissed it, and strode off, leaving her to stare after him, a dreamy look in her eyes while Marthe, who had just overheard the last few words of the conversation, pulled a large handkerchief from her sleeve and dabbed at her eyes sighing sympathetically. *"Ah, ma pauvre petite.* This horrible war."

Chapter 33

Marthe dressed her mistress with extra care that evening and, accustomed as she was to Isobel's beauty, she could not help exclaiming as she did the last button on the white satin ball gown. "Ah, but you look like an angel, *petite.*"

The Marchioness of Verwood drove Isobel to the ball, which was held in the converted coach house behind the Duke and Duchess of Richmond's in the rue de la Blanchisserie. "Verwood *would* insist on staying home in order to hear any news, which I told him is quite a ridiculous notion for anyone who is anyone will be at the ball. He will hardly hear anything sooner than Wellington, Maitland, Uxbridge, Hay, or Fitzroy Somerset and they will undoubtedly be at the ball."

Indeed, there was a predominance of uniforms of every kind when they arrived, and the room was abuzz with news which grew in severity as the evening wore on: the French were advancing, English troops were said to be assembling in the Place Royale, English troops were beginning to march toward the front. But Isobel had no time for any of it as she eagerly searched the room for one particular soldier.

Suddenly there was a hush, and then the buzz in the room grew louder as Wellington, his host, and a group of aides-de-camp appeared in the doorway. The crowd pressed toward them, anxious for details and a confirmation or denial of the rumors that had been flying all day. As the duke bent over to say a word in the ear of Lady Frances Wedderburn-Webster, Isobel caught a glint of candlelight on auburn hair, just behind Wellington's left shoulder. He was here, then! Her mouth grew dry and her heart began to pound. Would he notice her in all this crush of people?

At the moment, Lady Emily was chatting gaily to Lady Conyngham and Isobel seized her chance to escape. She had no very good idea of where she was going, just somewhere where Lord Christian could distinguish her from the crowd. Nodding and smiling randomly at people she encountered, Isobel edged her way toward the duke, who was alternately chatting with Lady Georgiana Lenox and other ladies gathered anxiously around him, and stopping to give orders to a variety of officers who kept hurrying up to him, exchanging a word or two, and leaving again.

Isobel watched as these officers went to seek out brother officers in the ballroom. Slowly and inconspicuously they began to leave in groups of twos and threes. Her heart beat faster. Something was most definitely amiss. Through the open window just behind her, she heard the tramp of feet marching toward the Place Royale. *Oh Lord,* Isobel prayed silently, *do not let him get called away before I have a chance to say good-bye.*

"Mademoiselle Isobel."

She whirled around to find Lord Christian right behind her. He had been forced to take a most circuitous route, but had reached her at last. "Oh, my lord"—she held out both hands—"I am so glad to see you. You are going, then?"

He clasped both her hands in his and held them tightly for a moment before raising first one and then the other to his lips. "I am, but before I do, I wanted to ask one thing of you."

"Yes?" The gray-green eyes were looking gravely down at her as though trying to tell her something, but what? She sensed that there was something he wanted desperately, but try as she would she could not guess what it was. All she could do was cling to his hands, feeling their strength and warmth. She wished she could give him something that would reassure him as much as his quiet, solid presence steadied her. "Yes, what can I do? Name it and I will do it."

He wanted to tell her how much she meant to him, how important she was to him, how he loved her. He wanted to ask her if she loved him in return and if she would wait for him no matter what happened, but he could not. It would not be fair to her, for how could a woman, especially someone as sensitive and understanding as Isobel, refuse anything to a man who might very likely die the next day? No, if he made it through the next few days alive and unscathed, then he would ask her, but not now. He wanted her to love him as he loved her, to long for him with the same passion as he longed for her, and not out of pity. He wanted her simply to love him for who he was without being blinded or coerced by the extraordinary events unfolding around them. But at the same time, he could not leave with just a simple good-bye. He wanted something to hold on to during the coming battle, something to remember during the worst moments of what was to come.

Still clasping both her hands in his, he led her gently toward a half-open door and out into a small yard behind the ballroom. A few paces away was a tree. Pulling her underneath it, he held her close for a moment, memorizing every inch of her face—the long, dark lashes, the exquisite triangle of her face with its high cheekbones, slender arched brows, and generous but delicately sculpted lips. "Sing for me, please," he whispered softly.

For a moment Isobel could not think what he meant. She was mesmerized by the look in his eyes, the feel of the broad solidity of his chest, the warmth of his breath in her hair. Sing? What could she sing? How could she sing when there was such a lump in her throat that she doubted she could even find her voice to reply, much less sing? But she must. She must give him something of herself to take with him, perhaps forever.

Slowly she disengaged herself and, drawing in several deep breaths very slowly, she began quietly, "I know that my Redeemer liveth." As the song swelled in her throat, the beauty of Handel's exquisite music washed over her and she sang as she had never sung before. "I know that my Redeemer liveth and that he shall stand at the latter day upon the earth." Tears streamed down her face as she thought of all that this man had done for her, all that he had come to mean to her, and how desperate were his chances and the chances of hundreds of thousands of men poised to fight one another.

The notes of her song, sung as softly as she could, were carried through some of the open windows of the ballroom, and more than one person heard the words "I know that my Redeemer liveth" rising above the hum of conversation. More than one anxious heart took comfort from their message. "For now is Christ risen from the dead, the first fruits of them that sleep." She ended her song and fell silent, captured by the spell of the music.

Again Christian gathered both of her hands in his and pulled her close. "I know that *my* redeemer liveth." He kissed her gently, worshipfully, and then put her gently away from him. "It is time, Isobel. I must go." He turned toward the ballroom to join the others who were kissing their loved ones good-bye.

"Do take care, I beg you." The blue eyes were wide with anxiety.

"I shall. After all, what is one battle to someone who has survived so many?" His lips twisted in an ironic smile. "If you will give me your address, I shall send word as soon as I can when it is over."

"Oh yes. Thank you," she breathed. "We are at Madame Hubert's in the rue du Musée."

"Then I hope I may call on you there soon."

"Yes, please."

Christian had reached the door of the ballroom and, standing in the golden square of light that poured through it, he raised his hand before being swallowed up by the crowd. "Think of me," he whispered inaudibly.

"Good-bye, my lord." Isobel was not even sure he heard the words as he disappeared into the ballroom. "Take care of yourself, my love." She leaned against the tree and wept. How could she bear it if he did not return? The tears poured down her face and sobs choked her until at last she had no more tears to weep. Delicately wiping her eyes with one gloved finger, she pushed her hair back into place, straightened her shoulders, and, drawing a deep, steadying breath, walked back into the ballroom, where the number of guests was rapidly dwindling. She need not have worried about her appearance, for there were few dry eyes in the room. Everywhere, sisters, mothers, wives, and sweethearts were clinging to one another, wiping eyes already reddened with weeping.

Lady Emily was one of the few not entirely overcome, but seeing her friend re-enter the ballroom, she hurried over to her and after one look at Iosbel's pale face, put a comforting arm around her shoulder. "Come, my dear. Let us be gone. Lord Uxbridge has already instructed all officers to finish their dances and return to their quarters. It is time we were safe in our own houses. Let us leave the streets to the troops."

Blindly Isobel followed her to the carriage. In complete silence, they rode the short distance to the rue du Musée, where Marthe was waiting. One glance at her mistress's tragic expression, and Marthe hurried her to her bedchamber and went to rouse the servant girl to heat up some milk.

Marthe had heard the tramp of feet, the clatter of sabers, and the clop of horses' hooves as soldiers headed toward the Place Royale, and there was no need to ask whether or not one particular soldier had been ordered to march. She brought the cup of milk up herself and helped her mistress into bed. "Do not worry, *petite,* Marie and I shall keep our ears open and we shall let you know the moment there is any news."

•

"Thank you, Marthe." Isobel climbed into bed and, clutching her pillow, lay listening to the distant thud of hundreds of hooves, the rumble of carts, and the occasional command that rang out in the empty streets. Her mind was in a turmoil. How could she have been so blind? She was in love with Christian Hatherleigh, and it was not until a few short hours ago that she had allowed herself to acknowledge it. Why had she not told him? She wanted to run after him now to tell him before it was too late. But would he have cared? By all accounts, a great many women had loved him; what did it matter that there was one more?

She lay for hours, holding her pillow and thinking that sleep would never come, but come it must have, for the next time she looked toward the window of her bedchamber, daylight, pale and gray, was flooding her room. She threw on her clothes and ran downstairs, where she met Marthe on her way to serve the duc his breakfast.

"The servant of Monsieur Creevey, who lives on the other side of the street, said that Milord, le Duc de Wellington, left town by the Namur gate half an hour ago," she reported.

And that was the last news they heard for quite some time. Isobel distracted herself by reading to her father some of Monsieur de Montaigne's essays and editing the most recent portions of his memoirs. From time to time she thought she heard the distant booming of cannon.

Later in the afternoon, a note was sent around from the Marchioness of Verwood, offering room in her carriage if Isobel wished to go watch from the ramparts, but Isobel could not bear to go. She preferred the solitude of her own drawing room to the constant speculations of the crowds in the streets or on the ramparts, and she wished to wait, alone with memories of Christian until she received news of his safety or, she could hardly bear the thought, of his death.

Day dragged into evening with no news until just before Isobel was going to retire when Marthe came to tell her that Monsieur Creevey's servant reported that a Colonel Hamilton had called upon her master with the news that a battle had been fought at Quatre Bras, and though he assured him that the British had distinguished themselves, he was unable to say who had won.

Isobel was forced to go to bed in a dreadful state of uncertainty.

The next day, a peculiar quiet settled over the town. No cannon fire was heard, and Isobel, determined to distract herself, spent much of the day at the pianoforte rigorously practicing the breathing lessons that Signor Spontini had taught her, running through scales, and singing all of her favorite songs except one.

During dinner that evening, the duc, who had remained silent and preoccupied most of the time, spoke at last. "Monsieur le Marquis de Juarenais stopped here this afternoon to say that the British are in retreat and the city is overrun with horses, men, and baggage. We must go to the king in Ghent."

For a moment, Isobel was too depressed by this news to reply, but Marthe, in the process of clearing the soup, came to her aid. "Monseigneur, it is said that there is not a carriage nor a horse to be found in all of the city. They have all been seized for military service. Besides, it has begun to rain most dreadfully. Monsieur Creevey's servant has just told Marie and me that Bonaparte has cut off communication between Wellington and Blucher and that none of the armies can move now because of the weather. As soon as it clears, however, a great battle will be fought."

There was nothing to do but wait, and Isobel and her father spent the rest of the evening reading quietly in front of the fire, preoccupied with their own thoughts.

The following day however brought activity. They woke to the sounds of horses, carts, and troops that had entered the city wet and bedraggled the evening before, heading slowly back out. Not knowing what this movement signified, Isobel called Marie to her side. "Run and see which direction the soldiers are heading." She turned to her father after the girl had sped off to do her bidding. "If they are going toward Antwerp, then indeed, all is lost, for Emily told me she overheard the Duke of Wellington warning Lady Frances Wedderburn-Webster to leave for Antwerp the minute things looked bad."

But an hour later, Marie returned to say that the troops were heading out the rue de Namur toward the army.

"Then we shall stay where we are and await further news," Isobel stated calmly and firmly. Not having heard from Christian, she had absolutely no intention of leaving the one place where he knew how to find her.

Chapter 34

While the hours dragged endlessly for those in Brussels, time was a blur for Lord Christian and troops on both sides of the conflict. Lord Christian had hurried back to headquarters after he left the ball. There all was confusion, but the duke, retired for two hours' sleep while his staff changed from their ball dress into their uniforms, conferred again, and were ready to join the duke as he rode to inspect the fighting at Quatre Bras. The rest of the day, Christian spent galloping from one battalion to another with orders designed to steady the troops and keep them holding their ground. By the time this had been accomplished, night had fallen, and Wellington had returned to the Roi d'Espagne inn at Genappe to eat and catch a few more hours of sleep. Christian, however, was only able to make sure that Ajax was given something to eat, blanketed, and allowed to rest before he also returned to the Roi d'Espagne to find what food there was to be had, splash some water on his face, and collapse in a vacant chair for what seemed only a few minutes before he was ordered to ride to Ligny to discover precisely what had happened to the Prussians the day before.

At about half past seven in the morning he returned to Genappe with the news that Blucher had had his horse shot out from under him and had nearly been trampled while his troops, who had been severely mauled by the French, had retreated to Wavre. Christian had barely reported this depressing news when Wellington sent him out again carrying orders to retreat, and then he joined the rest of the troops as, soaked by the rain that came down in torrents, they slogged back toward Brussels.

Unlike many others who were forced to bivouac in the rain and who had nothing but biscuits or rum stirred into oatmeal for breakfast the next morning, he was at least able to dry himself off in front of the fire at the inn at Waterloo and, once again, having rubbed down and fed Ajax himself, found a corner where he could catch a few hours of sleep.

It hardly seemed like morning when he next was awakened by another of Wellington's aides and sent to join the duke as he checked the defenses at the château at Hougoumont. From there, he was ordered to carry a message to the first battalion of the second brigade of Prince Bernhard de Saxe-Weimar's Nassauers, ordering them to reinforce the garrison at Hougoumont. By then, the first shots had been fired and the defenders, Colonel McDonnell's men, were under siege. The rest of the day passed in a fog of smoke and heat from the battle, cries of wounded men and horses, the shouts as charges were launched and men swore and cursed as they struggled to position guns. Christian galloped from one brigade to another carrying messages or bringing back reports, searching for the officer in charge of regiments where one commanding officer after another had been killed. Soon, time, men, animals, ceased to exist—only the mission of locating the next regiment where he was to deliver the message was all that mattered. Every time he returned to the elm where Wellington and his officers were most often to be found, the group had dwindled until it seemed there was hardly anyone left. In all his years in the Peninsula, Christian had never seen such carnage, never witnessed so many hours of unremitting combat, as wave after wave of French threw themselves at the English positions.

When the order to charge came at last and the British troops raced down from their defensive position on Mont Saint-Jean, he was too exhausted to share in their exhilaration, too worn out even to be surprised that he and Ajax were still alive. At the end, he could not even say how, his body aching from hours in the saddle, his mouth caked with dust, his nostrils filled with the smell of gunpowder, his face covered with sweat and grime, he found himself outside the farmhouse at La Belle Alliance as Wellington and Blucher greeted one another, barely able to believe the fact that victory was finally theirs, and overwhelmed by the price at which it had been bought.

Then, and only then, was Christian able to stop and realize that he was still alive and, except for a shallow saber cut across his brow, unhurt. *I know that my Redeemer liveth.* Despite his name, Lord Christian was not a religious man, but at that moment as tears of gratitude welled in his eyes, he thanked his Maker for allowing him to come through unscathed so that he could at last return to Isobel and tell her that he loved her. He pictured her at the

Duchess of Richamond's ball, how many evenings ago, he could
not even be sure. How pure her voice had been, how sad her eyes
as they had said good-bye. He must get back to her now that the
French were finally routed. The French—Auguste! The sadness in
Isobel's eyes had been not only for him, but for her brother and
every other soldier who had been prepared to sacrifice his life for
his country.

And now, as exhausted as he was, Christian knew he had to
find out what had become of Auguste. Outside of her father, Auguste was the only family that Isobel had, and Auguste would
have had no way to get word to her of what had happened to him.
For all that Christian knew, Auguste had no idea that his sister
was even in Brussels.

Christian turned Ajax around and in the fading twilight surveyed the field before him. Smoke from a few bivouac fires rose
to mingle with smoke from burning gun carriages and the last
final cannonades. Where in this vast wasteland was Auguste de
Montargis and how was he to find him? *He is with Ney?* he remembered asking that day in the park that seemed years ago. She
had nodded. Yes, Auguste had been in the cavalry, she had said.
Surely he would have been an officer. A cavalry officer under Ney
named Auguste de Montargis. It was not an impossible task, but
how was he to begin?

A band of French prisoners was led past him as Christian puzzled over this dilemma. "Wait one moment." He jumped down
and led Ajax over to the man in charge of the prisoners. "Please, I
am looking for an important French officer; let me speak with
these men."

*"Ya-t-il quelqu'un ici qui connait un officier de cuiraisseurs
sous Maréchal Ney qui s'appelle Auguste de Montargis?"*

No one answered. Christian cursed under his breath. It was
hopeless. Why had he been crazy enough to think it would possibly work?

"Monsieur." A grimy-faced man wearing the barely distin-
guishable uniform of a cavalry officer raised his head. *"J'étais
avec Ney. Je ne connais pas ce monsieur, mais je puis vous con-
duire à mon regiment."*

"Very well, my man, if you can show me where you were fighting under Ney, I shall take it from there." Christian turned to the
soldier in charge of the prisoners. "I am taking this man with me."

"Very good, sir."

Christian helped the Frenchman, who had suffered a flesh wound in the arm, onto Ajax and swung up behind him. "Now, show me where you saw Marshal Ney last."

The man pointed in the direction of La Haye Sainte and they rode off, picking their way as carefully as they could among the dead and the wounded.

At last they reached La Haye Sainte, where heaps of men, wearing the uniform of his guide, lay on the ground. His guide descended and, moving carefully among the dying, administered what little water that was left in the flask Christian had strapped to his saddle and questioned them carefully. At last he came upon a soldier with a bloody bandage formed of a cavalryman's sash around his forehead, who nodded weakly and pointed to a spot some ways away. Christian hurried over and helped to lift him onto Ajax and they made their way to a clump of men and horses. There, the wounded soldier pointed at a young officer collapsed against a dead horse, his foot thrown out at an awkward angle.

Christian carefully picked his way over to the man, whose dark, curly hair was matted with sweat, but whose aristocratic features were vaguely reminiscent of Isobel's. "Auguste," he whispered urgently. "Auguste de Montargis?"

The young man's eyelids fluttered and his unfocused gaze fell on Christian.

"Auguste?"

The young man frowned in concentration and tried to rise, but fell back with a groan.

"You are Auguste de Montargis?"

"The young man nodded slowly. "*Oui,* monsieur."

"I am a friend of your sister's. I have come to take you to her. Do you understand?"

"Isobel?" Alert now, Auguste regarded him in astonishment.

"Yes, but I am afraid it will be rather uncomfortable. Your leg . . ."

"*Oui.* I think it is broken, but except for that, and for this"—he raised a hand to the gash in his forehead—"I am unhurt, *grâce à Dieu.*"

Christian bent to put one of Auguste's arms around his shoulder and waved to his guide to take the other. With relatively little jostling, they contrived to lay Auguste over the saddle, next to his fellow soldier. "A bit rough and ready, I am afraid, but I believe it is better than riding astride."

Auguste, who was clenching his jaw against the pain, nodded feebly.

Christian grabbed Ajax's bridle, and turned to his guide. *"Au revoir, monsieur, merci, et bonne chance."*

The soldier waved, *"Merci, monsieur,"* and headed off in the direction of his retreating army.

Then began the long, slow process of returning to Brussels along a road choked with troops, carts full of wounded, and conveyances of every description. Passing a wagonload of wounded French soldiers, Christian gently lifted his other charge onto it, shifted Auguste forward on Ajax's shoulders, and climbed up behind him. Once mounted on Ajax, he was able to make better time, but still it was nearly morning by the time they reached the house in the rue du Musée.

Without a thought for the sleeping neighbors, Christian banged on the door and waited. He was forced to pound on it several times before Marthe, a candle in her hand, her cap askew, opened the door. *"Mon Dieu! C'est le milord Anglais."* Grabbing the shawl that had slipped from her shoulders, she opened the door further. *"C'est Auguste!"* She threw the door wide. "Oh, monsieur, you are the Savior Himself. Come in, come in."

Christian secured Ajax to a post, though by then the horse, who was as exhausted as his master, was unlikely to go anywhere, and slid the unconscious Auguste onto his shoulder.

Marthe pointed to the stairs. "This way, monsieur, there is an unused bedchamber at the back of the house. I shall throw off the dust covers."

They had just begun to mount the stairs when another candle appeared in the gloom. "Marthe? Whatever is amiss?" Isobel appeared, her green sarcenet pelisse thrown hastily over her nightrobe. Her eyes widened as she recognized their nocturnal visitor. *"Mon Dieu,"* she gasped as tears welled into her eyes. "You are alive, you are here . . ."

"And he has brought Monsieur Auguste, who is in need of assistance." Marthe gently set her mistress to one side as Christian and his burden reached the top of the stairs. "I am going to put him in the empty bedchamber but now you may do that and I shall warm some water, find some sheets for bandages, and get some brandy."

Still too dazed to think, Isobel lighted the way to the bedchamber, threw off the covers, and helped slide Auguste onto the bed. He groaned faintly, opened his eyes, blinking in the light of the candle. "Isobel? Am I dreaming? I was there on the battlefield. I thought I would die out there, but then an angel, an officer, an Englishman appeared. I must be dreaming. *Ce n'est pas possible.*" He ran a weary hand over his brow.

Isobel sank to her knees, the tears spilling over at last, and took his other hand in hers. "No, Auguste, it is true. And this officer, Milord Christian Hatherleigh, did indeed bring you back to us." She looked down at her brother, whose eyes had closed. "He has fainted again." Gently she stroked his cheek, then rose and held out her hands to Christian. "How can I ever thank you, my lord?"

He covered her hands with his for a moment, feasting his eyes on her face, then gently lifted them to his lips. "To see you again is more than I could have ever hoped."

She pulled one hand away and reached up to examine the saber cut. "You are hurt."

"'Tis the merest scratch."

"But if it had been deeper, you might have—" She broke off and buried her head in his chest, her shoulders shaking.

He pulled her close, reveling in her softness, her warmth, the scent of rose water in her hair, which was soft as silk against his cheek. He was alive, he was with her. Life had never felt so complete, and he wanted it to stay like this forever.

Christian had stood motionless for so long that Isobel pulled away to look anxiously up at him. "Are you feeling all right, my lord?"

"Never better, but . . ."

"But?" Her eyes widened with concern.

"Before I left, at the Duchess of Richmond's ball, I asked you if you would do something for me, do you remember?"

"I remember every minute of that evening. You asked if I would sing for you."

"Yes I did, but I wanted to ask you something else."

"What? Anything." She could not bear the worry she saw in his eyes. Having lived through this terrible battle, what else could he possible have to fear?

"You say that, but . . ." He had said it so many times in his mind, why was it so difficult now? The truth was that he was afraid, more afraid than he had been of the cannon fire, the death, and the destruction that had surrounded him all day. What if she did not care? How could he face life without her?

Isobel reached up to cradle his face in her hands. "There is nothing you can ask that I would not want to give you. My life is yours."

"It is not your life I want, but your love. I love you so, Isobel." His voice, already hoarse with emotion, broke.

She smiled at him tenderly. "And I love you."

Christian thought he had never seen a woman look more beautiful. He crushed her to him, his lips seeking hers, gently at first, as he traced them with his own, and then passionately as her mouth opened beneath his and he felt the warmth and softness of her skin under his hands as he traced the slender column of her neck.

The creak of the floor behind them brought them back to reality as Marthe reappeared with bandages, brandy, and a basin of water. Her wrinkled old face lighted up as the two fell guiltily apart. *"Eh bien, mes enfants, c'est bien."* She pulled a chair to the head of the bed, and after surveying her patient, gently began washing Auguste's face. "Let him rest now. In the morning we shall see if we can find a surgeon to set the leg. In the meantime, what my poor Auguste needs most is rest."

There was another creak of the floorboards and the duc, clutching a brocade robe around his frail frame, appeared in the doorway. Isobel and Christian fell back, but he had eyes only for the figure on the bed. *"Mon fils,"* he whispered so low that Isobel was not even sure she had heard him.

Slowly he made his way to the bed and sank into the chair beside the bed that Marthe had just vacated. Tentatively he stretched out one thin, blue-veined hand to brush the dark curls off his son's forehead. A tear ran slowly down his gaunt cheek. For some time he sat there, so immobile that Isobel could not be sure he was even breathing. At last he rose. "My son is alive. For that I thank *le bon Dieu,* but he is still a traitor. When he wakes I will not see him."

Slowly he rose and turned back toward the door, but Isobel stepped into his path. "Please, Papa, he . . ."

"I have spoken."

"I would have thought that a de Montargis would admire devotion to one's honor and duty, no matter what the cause." A firm voice spoke quietly from behind Isobel. "If I, who fought against him and countless other gallant souls today, can honor a brother officer, surely you might find it in your heart at least to acknowledge your son."

The duc looked at the battle-weary officer in front of him, whose face was black with powder, his brow crusted with blood, one epaulet missing, and the shoulder of his jacket ripped where a spent ball had glanced off it. There was a light in his eyes, a ring of conviction in his voice, and an air of pride that commanded instant respect.

"We shall see. We shall see," the duc murmured vaguely before making his way back to his own bedchamber.

"Thank you, thank you." Isobel lifted one of Christian's hands to her cheek. "You have done more for us than we deserved today. Now you must let us feed you and then you can rest."

"I thank you, but I need rest more than I need food, rest, and the chance to say I love you." He bent to kiss her one more time before leaving for his quarters in the rue Montagne du Parc, where, fully clothed, he fell into bed and the deep, dreamless sleep of exhaustion.

Chapter 35

It was the better part of a day before Christian could make it back to the rue du Musée, and when he did, it was to discover Isobel sitting with her brother as he ate his luncheon.

"Never did I think to taste Marthe's good cooking again, and I owe it all to you, my lord, not to mention that paltry item, my life." He greeted Christian.

"Think nothing of it. I am always glad to help a brother in arms, especially one who is the brother of the woman who saved my life."

"Oh?" Auguste turned to his sister and raised a quizzical eyebrow.

"He is exaggerating, Auguste. I have done nothing for him except sing."

"Nothing except sing like an angel, an angel who brought beauty and ideals back into my life when I had begun to doubt that such things still existed. Your sister gave me something to believe in again."

"That is rare praise indeed, my lord."

"And your sister is a very rare and talented creature."

"That she is. She tells me that some of that she owes to you, for without your introduction to Signor Bartoli she would never have improved as much as she claims to have improved, and which she plans to demonstrate as soon as I am able to hobble to the drawing room."

"It was little enough to repay her for the beauty she brought into the life of a battle-weary soldier."

"Ah, yes, I know that feeling. But tell me, she says you were at Vitoria. I too was there, though naturally, I have a slightly different view of things than you do."

The two men launched into a discussion of various campaigns throughout Spain and Portugal and Isobel, seeing they were no longer even aware of her presence, crept silently from the room.

Under Marthe's expert care, Auguste improved daily, and soon he was able to hobble into the drawing room as promised. It was there one morning that he came upon the duc at his writing. Before his father could think about escaping, Auguste settled himself into the chair and stared at the duc, willing him to look up, until his father could stand it no longer and was forced to look him straight in the eye. "Papa, if you had not taught me that my honor was my most prized possession, and that my duty was to defend my country with my honor, I would not be limping before you as I am today. If France is to remain strong after this terrible war, it must grow and change. It needs both of us. It needs our family, the de Montargis, father and son, upon whom it can depend. Please let me be your son again. Let us restore our lands together, for France."

The duc was so silent he resembled the marble bust of his grandfather that had graced the entrance hall of the de Montargis château. At last he held out one hand to Auguste, who lifted it gently to his lips. *"Mon fils."* was all he said.

Standing in the doorway, Isobel gulped down a sob of joy and ran to share the good news with Marthe.

The next day when he came to call, Christian found all of the de Montargis in the drawing room as Auguste sketched out the battle from his perspective while Isobel played quietly on the pianoforte. "You can not imagine the bravery, the heroism on every side, Papa. It truly was one of the most momentous battles in history."

"But the Prussians, how were they able to march from Wavre?"

The two were so involved in their discussion that it was Isobel who first noticed their visitor. She rose and hurried joyfully to greet him.

Auguste, already curious about the tinge of pink that warmed his sister's cheeks every time the Duke of Wellington's aide-de-camp was mentioned, was now able, as he interrupted the speaking look that passed between them, to confirm his suspicions. His *petite soeur* was in love. In fact, he had never suffered under the illusion that Christian had saved him merely out of the desire to do a brother officer a good turn. It was because Auguste happened to be the brother of a particular sister that he owed this man his life. "My lord, I hope you will forgive me for not rising to greet my savior, but . . ."

"I forgive you anything when I see you doing so well. The question is are you well enough to drive in the park. I have prevailed upon an acquaintance of mine to lend me a barouche and I had hoped to convince you, your sister, and Monsieur le Duc, if he so desires, to take in some fresh air."

"How delightful." Isobel jumped up. "I shall just go fetch my pelisse.

"I thank you, monsieur, but my daughter is not in the habit of accompanying young men on such outings." The duc spoke mildly enough, but his posture and his expression clearly registered his disapproval.

"Papa! We owe Auguste's life to this man, besides which he is perfectly unexceptionable."

"Unexceptionalbe is not enough. My daughter, sir, is a well brought-up lady of France, and as such, she owes it to her reputation to be seen only with men of her station."

"Papa, please. This is absurd. Lord Christian *is* of my station, only he is English. How can you say that we can only associate with the French? After all, Marie Antoinette was not French. Besides, he is not asking for my hand in marriage, merely for a ride in the park."

"No, actually"—a secret smile hovered at the corners of Christian's mouth—"I *am* asking for your hand in marriage."

"You are? Oh, Christian!" Completely forgetting her father, who looked on in horror, Isobel held out her hands.

Christian took them in his strong clasp. "So you see, sir, you are right to fear that I have designs on your daughter's future, I do. But they are honorable designs; I mean to make her the happiest woman on earth."

"Non, absolument, non."

"Now Papa." Auguste laid a calming hand on the duc's sleeve. "Isobel has told me what an honorable gentleman this Lord Christian is and he is related to half the noble families in England. He owns several valuable properties in his own right, besides which, he loves her and she loves him. Having talked with Isobel a good deal myself in the past few days, I would say he is a most admirable fellow."

The duc rose majestically from his chair. "My son and my daughter vouch for your noble lineage and your gentlemanly conduct, monsieur, and I thank you for all you have done for the de Montargis, but a marriage between my daughter and you is out of the question. I have made arrangements for her to marry someone of her own kind."

"Papa, you know that is not true, for you had not decided between the Comte de Pontarlier or the Chevalier d'Entremont, and besides, Lord Christian is my own kind." Seeing that there was no sign of weakening on her father's part, Isobel played her trump card. "If you do not let me marry Lord Christian, I shall return to Paris to become an *actrice d'opéra*."

"What? You will do no such thing! Bah, I do not worry. It takes training and extraordinary talent. After performing for a few friends you think you have the skill to perform at the opera, bah."

"I might. Signor Spontini has offered me a position at le Théâtre Italien any time I wish, and Signor Bartoli said he could make me greater than Catalani. I can support myself in greater style than we lived in London. You will see . . ."

"And you would let her do that?" The duc appealed to Lord Christian.

"Not if I were her husband."

"But . . ." Isobel opened her mouth to protest, only to be silenced by a meaningful squeeze of her hand.

One glance at his daughter's stubborn face and the duc knew he was beaten. She had a will of her own. Her grandmother Châlet-Gonthier had never given in, and he could see she would not either.

"*Eh bien,* at least I have my son to marry a French woman. Come, Auguste." And with that parting shot, the duc held out his arm to his son and the two of them slowly made their way from the room.

Isobel turned to Christian. "But you might let me sing at least once in a concert with Catalani, mightn't you?"

Christian pulled her into his arms. "I might if I ever stopped kissing you long enough for you to sing at all." His lips came down on hers and Isobel forgot about everything, but the love he had brought her.

SIGNET

REGENCY ROMANCE

The Irish Rogue by Emma Jensen

Ailís O'Neill is not the average Dublin debutante. She spends time teaching English to Gaelic peasants—and painting the local wildlife. But with her brother running for British Parliament on behalf of Ireland, Ailís is expected to socialize with the political set. Her disdain for the English partisans is evident, but no more so than for Lord Clane. And she knows nothing of Lord Clane's notorious past—or that his future includes plans to steal her heart....

0-451-19873-5/$4.99

A Fine Gentleman by Laura Matthews

Lady Caroline Carruthers was enjoying her visit to the Hartville home. But one thing made life at the estate complicated—Lady Hartville was intent on convincing her son that Caroline would be the perfect wife for him. Who could think of marrying such an obstinate, infuriating man as Richard? But an unexpected surprise arriving on the doorstep turns a far-fetched plan of wedding meddling into startling possibility....

0-451-19872-7/$4.99

To order call: 1-800-788-6262